# Praise for Je
# & Skullcrack City

"*Skullcrack City's* blend of genres, breakneck pacing, brutality, and dashes of philosophy and social critique serve to cement Johnson as one of the most exciting voices in contemporary fiction. *Skullcrack City* is a smart, incredibly well-researched, and painfully plausible look at our immediate future. Jeremy Robert Johnson's work has always tested the limits of both genre and literary fiction and this novel proves that there's still new ground to tread and that he's already on it."

**—BOOKSLUT**

"Fucking incredibly well written and really entertaining the whole time. Wholly original—it's a gem. Without question a FIVE STAR book."

**—BOOKED**

"Jeremy Robert Johnson is a madman. [*Skullcrack City*] was worth the wait...the end is both unexpected and rewarding."

**—WILLAMETTE WEEK**

"Like James Ellroy on meth, explosive and ultraviolent. The weird and strange are heavy-duty in *Skullcrack City*, fostered by a solid mythology that makes the Illuminati seem tame by comparison. Readers will find this book to be an entirely different beast, imaginably raising the bar for horror-fueled nightmarish paranoid fiction."

**—THIS IS HORROR**

"This book is a little bit science fiction, a little bit horror, a little bit everything really, with a dark, literary angle throughout. It's a must for fans of body horror, intricate conspiracies, David Wong/Don Coscarelli's *John Dies at the End*, or just plain great story-telling."

**—HORROR NEWS**

"[T]his book is singularly original. Certainly, it takes cues from Philip K. Dick and William Burroughs. It feels like it could be put on a shelf next to Warren Ellis' Supergod, Grant Morrison's *The Invisibles* and *The Filth*, and David Wong's *John Dies at the End* and be perfectly at home there. Despite its bleak setting and tormented characters, this book is very, very funny. And ultimately, it is a book about hope, and love, and redemption, and the human will to adapt and survive despite insurmountable odds."
**—INTERNAL SHIRT**

"This is a staggeringly well-written and amazing book. The scope, the skill, the story, everything about it is just fantastic. Deep and complex, yet funny. Gory and scary, yet heartwarming. It's a cyberpunk Lovecraftian gritty horror thriller screwball cult action comedy conspiracy with elements of romance and family drama... the ultimate combination of so many awesome things."
**—HORROR FICTION REVIEW**

"This book is like nothing else you have ever read... If forced I would say it felt like a way weirder take on Carpenter's *They Live* if William Burroughs and Clive Barker worked on the script and Cronenberg directed."
**—POSTCARDS FROM A DYING WORLD**

"A far-out hilarious genre-bending thriller. Like a bizarre *Blade Runner*...Jeremy Robert Johnson writes like a dream."
**—TRAUMA (Denmark)**

"An absolute mind bomb of a novel...hilarious, dark, dramatic and bizarre...moves along at a breakneck pace. Like David Wong's *John Dies At The End* in that it seamlessly blends a streetwise mean streak and rough and tumble violence with a sharp and incisive wit all while pouring on the weird gravy..."
**—DIRGE MAGAZINE**

"*Skullcrack City* is one hell of a paranoia crazy train. I read the thing in one sitting. 5 out of 5 stars!"

—**KAFKA REVIEW**

"With its sustained paranoia and freakishly malevolent entities of mass control, *Skullcrack City* recalls the work of Philip K. Dick. Additionally, the novel is given a contemporary punk-ish wash that brings to mind *The Matrix* via Warren Ellis with some Chuck Palahniuk-styling. But really, Johnson's voice and mission are entirely his own...So yes: there are drug fugues, cyberpunk-Frankensteinian creatures, capitalist monster hive-mind villains...but above all, sharp and hilarious prose and an overarching love of humanity. An off-the-beaten-track thrill ride packed with humor, intelligence and a hard-won compassion."

—**POP CULTURE DESTRUCTION**

"There are no words for this behemoth. When you think you understand it, you discover that you've got no idea. [T]his is a book without boundaries. It isn't bizarro or crime or science fiction but it is all of those things and more, something you've never experienced before. Something you need."

—**SPINETINGLER MAGAZINE**

"What makes JRJ's work stand out from his contemporaries' is the strange sense of empathy—in that regard he is not unlike David Foster Wallace's wicked and perhaps deranged younger brother. Sometimes the horror is so understated that it's deadly. JRJ has the ability to balance sheer humanity with sheer grotesquerie."

—**21C MAGAZINE**

"Johnson weaves vivid and fascinatingly grotesque tales."

—**BOOKGASM**

Coevolution Press

ISBN: 978-1-7367815-0-0

Second edition

# SKULLCRACK CITY

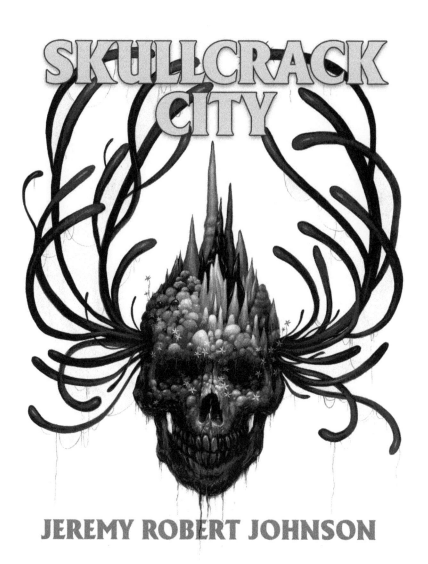

## JEREMY ROBERT JOHNSON

Coevolution Press

To Jessica,
for your wisdom, courage, love,
and occasional total restructuring of reality into a new, more
beautiful form.

"It is pretty obvious that the debasement of the human mind…is no trivial thing. There is more than one way to conquer a country."
—**Raymond Chandler**

"The human mind will not be confined to any limits."
—**Johann Wolfgang von Goethe**

"It's a lovely day to go Blitzkrieg, isn't it?"
—**El-P**

# PROLOGUE

# Welcoming Mr. Trasp

Yes, that is your body on the ground. On behalf of everyone involved in your murder, we'd like to apologize.

If you need a moment to mourn, we totally understand. But global revolutions don't really allow down time. Will it help you move on if you realize you're not really dead?

It's confusing at first. We know. Because the person you thought you were is right there on the floor, a body growing cold. This place is tidy so the blowflies won't get a shot at you, but the bacteria and mites have already heard the dinner bell. The You Buffet is wide open.

And, yeah, within 48 hours the net will be flooded with obit's and R.I.P.'s. grieving the loss of a great scientific mind. "Nobel-Winning Physicist Henry Trasp Dead at 91." Book sales for *Our Galaxy, Our Mind* will soar. Old *Charlie Rose* interviews will resurface on public media. Colleagues will post heartfelt essays about how you changed everything, forever. You know the drill.

If it's any consolation, you barely felt a thing. A pin prick, the flutter-panic of a heart shutting down under just the right dose of remifentanil. *Maybe* the surface vibration of the drills and saws as we created the bone flap.

We wish that we'd been so lucky. This trauma was some low hum lullaby next to what happened to us.

Hell, we even sutured your dura and scalp back into place. Your relatives won't be shocked. It's not like one of those gorilla-jawed skullcrackers got hold of you. Goddamn do they make a mess of the human head....

Sorry, Henry. That's not the point. We can't worry about them at present.

The more important fact is that you're free now. No more wheelchair. No more retina-twitch typing rendered as robo-speech. Think of this in hermit crab terms: you've shed a too-small shell and upgraded to a conch condo. But your consciousness is a little soft in here. Too used to human limitations. We'll help you grow.

It's a delicate process. We lost a few minds before yours, but you'll be integrated slowly. No blowouts. The last thing we need is one more charred genius.

We'll be working in the background, Henry, uploading You. Your theories. The precise interlocking memories which led you to believe you existed. Once you're in here the corridors of our knowledge will be open to you. But travel lightly. There are atrocities inside us. War criminals have *very* vivid memories. Not all scientists worked with theory. Some worked with flesh.

*Enough. His ego still desires. He needs purpose.*

You're right. Henry deserves to know why he's here.

The truth, Henry, is this: humankind is on its way out and our world is coming to an end.

4

We'd like to speed up that process, and we need your help. It's a symbiotic set-up and if you do your job properly, there's a reward beyond even your imagining.

We've got a two state drive to the next acquisition. Does that euphemism make you more comfortable? You're still thinking of murder as a crime.

It's not. Not anymore. Not in this new world.

You'll understand once you've heard our story.

Before there was an Us, before the skullcrackers roamed the city, long before we had this machine attached to our back, and way, way before we realized it was a really great idea to murder you, there was just Me.

My name was S.P. Doyle, and I was a subhuman parasite buried deep in the flesh of a dark god.

Hey, you guessed it.

I was a banker.

Please forgive me.

# ACT I
# ISOLATION

# CHAPTER 1

# The Fuck It Tsunami

No one chooses to become a banker. It just happens, like cancer, and then you try to live with it for as long as you can.

After thirteen years in the industry, I was damn near terminal. With each step up the corporate ladder I received a slightly smaller laptop, a slightly-harder-to-adjust office chair. To compensate they offered free donuts and coffee cards. Weekends off. 401K vesting. Medical insurance that I had to have because they were turning me into a half-blind hunchback with diabetes.

The illusion of safety and security kept me hooked, but every two or three years the veil would be pulled aside and some egregious fraud or pyramid scheme would nearly topple the bank. Then, after a series of Fire-Day Friday culling events, our stock would get low enough to bait some bigger finance fish to swallow us whole.

It felt good to survive those Fridays, but—just in case it was your turn on the chopping block that week—you kept your photos and desk plants in a cardboard box so you could easily escape the cubicle village before you started to shake from the shock of termination.

I never understood the folks who sat outside the bank and cried on the curb. To me, that was like a cow lowing and brushing against the steel doors of a slaughterhouse from which it had been released.

I collected promotional mugs for all eight of the banks which collapsed beneath me. I lined them up in each new cubicle like heads on poles outside of a cannibal village. My resume was a graveyard of once powerful institutions. I felt like a jungle vet and had the ugly stories to go with the vibe.

If you're a young man and they put you in a tie and a cheap dress shirt and some khakis and tell you you're doing a great job, you might buy the propaganda. You might have to, so any of it can matter. So you can survive Fire-Day Friday.

They told me I was a man on the move. An asset to the corporation. I believed them.

I foreclosed on a family farm even after the eighty-year-old matriarch brought me a bag of free cucumbers and begged me not to take what had been in her family for generations.

I shredded files which showed our northernmost office had been issuing racially-based loan denials for years. They'd even created an inter-office spreadsheet to track and remove the applications. Rest assured we deleted any knowledge of "nowaynigger.xls" to the depth of our hard drives. I heard they sent Dale Pritchard to the actual branch to destroy their systems with thermite.

I filed customer letters promising suicide—"You have given me no other choices."—in our newest batch of collapsing mortgage portfolios. After a while these notes got backed up and we had a Sunday pizza party to file them down.

I forgot to mention all the free pizza.

The banks were experts in the kind of stimulus which dulled desire. They never paid anything near the scale of what the upper echelon and stockholders were raking in, but they made sure you had enough money for a commute vehicle and junk food and internet so fast you could run five porn browsers at once. They'd offer you discounted smart phones so you'd never have to spend too much time thinking.

Thirteen years.

I should have known better.

After all that time, all that casual corruption and money-mongering on display, I should have been wise enough to re-fuse their last offer: a position as Primary Compliance Officer.

They wanted me to preach civility to a pack of wolverines. Sure, they were upright and drove whatever the newest BMW was, but still…fucking wolverines.

I'd been a steadfast grunt for so long they had me pegged as a Company Man. "Think you can keep these cowboys in order, Doyle?" And then they winked. They *winked*. Like Santa Claus in Just Our Secret mode.

The role and its implications were clear. Keep the files clean for the Feds. Give our bank the appearance of utmost propriety. And never, *ever* get in the way of our money.

I used to believe there was a part of the human brain we couldn't quite excise, and its sole purpose was to encourage self-destruction. Someday, I thought, the guys working on the BRAIN Initiative would push aside a contour in the gray matter and find a pulsing, jet-black spot. They'd insert a probe into the patient's head to press the nodule and the patient's immediate response would be to shout out, "FUCK IT! WHY NOT?"

It's this spot which I blamed for my entry into the banking field in the first place.

I met a beautiful girl, but she was crazy—ferret-owning, new-piercing-every-week, irrational, knife-toting, porno-contortionist crazy.

FUCK IT! WHY NOT?

She asked me to move in with her six days after we'd met.

FUCK IT! WHY NOT?

She said, "You don't make enough money at the newsstand. You should quit and get a job at that bank across the street. They have money."

FUCK IT! WHY NOT?

And then it's thirteen years later, twelve since that girl put a knife through the thumb/forefinger junction-meat of my left hand during a one-sided break-up, and there's a smiling wolverine in a dark blue suit asking me if I can keep the cowboys in order.

FUCK IT! WHY NOT?

And that same part of my brain, that inky tumor of bad impulse that had led me on Hexadrine blowouts and bottle-draining binges, threw me a flash image of the weeping grandmother whose farm I'd taken on behalf of these bastards. I pictured her bag of cucumbers and how we'd just left it to rot on our lunchroom table. And I swear I thought, with great earnestness, "I'm going to clean up this bank. And if I can't, I'm going to take it down from the inside."

Now if you go back to the prior statements and change "clean up this bank" to "fall into a state of deep acquiescent hopelessness followed by fits of drug-addled paranoia" and "take it down from the inside" to "place my life in immediate danger by stealing a serious chunk of money using a weakness in their general ledger database" you'd end up much closer to the truth.

Hindsight can rob you like that. Turn your pride to hubris, force to foible.

But I had moxie that day. I accepted the gig, started to dig. Took to typing as quickly and loudly as possible and yelling, "I'm in!" when accessing basic programs. Made me feel like a hacker. Made me feel something.

My wages bumped upward in an appreciable way. Bought my first real suits. Quadrupled my coffee intake, amped my anxiety and sleeplessness. Paranoia helped me see patterns: intersecting clients, brokers, financiers. COLLUSION. GRIFT. THOSE BLOODSUCKERS.

I wasn't sure what percent of any of my theories were legit, but based on prior experience, they sure as shit were up to something. And I knew I would find it.

I was upgraded to an office. A wraparound desk, cherry oak with a glass top. A contained space I filled with caffeinated hyperventilation exhaust.

My new laptop had a seven inch screen—the better to hunch into. My head the dot in the mouth of the world's slowest chomping Pac-Man. Screen radiation drying my eyes.

Once I had a door I could close to the rest of the office, I integrated my own offline database: pad and pen. The notebook that would bring down their house of lies, or, if reviewed by a state-licensed psychotherapist, have me institutionalized.

I kept my emails obsequious. Every word you type is accessible to your higher ups. The content of your emails is corporate property. They had systems reading correspondence, testing tone and syntax to predict future malfeasance. The tiny microphone dots next to the webcam lens were also bio-analysis ports taking in exhalations—you consent to drug testing on day one.

Hindsight might interrupt here with a pertinent question: Why didn't I notice the camera mounted in my office's lighting ballast? And why wouldn't I assume that such a camera might be able to train in on hand-written content and translate that into digital text?

Well, Hindsight, have you ever heard of the term Busy Idiot? Have you seen the footage of the caffeine-injected spider whose web was riddled with massive holes?

I'd been on the job three weeks. I spent hours in my office chair just wiggling and worrying and mapping conspiracy. I was easily as effective in the position as, say, a barely sentient Jell-O sculpture of me.

I made a wall of files around myself and peeked over suspiciously. I only came out of my hole on Free Pizza Fridays (which is what banks do with their Fridays when they're not liquidating staff).

For all of my digging, even after a weekend search of files about to be shipped off to the archives, I'd found nothing. Had the bank gone clean? What portfolio had I neglected? Which massive risk were we pretending didn't exist?

The lights were on in the bank. The sign outside the entrance said, "OPEN." We had to be lying about something.

Worse—my compliance reports received kudos from upper management. I was telling them what they wanted to hear. All was well. Profits were up for the quarter.

I'd cleaned up nothing. I'd maintained the status quo. I'd

always been a cog in this machine, but now I was a component in the vocal apparatus of the beast, telling our future victims, "Don't worry. These cowboys are all in line. Nice, law-abiding batch here, only want to help you reach your dreams. They're nothing like that last group who rolled through town with branding irons and rape-trusses and shotguns. These are the good guys."

Cue new waves of rolling cold-sweat anxiety. Cue the 3:00am wake-up gone chronic. Cue the real kind of deep insomnia which allows the Bad Idea Bundle in my brain to think something like:

Maybe I'd be more focused if I bought some Hexadrine.

FUCK IT! WHY NOT?

But there were plenty of WHY NOTS when it came to Hexadrine, and I already knew them intimately:

1. Hexadrine (aka Hex, Hexadrizzle, Silvertops, Pounder, etc.) is a Street Drug the way getting stabbed in the face is a Street Game or the desiccated body of a plague rat is a Street Snack. This wasn't some 6-alpha-chloro-androst-beta synthetic with euphoric/stimulant benefits at abuse dosage. After developing a reputation for fuck-uppery not seen since the heyday of bath salts, FDA approval for Hex was never, *ever* pending.

2. Hex was firmly entrenched as a Schedule One controlled substance, based solely on anecdotal evidence about physiological effects. The real ingredients in Hex eluded government chemists because the real ingredients kept changing. Hex's ability to render the same effects despite the wildly divergent pill-to-pill chemical make-up gave scientists

the worst paroxysms of confused anger since we discovered matter slowing its velocity in outer space. Which brings us to WHY NOT #3.

3. That shit is cursed. Bizango Voodoo/Santa Muerte/The Mennonite Underground… nobody knows. Somebody's mojo is all over it. That mojo is what hits you first—a blood rush tingle from head to toe, the sound of a children's choir trapped in a giant metal blender, a silver-squiggle aura on everything. After that you're swimming in speed-brain momentum and there's this inescapable sensation of a presence being with you. Some people describe it as a black wolf. It's a weight on your left shoulder, persistent in the same way heavy indica will magnetize you to a couch. And that presence, somehow, is *watching*.

4. "Severe genital engorgement" is how the government site denotes one of the side effects, because they can't post a sentence like "turns your clitoris into a hot massage stone or your dick into an all-steel sure strike hammer." Some hardcore male Hex tweekers had taken to fashioning a softer second belt for hard-on tuck-up. Emergency penile reconstruction surgeries were on the rise. However, the same public which adored the DEA's Faces of Meth campaign decades prior found zero enthusiasm for the post-priapic After Hex Dick Wrecks photo series launched via third party sockpuppets.

5. If you're anything like me, Hex may not actually be beneficial. You might think you've found the Light and the Truth and then you wake up the next day and the notepad in your living room is filled with tic-tac-toe games and in your

bathroom there's a mound of hair gel with clear bite marks and a post-it reading, "WE CAN END THIS!" You might jerk your dick so often you have to use lube to keep from peeling off any more skin. In fact, you might be so obsessed with stimulating your all-steel sure strike hammer that one night you come and all that erupts from your dick is a puff of what appear to be dehydrated milk particles which drift slowly down to your abdomen like the saddest first snow of winter. You might even find yourself in a doctor's office wondering why scar tissue is bending your dick like a balloon animal, and end up leaving the hospital with a prescription for Vitamin D, cocoa butter, and a halt to your overblown onanism. And maybe, just maybe, one particularly agonizing night, you might decide to launch a one-man ska/dubstep mash-up project called Skunkwave Bass.

6. Seriously: Skunkwave Bass.

7. Remove your heart. Flatten it with a meat tenderizing mallet. Place it back in your chest. Now you know what the comedown feels like. But, hey, why come down?

8. Acquisition could be troublesome. Weed and booze: as close as the local market. Cocaine and oxy analogs: easy online scores. But Hex…the dealers are a rare breed. Maybe it's the difficult clientele, hopped-up, hard-dicked and hallucinating in the throes of sleep dep. Maybe it's the secrecy of the manufacturers. Maybe it's better you don't know. Because…

9. The Hex trade ain't pretty. I avoid the articles about Hex because half of them are clearly bullshit. And the other

half, talking about blood cults and human sausage and that farm they found in northern Canada...well, in college I took an Economics course and learned an important term: Externalities. Basically, anything that isn't a business making a product or me buying and consuming said product is an Externality. So when you're in the middle of a binge and you decide for the tenth time that week that you're quitting and you call your mom to tell her you've got a problem with Hex and then she says she just *knew* something was wrong and she'd come right over if she wasn't states away and then she sees fit to segue into implications and how you're probably funding human trafficking and she says, "You know they only found pieces of those kids on the farm," and her voice echoes in your mind in a way that tells you this call was the worst decision you've made in a long trail of them, you can take comfort in that term. *Externalities.* There you are at the center of everything. Take what you need. Somewhere, floating in a muddled abstraction beyond your existence as a generally good person, are the Externalities. Fuck 'em and God Bless 'em. Hang up and grab some bottled water and, shit, that's mom calling back but you pop another Hexadrine and the mangled choir is louder than the phone and your hands are trailing mercury and everything but You is an Externality.

So, sure...I had my share of WHY NOTS.

But my time as a Primary Compliance Officer had me riding a tsunami wave of FUCK ITS. Once I catch a serious FUCK IT wave, I ride that thing right up to the sand. "Sand" might be a loose metaphor for "point where I'm almost dead and filled with the kind of regret you have to actively forget in order to continue on as a human being." But I'd convinced myself that this time I'd harness the speedy authority and constant action of the Hexadrine and that it would open my field of vision and let me see beyond the structured absurdity of my daily grind.

Because *this* was the view from my office, every day: A field of beige cubicles under buzzing neon tubes, a hive of pizza-fattened service drones harvesting interest.

The thing I couldn't see but always felt coming from my laptop: Queens and soldiers, sated and slow from gorging themselves on what we'd made for them, biting each other's faces as they fucked in babyskull BMW's.

I saw them clearly once—looked beyond my spreadsheets, about an inch through the crystal display. They felt my eyes on them, separated their latched mandibles, rotated hundreds of compound eyes to see who had dared disturb their reverie.

They could read the look on my face: Why does it have to be like this?

A buzz filled my head, a vibration from inside the oldest part of my mind.

They were laughing.

The thing closest to me spoke. The high tone of royalty.

*Who are you to ask?*


That vision came on a Friday. There were free donuts in the employee lounge.

I ate three bacon maple bars in lieu of a real dinner. Washed out the sugar shock with a mug of jet-black French roast sludge in a World's Greatest Bank mug.

A cowboy behind me, one of our best earners (and a hell of a golfer if you asked him or his mama, hohoho) dropped his newspaper and sighed.

"Another day of busting our chops, huh?"

He winked.

I returned with a, "Well, you know how it is," shrug/smirk thing that felt like betrayal.

The old buzz from my vision set my bones to shiver.

"I read your last report, Doyle. You were kind of rough on the girls in loan processing. I don't think they're used to being watched so close. They'll follow your suggestions, though, I mean, we all have to toe the line. But we have to keep those loans moving too. Used to be, before all this nanny state b.s., pardon my French, but it used to be that *that* was the main thing. Used to be an 'Easier to beg forgiveness than ask permission' kind of set-up, and you didn't get hit with a colonoscopy so long as the deal closed."

I feigned amicable but concerned. "Yeah, I think after the Third Depression the Feds decided we'd been a little too reckless."

The cowboy rolled his eyes.

I remembered a file photo from a home we'd foreclosed: The owner's body gone to fat soup in a tub, both arms razored from wrist to bend, SORRY ABOUT THE MESS! written on the wall in dark smears.

"Shoot, it was the Feds who cleared those damn mortgage products for three years running before they decided to start making examples out of us. You ask me, a little less government involvement and we could have set that ship straight."

This cowboy was using a cognitive dissonance lasso to rope

me out of rational response. I was dazed. I took a blind swing. "Do you really think we were doing the right thing?"

His nose wrinkled like I'd just shit myself. His eyes left mine and focused on a spot on my forehead, where I'd imagine he was picturing a smoking bullet hole.

"Well, I'd say we were doing our best to survive in a free market."

He snorted. His newspaper came back up. The message was clear.

*What's your fucking problem, man? And who are you to ask?*

Jesus. My hands were shaking. Too much coffee. Too much of this place.

I'm certain that as of that evening—after some kind of corporate cowboy klatch—my surveillance status had been elevated to whatever code they use for Fucking Limp-dick Capitalism-Hating Socialist Snitches.

Probably Code Pink, right?

And I think I would have noticed how large a blip I'd become on their radar if that hadn't been the same night I set to the streets in search of an elephant-overdose-sized stash of Hexadrine.

If you want to destroy a wasp nest you approach slowly at the cool of dusk with the right poison in hand. What you *don't* do is wait until the hive is wide awake, chug a jar of moonshine until you're blind, strip naked, cover yourself in alarm phero-mones, and bum rush the nest with your bare fists. Doing that kind of thing might create a mess you can't fix.

Doing that kind of thing might just end your life as you know it.

# CHAPTER 2

# The Most Magical Key

Zombie drive time, the dead-eyed commute from the office to home to dig out an old, busted-up phone with Hungarian Minor's number stored in its guts.

*Are you really going to call him? There's got to be somebody else with a hook-up. Somebody with more fingers and less knives.*

But my social circle had dwindled. Hell, all I had was a social dot—just me on a one man continuum. My last round in the Hex rodeo had thrown off most of my old friends, and after I got clean I had to shake my new acquaintances to ensure I stayed alive.

I mean, I had my turtle Deckard, but his lifestyle consisted of sunbathing, eating goldfish, and—somehow I just knew this—silently judging me while I masturbated. I'd taken to covering his tank with a thin blanket, but still…he knew.

Home: a one bedroom apartment three blocks short of the really rotten side of the city. When I'd moved in I felt a certain naïve thrill, being so close to the reddest part of my city's crime maps. Stabbings just a few streets away! I was fearless, a man of the people. A saint, maybe, moving among the fallen.

Plus: super easy access to drugs.

My brain woke from auto-hypnosis as I neared my apartment's parking garage. A cop car whipped by as I pressed enter on the security key pad. The sound of sirens had been rendered dead stimulus after years of constancy. It was like living next to a waterfall of alarm.

Driving in, I noticed the increasing number of bum barrel bonfires in my neighborhood. Probably time to find some fresh real estate. The number of homeless still rocking dress shirts under brightly incongruous mission-granted hoodies told me that some of the newest barrel buddies were likely fallen comrades.

My sedan made an ugly rumble as I pulled into my parking space. The thing was dying. Every morning I closed my eyes and shot a silent prayer out of my forehead before turning the ignition. Every evening commute I turned up the car radio to avoid the new noises the sedan made as it fell apart.

Time for a new place to live. Time for a new car. New debts. Time to grow up and sign paperwork saying, "Sure, I'm comfortable with this grind for the next thirty years or so. And what a great rate!" Time to let the bank own each and every facet of my life.

I considered going off grid, but where was "off grid" anymore that didn't require me to know how to kill an elephant seal and live off its blubber? And where could I even set up a nature camp, now that the ProTax Drones had become so wide-ranging and effective? Public assistance programs needed your Social—thus placing you firmly back on the grid—and ran weekly drug tests. The government's health care system was still a shambles since the ShellPharm testing scandal broke and all of the parents of short-lived jellyskin babies got their class-action going. Alternative economies in New Hampshire and Boston flopped under old school COINTELPRO disruption. And after the bitcoin Digipression almost negated the global value of the US dollar and the Yen, no other agreeable survival systems had been forthcoming.

I'd still have a nice stash left from dad's life insurance—we lost him to a donorcycle accident before I was even old enough to remember—but mom's fight with a rare case of Pelton-Reyes Syndrome drained the war chest. I couldn't sing, dance, play sports, or produce any kind of art you'd want, and my student loans didn't seem to go away no matter how many petitions I signed.

I considered sex work, but then I bent over and looked at my asshole in a mirror. Nobody was going to pay me for access to that thing.

So the bank owned me. But not for long.

I'd call Hungarian. Hook things up. Get focused. Find something. Something BIG.

And then what? Tell the Feds? Then they take the bank down, I'm out a job, and nobody hires a whistle-blower.

Or worse. Maybe the bank decides I'm an Externality. Maybe I have a mysterious heart attack. Strange for someone in the prime of their life. So sad.

No. I knew that taking it to the government was a dead end. Instead I'd play the bank's game.

Everything is commerce. We weren't the only multi-national mega-bank in town. Whatever I found, I'd sell at a premium to the biggest buyer I could. They'd respect me as a rogue, a high-finance info-pirate. I'd push for my price, the shark-feeder's fee.

And then I'd do it all over again. New bank, new gig, maybe the first shark I feed finances a fake identity. Bank after bank collapses.

At the end of it all, my fortune well-secured, I turn on the bloated old bastards I've been working for and release all their attack info to the public. The Fed is forced to act, anti-trust laws kick in, deep corruption is made public, and maybe this time instead of "Too Big to Fail"—and its latter sequel "Still Too Big to Fail, Seriously, You've Got to Trust Us On This, Guys, Just Roll With It"—*maybe* the people rise up and tear that last bank to pieces.

This was my mission. My heart was filled with a newfound righteous fire. One man against a corrupt system and I knew I could win!

And Hindsight would like to point out I wasn't even on the really hard drugs yet.

I'd been stabbed twice in my life, which is precisely two times too many. The first knife-wielder was the aforementioned, now restraining-ordered ex-girlfriend. The second person to stab me was my Hex dealer Hungarian Minor, the man I'd become desperately anxious to locate. My brain tried to apply logic—*Do you even still own that old phone? This seems unwise. The dude stabbed you.*—so I quickly countered and convinced myself that sometimes a guy might deserve a little cutting, maybe even a two-inch flip-knife stuck in his left butt cheek after almost pushing his dealer in front of a speeding cab.

Eight absorbable stitches. A thin white scar which developed a red rim and phantom stab syndrome on cold days. Hungarian eighty-sixing me from his services, saying next time he saw me I'd end up with a "blood moustache."

I didn't even know what that was, but I got the message. ER with an ass wound, ostracized even by my sketchy dealer, fearing a mysterious injury—that was my last rock bottom.

So calling Hungarian was not ideal. But I was a man on a mission. Some risks would be required. And I knew my old phone was somewhere in my apartment.

I hit my fridge for a new round of cold-filtered coffee and a handful of earthworms. Pounded the coffee, slipped the worms into Deckard's glass enclosure. I moved too fast—he retracted into his shell and hissed. Five years together and he was still hissing at me.

"I love you too, bitch."

I gave his shell a water spritz from a spray bottle—marked YOKO H2OHNO! during the late hours of a bender—and lightly touched the top of his head with my index finger.

I knew he couldn't really smile, but I liked the look on his face. Loneliness is a hell of a drug. A week prior I'd misted up when a grocery clerk told me, "Take care."

"Have you seen my old purple phone, Deckard?"

No response. Just a dry shuffle indicating he'd noticed the earthworms.

"Go get 'em, Deck. Fuck 'em up."

The earthworms died quietly, as always. Bisected, gut trailing, trying to wriggle away from the maw. Soon enough their friends would be filtering through their turtle-rendered remains.

I flipped on all the lights in the apartment. Too bright. Drank that coffee too fast. Cracked a twenty-two of stout to counter-balance—I rode the chemical teeter-totter roughshod, all day. I assumed the ride was over when I was asleep, but I often woke to soaked sheets and a sore jaw which said otherwise.

Digging in my bedroom closet yielded a thin collection of suit jackets, dress shirts and pit-stained undershirts, a few pairs of crumpled jeans, and external hard drives marked "Turtle Movies," "Family Pics," "Kung Fu," and "Big Booty Only Vol. 1."

The kitchen was even more spare—a randomized collection of Tupperware, plastic plates, and mismatched utensils. All the same stuff I'd looted from my parents' house when I got my first apartment over a decade ago. Flashlight search under the fridge and stove revealed dried old Choco Loops and uncooked macaroni. When I was dating someone, it was very much about going to restaurants and staying at her place whenever possible. I wasn't a hoarder, but I knew my place gave off a Feral Child Hidey Hole vibe.

Foyer closet—one pea coat, one snow jacket, three stolen bowling balls with other people's initials engraved. Oh, and under a pair of winter gloves, my prized "Big Booty Only Vol. 3" hard drive—such a glorious rediscovery that for a moment I almost forgot my search for the phone.

Under the coffee table? Bupkus. Behind the entertainment center? Some kind of dust bunny civilization creating grand structures from dander.

Hit the streets? Head to Hungarian's old haunts?

I was hoping to make a call first. Verify he was still the right guy. Apologize profusely. Try to defuse any future stabbing urges. Avoiding answering the question, "What is a blood moustache?" seemed paramount.

Frustration made my apartment feel smaller, the air more reptile-tainted.

*Maybe it's time to cool down? Are you sure this is the right move, pal? Have another beer. Turn on the television. Check your accounts. Let Deckard out for a roam. Maybe you just need a relaxing weekend. Sleep on it.*

That voice. Always preaching reason and paths of least resistance. The gear pin locking me in place.

No. I looked at myself in the mirror above my entertainment center. Bloodshot eyes, hunched back, neck tie still in place. Decades would pass—an ever-faster whirlwind of free donuts and supplications and the gradual crushing of whatever the fuck I was supposed to be and night after night I'd sleep on it until one day I woke up in Willy Loman territory with an elderly turtle as my only heir.

"Deckard, I've got to head out for a while. Keep this spot on lockdown, okay?"

No response.

I grabbed a can of Hi-Pepper Bear Spray—a vestige from the week after I read *Walden* and decided I'd redefine myself as a woodsman—stashed on top of my fridge. It was the closest thing I had to a weapon, a provisional measure in the event Hungarian decided I was still persona non grata.

I turned on Deckard's heat lamp and dropped in some TetraVit flakes for him. He stared straight at the flat rock corner of his enclosure where half a worm was trying to find purchase on a glass wall. The gutted worm flopped toward me, as if to say, "Hey, buddy, can you help me out of here? I think the big guy over there's going to eat me."

But I knew his situation was even worse. Deckard was full. The half-worm flopping himself to a slow death was the night's prime time entertainment in turtle town.

I know it's irrational to anthropomorphize a feeder worm,

but it was an ugly way to end. My heart went out to that worm chunk like he was an elderly woman who had to stop for walker oxygen every third step. I reached in to crush the guy with my fingers. Deckard hissed. I snapped back to the now.

I drained my stout, threw on my pea coat and left my beautiful brute of a turtle to revel in his homemade snuff show.

The moment your car reaches 45th Street, you lock your doors. Even a tourist who accidentally strays into the red zone can feel it in their bones. This is not a safe place.

Since 45th was a major thoroughfare the city council pushed to have it rechristened "The Street of Flowers" and devoted taxpayer money to developing curb planters and medians full of roses and lilies.

It took the residents of 45th exactly ten hours after ribbon cutting to strip and re-sell the landscaping. Medians became dealer/whore islands, curb planters became impromptu biohazard bins blooming with needles.

I had walked to 45th. I had no car doors to lock in protection, and a pocket full of anti-bear spray so old I wasn't even sure it would work. My jacket and tie sold me as square, but it also said I was looking to buy. My face wasn't busted open and my hands weren't shaking, so the dealers and pros knew it was likely I hadn't been robbed yet. That made me a mark.

I wasn't close enough to the chaos yet to make a venture at Hungarian's location. The stretch of 45th closest to my apartment was refreshingly low on tweekers. The drug trade here was more rigidly enforced, and the arbitrary shitbird behavior of the Hex clientele brought too much attention and risk. If you were moving Hex here, you did it as a tangential, on the low and at great danger. The Kept Squad played this territory tight, and the rumor-mill put them at the center of last year's anti-Hex art installation: One dealer, one tweeker, barbed-wire bound at the torso, eyes plucked, arms slashed, left to bleed out on an intersection roundabout. This wasn't the kind of art open to subjective interpretations. Hex heads got the message. I'd have eight blocks or so to walk before I had a shot at finding my guy.

The Kept Squad blocks reminded me of the office. Plenty of slow/sad grinds. Plenty of getting by. But Fire-Day Friday down here was far more likely to put you in the ground.

I clutched my bear spray tighter, felt nostalgia for the quiet warmth of my apartment.

In my twenties, slumming down here had a fun edge to it. That kind of edge gets sanded right the fuck off the first time someone puts a gun to your head and says, "Your wallet. Now. No joke."

Shit—I'd kept my wallet on me. Car and house keys, too, when I could have just key-coded my way back in when I got home. I was forgetting the old protocols: Bring nothing you don't want stolen. Dress down. Walk fast. Head aimed at the pavement three feet in front of you. Ignore everything. Hear something, shrug it off. See something, shrug it off. Eye contact is a liability unless you suddenly need to sell yourself as crazy (and then you better be ready to fill that bill of sale in an ugly way). Quiet customers get served first. Empathizing with hunger is not the same thing as living inside of it. Do not make assumptions. Don't laugh, even if it seems okay—that flash of bared teeth reads SUBMISSION.

This wasn't anything I was proud of knowing. These were

lessons I learned by being stupid and lucky and knowing that same luck runs out.

I was out here on a series of questionable assumptions: That Hungarian was still in the Hex game, that he was extant at all, that he'd be willing to extend his clientele list to include a man he'd last sent away bleeding. I heard alleyway sounds, the kind of muffled, fleshy smacks which could only be producing a variety of traumas. A far-too-young tranny pro dressed in an American Flag bikini and faux fur coat called out "Kirby on the block," which I assumed triggered cop watch. Had it been so long? Was I now reading lawman instead of twenty-something fuck-up? Maybe my hints of gray hair popped in the streetlight.

I picked up my pace. I was already drawing too much attention.

Another block, a slight shift in demographic. Gutter punk kids spending the day's spare change getting blasted. Gassing hard like they had auxiliary brains on back-up. I'd tried gassing once—face locked inside a gas mask with spray paint-soaked filters—and got a concussion and a three day headache for my interest. Never again. I'd learned to apply my bank brain to drugs, running a cost/benefit analysis, determining return on investment. Gassing paid zero dividends next to something as transformative as Hex.

Next block, and I knew I was headed the right direction. More punks, two of them pointing at a friend who was punching himself in the groin and shouting, "This is the steel forged in Valhalla!" He ran over to a burn barrel and started baboon humping. "I will impregnate the Earth's core!" His buddies were dying, tears from laughing.

They spotted me watching. I was rusty. I blew it. I smiled.

Maybe camaraderie would play?

"Whatchu creepin' on, faggot?" Guy with a bullring in his nose pulled a hammer from his back pocket.

I decided to keep my teeth. Head down. Damn near running. Two more blocks and I heard the call.

"Toppers. Benzos. Twoferfiddy over here."

Normally I would have a pre-set amount of cash ready and folded for fast hand-off. This time I was going to have to pull my wallet. Perhaps I should have just worn an LED-wired jacket flashing, "Rob me."

I scanned the street, found my guy. Got the single nod in response.

I moved toward him slowly, remembering the pro pegging me for a cop, remembering Deckard hissing. I stepped close enough for him to speak. Everything was a delicate ritual.

"Fuck you need, Kirby?"

Shit, I was blowing it without opening my mouth, and copping from this guy would be so much easier than dealing with Hungarian. I decided on eye contact, so he could read my face. He needed to see real exhaustion with a side of desperation. He squinted, taking me in with all-black eyes. Looked about twice my size, a Viking amount of man. Maybe ten years my younger and he'd had his irises removed. Head shaved and tattooed. Beard like a lumberjack soup trap. A slice of his septum missing to make his nose more of a nozzle. The standard freak show chic bullshit which had beset the generation after mine thanks to a string of wildly successful reality shows centering on competitive body modification.

I'd had fun watching *Manual Mutants* and *Oddfellas* when they first started, but then *The League of Zeroes* came along and made things too grotesque. They lost me when Rectal

Rachelle died on the table during her ass-neck implant surgery. She was just a kid, barely eighteen. How many assholes did she need for us to love her? Tough not to feel complicit in her death. I hadn't watched in months.

Still, I'd read an episode recap during lunch that day. I knew enough to take a calculated risk.

"You watch *League of Zeroes* last night?"

Cue a heartfelt can-you-believe-this-motherfucker snort. "Man, that's *my* business. What's yours, Kirby?"

"I just...I mean, I thought it was kind of lame how they kicked AsparaGus out of the Big Top."

"Yeah, well, Gus was always a third rate SaladMan knock-off. I wouldn't have been able to live with that smell, either, but...listen, man, you think 'cause we watch the same show that I don't see your wallet bulging out of your pocket? Maybe some pepper spray on you, too? How many of your buddies are watching us right now?"

"None. I..."

"Basically the only thing that would make you a worse undercover would be a moustache. Maybe a badge glued to your forehead."

"Man, I'm not a cop. I swear. I have a project I'm working on and I need a boost. Just a little bit of Hex to help me see things straight."

"Sure, buddy. Move the fuck on." A shift in his posture. A friend of his I hadn't noticed stepped forward from the shadows.

Shit. I played the only card I had left.

"I used to buy from Hungarian Minor."

His eyebrows went up. The name registered.

"Oh, did you now, Kirby? You hear that, Port. This guy

says he knows Ol' Hungo."

His buddy stepped back into his preferred shadow. His voice came from the darkness, the slightest tint of fear to it. "That the blood moustache guy?"

"Yup, that's him. Motherfucker is crazy. I heard that right before he disappeared he'd moved down into the fucking sewers. Like camping out. He kept telling everybody that they had to move to the conduits. 'Only the conduits are safe.'"

*Disappeared?* Hungarian was gone and this guy had already written me off. Goddamn. This was a blowout. I couldn't even execute bad ideas properly.

My face dropped, the saddest attendee of a one-man pity party. Time to head back to the bank. Time to buy a gun and call it a life. But then Deckard would be alone, all alone. My name would become a cowboy punch line for a week before being forgotten. Fuck.

And the look on my face had finally reached Desperation Point. No cop could feign this kind of pain at hearing about the disappearance of a jacked-up Hex dealer.

The big bearded guy's lips pressed together tight and his eyebrows crunched down. He was making a decision.

"Listen, pal. If you used to buy from Hungo then you probably have some kind of proof."

Yes—I jumped. "Yeah, he was about my height. Long black hair. He was missing a couple of fingers on his left hand. Usually had a belt with two or three knives on the thing. He…"

"No, pal." His patience wearing already. "I'm saying that if you used to get the good shit from Hungo, then you probably have some tweeker tracks."

"Oh, well, I always did the pills. I never shot or…"

"What about your dick?"

"What?"

"Your dick. Your junk."

He was smiling now. Playing a game. I could feel his buddy Port smiling from his outpost. They were still fucking with me. This was a preamble to a robbery, them regaining compensation for time lost. Watching half a worm chase escape.

He continued. "What I'm saying is that most guys who buy Silvertops end up mistaking their junk for an enemy at some point."

And I laughed, because he was telling the truth and because the scenario was just past the point where even the most strident FUCK IT! WHY NOT? would normally carry me and yet I could feel something insane about to happen. And it felt good.

So I looked him right in his unreadable all-black dead doll eyes and I whipped out my dick.

Hindsight would like to mark this moment with a special sticker reading, "All Is Lost."

Then we're both looking down and laughing. There's a little embarrassment in the air, because it was cold and we were both staring at my penis, but the predominant tone was shock and recognition.

"Oh, man—you fucked up your homeboy something fierce. Jesus. Shit's like a hockey stick."

Port stepped forward, curious. "Dude, you broke your dick's neck. Daaaamn. If you threw that thing it would come right back to you."

Exactly how long can you stand on a street corner showing two drug dealers your scar-tissue-induced radical penis curvature? The answer is twelve seconds. After that it feels weird.

But those twelve seconds of busted-up dick made all the difference. It was as if I'd inserted a magical key into their minds and unlocked all the trust in the world. They were going to let me buy.

Hell, Port even stayed with us in huddle formation so I could safely pull my wallet without being scoped. And the big bearded guy told me his name was Egbert. I knew Port and Egbert probably weren't their real names, but some childish part of my mind instantly catalogued them as "P & E: My Buddies."

And I'm guessing some part of their minds instantly catalogued me as "Customer: Bent Dick Guy." Still, I had a hard time not smiling on the way home.

The blocks back disappeared like nothing. I raced to my apartment with six Hex pills in my pocket and anticipation as an engine.

The night was vibrating with new potential, the beautiful after-haze of adrenaline and bad ideas fully embraced. Ugly thoughts crept in, forcing me to write off a growing list of concerning data: My old dealer gone mad and roaming the sewers; Egbert's hand—notably short on its middle and ring fingers—reaching out to me with three tiny pill baggies; gas-masked kids dodging conscious thought like a plague; a trafficked tranny more concerned with evading cops than finding love.

Tried to pay it no mind. Externalities.

And then I'd made it home. Confirmed Deckard was passed out under his lamp. He slept with an enviable peacefulness and resolve.

On the opposite end of the spectrum: Me, giddy, a pile of pills singing my name from the coffee table. I forced restraint, grabbing a beer and a carton of leftover kung pao. Flipped on the news and it was more bad buzz.

"…a second murder in the beleaguered Street of Flowers district. Police have confirmed that both have been listed as homicides, and that the second case shares the same cause of death. Official details have yet to be released, but we spoke with the neighbor who found the body from today's murder. A warning to our viewers—what you're about to hear is very graphic."

A street kid was on my screen. Did he have strap marks along his jaw from gassing, like the gutterpunk version of pillow face? The kid had shock in his eyes, but he was excited to be on TV, maybe hoping for some compensation.

"I found his body and I thought, you know, corner [bleep], typical. Maybe he tried to step somewhere he shouldn't. But then I noticed the top of his head was just *missing*, like dude who got him used a shotgun. But the weird part was, no brains. They should have been all over the place. You know. BLADOW! PSSSHHH! Brains everywhere. But there was nothing coming from his head. [Bleep] was empty."

I couldn't have grabbed the remote fast enough. I turned off the screen and immediately set to forgetting what I'd just watched.

*You've seen that kid before, when he was even younger. With Hungarian.*

No. Fuck that. Nope.

I had my Hex score. I had bankers to bust, secrets to sell. It was time to get focused.

It was time to bring down an empire.

# CHAPTER 3

# Headlong Into Conquest

The first pill tasted distinctly of human blood, but I chose to write off the flavor as a mix of ocean water and barbecue sauce.

Not that a pharmaceutical, even one as black market as Hex, should taste like any of those things, but that was the mojo in these pills. So the first wave was alien, a mouth filled with blood, and I flinched thinking I'd been busted in the chops. Then the second wave rolled in, throwing shivers across every inch of my body like an all-skin orgasm, followed by the sound rush, a beautiful child screaming from the depths of a corrugated metal well, and my eyes were painted silver and my fingers trailed melted aluminum tendrils and EVERYTHING IS HAPPENING RIGHT NOW.

The feeling was like this: Imagine your legs are spring loaded. Imagine every breath you pull is processed at maximum efficiency, pumping pure light to your extremities. Everything is vital. Everything is important. None of it can hurt you. A thought translates to action before you have time to remember the thought. If you were at a baseball game and engaged in deep philosophical conversation with a beautiful girl and you heard the crowd roar, you'd be able to tell by the shifting streams of audience noise that the ball was headed your way. And you might catch that home run ball without ever turning away from the truth you were imparting. Everything is possible.

The reality was like this: You clean your kitchen. You drink a gallon of water because you can feel it moving through you all the way down to your stomach. You jerk off, a sacrifice to the newly unearthed Goddesses of *Big Booty (Vol. 3)*. You light candles to unknot the spunk and turtle smells that suddenly rope in your senses. You clean your bathroom. You jerk off again and it shouldn't but your scar tissue feels so good. You realize you didn't pack your Top Secret bank investigation notebook in your briefcase, but urgency and movement erase panic. You admire your turtle, quietly. You clean your bedroom. You clean your garbage disposal interior without flipping the switch at the fuse box. You wish you had robotic prosthetic hands, an end to the weakness of the flesh. You jerk off until the morning sun peeks in through your drapes, murders your mechanical hypnosis. You try to ignore the heavy weight on your left shoulder, the warm breath of a snorting animal on your ear, soft black earth crumbling from its paw to your skin.

The weekend disappeared. I didn't even make it to work the next Monday. Called in sick with plans for an epic blackout sleep session. The cowboy on the phone played it cool. Told me, "Take 'er easy, bud, and we'll see ya when we see ya."

I was certain, though, that the empire was trembling.

# CHAPTER 4

# The Hungarian Situation

The terrible loop began on a Tuesday and didn't end until the day I saw a skullcracker swallow the brain of a bank-hired assassin.

I'll try to explain how I got from here to there, but even now the memories are a series of frenzied fragments, a Hex-infused panic parade of questionable content. The subjectivity of anyone's recollections is already suspect. When you add Hexadrine into the mix, in greater and greater quantities, "reality" becomes a punch line.

Work began in earnest, and it felt great. Discipline. Empowerment. Hundreds of loan files cracked and scanned for corruption. Real progress on my mission.

The Hex gave me the laser focus I'd desired. My eyes became X-Acto knives, stripping the truth from purposefully obfuscated underwriting docs. Glowing silver threads appeared, underlining passages of interest. Our portfolio for a medical supplies conglomerate developed a shimmering, smoking aura which smelled like a burned-out electric socket and throbbed with my heartbeat: Delta MedWorks sat atop the surgical tool empire, a three-eyed goat with a rib-spreading device for a mouth.

Plus: Found a barely used men's bathroom on the fifth floor of the bank building, perfect for satisfying my most persistent urge. Only two employees—one male, one female—were on the whole floor, processing just enough state-subsidized small business loans to allow us to put the words "Equal Opportunity" in our marketing. Within three days of likely less-than-casual observation I'd charted the guy's bathroom timing, and knew when to turn it into my Hex Stroke Session Chamber. For every contact number in my phone, there were twelve film files featuring well-oiled ass. Sometimes I could close my eyes and still see the outline of heart-shaped booty in an eternal cycle of rise and fall, a retina burn more beautiful than any sun. I carried a small spritzer of air-freshener to cover the smell of atomized Astroglide.

I amped up security in my office, stacking the Delta MedWorks loan file wall to a height of four feet around the periphery of my desk, making it difficult for them to tell if I was present at all. I'd made a small cabin, my usurious Unabomber enclave. Felt safer. Theorized my visual absence comforted them. Perhaps they'd grow complacent and slip up.

I had them on the ropes.

Of course, if you change "on the ropes" to "watching me with ever-greater concern" then you're probably closer to the heart of it.

My first notebook filled in two days. I didn't trust my

briefcase since the bank had purchased it for me, so I had to sneak out my secret file tucked into the back of my khaki pants. Sweat caused the ink to smear on the first page, but I was able to interpret what remained. Besides, most of the first page was just a list of my favorite foods and where I'd first eaten them (e.g. shrimp burrito with sweet whiskey sauce/ country jamboree in Montana). The investigation had gotten off to a rough start.

Not anymore—now I was playing the world's greatest game of bank fraud Tetris, and everything fit no matter how fast the pieces fell.

Delta MedWorks was the black heart at the center of this beast. I could feel it. They had subsidiary arms in medical testing, pharmaceutical distribution, prosthetics, dietary supplements, and something called bioballistics. Their subsidiaries had national supply chains under them, and it took me two days of net searches—at home only—to link them to a series of elder care facilities launched during the heyday of The Great Loss (which the Boomers, of course, had themselves named before perishing en masse).

Most of our clients had only one loan officer assigned. Delta had twenty-five lenders in offices across the country. With each, Delta was their sole client. Word was they all drove vintage Jaguars, received shortly after the Delta-SynthroTec merger closed successfully. Unless those Jags cost thirty bucks, that's a gift well outside federal guidelines. But the car thing, however transparent, however traceable those sale records would probably be, wasn't the silver bullet I needed. It was closer to Business As Usual—*C'mon, pal, these guys work sixty hour weeks for the company, taking care of our largest client, and you want to begrudge them a nice car for their commute?*

No, I needed a Bank Destroyer. A foundation crumbling bunker busting violation they couldn't justify.

Delta MedWorks had to be the key. Its convolutions and intricacies would have stymied me in the past, but now I was jacked in.

Jacked up.

Fucked up.

Thirsty all the time.

Talking to Deckard in three hour shifts at night, running down theories while he slept under a flickering heat lamp.

Upon waking, Deckard would blink slowly with heavy lids, just like a human. He was a good friend. A great friend! I bought him extra feeder fish to let him know I loved him.

Mom called every Sunday. I didn't pick up. She'd *know*—every conversation on Hex is a series of shouted interruptions, followed by an apology, followed by an interruption, ad infinitum. She had enough to worry about. I'd call soon, once the Delta MedWorks Scandal had been packaged and sold to a rival bank. I'd tell her about the new job, promotions, but not exactly what I was doing. Couldn't put her at risk.

Deckard knew my grand plans. I told him one night, after singing him a song about whales which I remembered from attending Science Camp Kiwanilong when I was eight.

"So, what do you think, Deck?"

And I looked in his enclosure and he had shed a single, milky tear. Was it the beauty of my song? The brilliance of my plan?

I discovered later that it was a defense mechanism—his body shedding excess salt from all the extra feeder fish I was giving him—but at the time it felt very important.

Everything was important.

Everything was silver. I started stacking Hex, lighting the next high off the still burning butt end of the last.

Pick up runs to Port and Egbert hit every three days, no matter how much I'd previously acquired. Demand kept exceeding supply. Purchase protocols were back in place. Old patterns returned to sense memory.

No one saw me as Kirby anymore. I'd appropriated the right look. A sheen of sweat, the smell of accidental neglect and starvation on my breath.

Egbert nicknamed me. "What up, Crooked D?"

Port laughed from the shadows. He stayed back there, though—I picked up new nerves from him, imagined he kept his hand on his pistol when I approached.

"Same ol' same, Egs, plus two more packets."

"Shit. You setting up your own shop? You know it doesn't work that way with Hex…"

"No. No. No. These are all for me. I'm right on the verge of something important. I don't want the tank running low."

And I knew then that he would ask Port to follow me. Trust was an idea not permitted here. The rumors regarding the Hex trade were never just rumors. I'd seen the documentary *Hexposé*: Folks who tried to deal Hex without the right contacts and suppliers in place lost their eyelids and lived forever fearful lives in mist-goggles.

Blood rituals to show loyalty? I could see it. The missing fingers on both Hungarian and Egbert? Maybe the trade was tied into the Yakuza (or just a big fan of their marketing).

I rushed home that night with nary a swerve or glance which could be perceived as me reselling Egbert's merch. Hoped Port was satisfied with what he saw.

Home safe, seeing the invisible.

They saw everything. The infrared eyes of the surveillance state created a constricting red web across my skin.

Picturing it as One Large Eye would be a mistake. One Large Eye could be deceived. You could hide outside of its view or hope to blind it. Instead I imagined the air as a silver ocean filled with bioluminescent krill, each tiny organism trained to receive one type of data. The motion of a hand sent out purple ripples modeling the likely cause and purpose of the movement. The eye twitch of REM slumber triggered tiny green waves resulting in Common Sleep Patterns of Subject. Yellow waves followed sexual activity, determining possible needs for future hospital care or progeny-based loans. And the corporate Overlords owned the Blue Whales, massive cloud beasts fused together from drone-extracted data and evolving algorithms. Only our masters could understand the alien song of their information behemoths.

This knowledge was buzzing inside my skin.

Someone was reaching for god-like power.

But who? And why?

The default response, emitted from cell towers at frequencies below conscious perception: *Who are you to ask?*

I decided my best option for evasion was to hew to understandable consumer patterns while displaying just enough randomized behavior to allow a few moments for escape if they decided it was time for my termination. If I couldn't predict what I'd do, how the hell would they?

Went to the SavMart and spent one hundred dollars on baby carrots. Abandoned those carrots in the jewelry section at Macy's.

Every Monday I bought a cheapie cell, logged it into a social site under my real account, broke the screen, then tossed the phone into bum carts/baby strollers/train cars.

Triangulate that shit, Blue Whale. Where can you expect to find me on a Monday night?

Work emails were responded to promptly. I ate three slices of pizza every Friday, though I had no appetite. "Marathon training" was the catch-all lie to diffuse concern over weight loss and triple black bags under my eyes. Reports were filed in which new loans to Delta MedWorks were listed as "perfected and well-secured." Meets All Requirements.

Beats All Machines. For now.

Even with the Hex in constant rotation, I knew this was a rigged game. But I was convinced they could tell I was changing. I was joining their team, playing commerce games in the only way they respected: Pure Cutthroat. I was evolving fast enough to survive in their world.

Fear made me wise. Hex fed me opportunities and the courage to take them.

See an open semi-truck trailer? See the driver rolling in the warehouse bay doors with a pallet that will take at least ten minutes to unload? That's an opportunity.

That's me with three boosted laptops. The first got burnt two cities away—researched undernet set-up then sent it swimming in the river. The second bought the extra computer gear I needed and had it shipped to an abandoned house across town. The third, finally, was wired in at my place, encrypted enough to let me research Delta MedWorks and all of its tendrils without fearing immediate reprisal.

Plus: Even better porn access.

Learning how to force something broken to continue to perform its primary function is called a workaround.

My "Crooked D" needed some help. New faces, new

lubricants, new hand positions, varying times of day, trying my best to remember my scar tissue treatments. Workarounds. Necessity is the mother of... well, let's not use the word "mother" in this particular conversation.

I'd finally found a way to pull off the phone calls from mom. Fear of needles and concern over the ultra-questionable nature of Hex interactions kept me from actual speedballing, but I found a suitable alternative in chugging a glass jug of table wine. The combo left me with a woozy forty-five minute paranoia suppression window.

Pop. Chug. Call. Listen. Say "I love you, mom" the moment I heard the clicking mandibles of the sonic transmission mites. "Next week." "Sure, mom." "Bye, honey." Hang up. Throw up if needed. Cry as a defense mechanism to shed excess shame and confusion, if needed.

I could feel time running out, but on whose clock?

I didn't notice my money running out until the pet store clerk asked me if maybe I had another card I'd like to use.

Six weeks since my first pill and I was tweaking on credit. A cash advance is not the first, nor does it do the latter. I knew that from years of watching clients drowned under their own waves of need. And I knew I needed my own bank to extend me enough credit to allow me to complete my wholesale destruction of their institution.

I assumed whichever marauding bank took over and hired me would be willing to write off the debt. Such was my voyage across the Delusion Möbius Strip.

My trips out to the Street of Flowers started to feel like work. Buying Hex at twenty-five percent interest was double-ugly. But I'd pay them back. There'd be loads of payback. I'd found some very strange foreign wires to Delta's overseas pharma testing facilities. Massive amounts of money which had conveniently avoiding federal reporting. And there was something happening right here in town, too, a single doctor's office—Tikoshi Maxillofacial Surgery—being funded via zero balance account transfers from twelve different businesses I knew pledged Delta allegiance.

I was so close to something real. There were a few pins left before the tumbler lock clicked over. I had traction. Momentum. Meaning.

And then the news hit: The identities of the bodies in the "gruesome missing brain murders" on 45th had been released.

The first was a nobody, some punk whose finest hour was a series of arsons, lighting up hospital restroom trashcans for kicks.

The second was a dealer with suspected drug gang and occult ties named Kevin Pendergast.

Street name: Hungarian Minor.

No, it was not good news. Especially since my Hex stash had me just four pills away from a rhino rape of a comedown. I popped sick sweat at the specter of the thought. Not an option.

I had to run containment. My hyper-consumption had already put Egbert and Port on edge. This Hungarian situation would have them on full alarm.

Worse—I'd received an email from the bank. The extension of my credit line had been denied. Debt-to-income ratios were insufficient for our new, stricter lending standards. My revolving account balances had been too high for too long.

"Too high for too long"—*What did they know? Was this a warning?*

The cowboy who'd passed my file to underwriting stopped by my office the next day. "You know how it is, Doyle—Fed's got our credit standards tighter than a nun's butthole. We'll have Nancy in QC review your file and then seal it in employee archives so it's not floating around the bank. Nobody needs to know your business."

A pat on the shoulder. A Sorry Pal concern face he'd perfected over decades. But he was smiling by the time he rounded the corner out of my office—the sweet, sweet taste of schadenfreude.

I pictured him hovering over a burn barrel on 45$^{th}$, trying to figure out how he'd ended up there after all his years of service to the bank. Gas punks with quarter roll fist packs approached him from behind. The snarl of a black wolf rolled in low past my left ear, giving my Hex daydream a new authority—*Make them hurt*. The punks did their work. Fists swinging. A face transformed, the sound of falling coins and snapping bones. Future me as witness, shrugging right by.

Fuck This Bank.

See how the bank still hasn't employed anyone to fill their Bruxton 505 compliance requirements? See how that means the Foreign Transit Comp General Ledger is being reconciled only once every quarter? That's an opportunity.

Any deposit or transfer into my account for greater than ten thousand dollars would automatically be flagged for review. Any funds received from an internal GL other than payroll or benefits was sure to end up on a security screen by nightfall. But by the close of my extended lunch that day— rendered overlong by a round trip commute to and from my undernet connection—Client Rep Stephanie Richmond had received an email request for the addition of one "Martin S. Peppermill" to the MK-Oil travel account.

Would you be surprised to find that when we dealt with

MK-Oil—a US petroleum product distribution arm for one of the big four—we neglected our federally mandated due diligence with regards to new account set-up? Billion dollar balances turned rules into polite suggestions.

See how Client Rep Stephanie Richmond abandons all of her other projects to set up a new MK-Oil account based on the barest of information? See how she orders Card Services to express issue an ATM card—with a withdrawal limit override encoded—shipped to an address one city away? I could see it. I saw that kind of thing every day, but always as a begrudging bystander, a silent witness in need of the next paycheck. Now I was playing the game.

The sensation was like jumping into a rocky swimming hole on the first truly hot day of summer. Everything was fear and concern and hesitation, but once I committed and dove and surfaced all I could feel was exhilaration and bewilderment as to why I hadn't jumped sooner. And I was filled with the desire to do it again.

So I transferred funds from the Foreign Transit Comp GL—an amount small enough and odd enough to appear non-material to anyone concerned.

So I drove to my appointed drop spot and copped Martin S. Peppermill's ATM card just two days later.

So I used a third party bank's ATM—jutting baseball cap and tilted head concealing the majority of my face from the fish-eye lens—and scored enough cash to lock down another week of Hex and ensure that my mission continued at full force.

Waves of paranoia crashed against a new bulkhead of confidence.

*Are they watching? They're always watching. But maybe now they respect me.*

I saw myself as an amusing anomaly, a now-larger blip on the Overlord radar. I told jokes to the empty air during the commute home. I could feel them listening, disarmed. My data was highlighted, a tiny Blue Whale was assigned solely to my life patterns. I did fifty push-ups before jerking off, hoping the infra-red surveillance footage would be arousing.

I decided Deckard was the most handsome turtle who had ever lived. I posted new turtle photos to my online accounts every day.

Realizing I had access to money whenever I needed it had freed me intellectually. I devoted more time to investigating Delta MedWorks, until I had a near perfect copy of our bank files in my apartment. It became easier to ignore the physical realities—bloody noses, head and toothaches, deepening wrinkles, backed-up pipes, a mangled penis subjected to the Spanish Inquisition of self-abuse. My body was an Externality until the moment the Hex started to wear off, and then it was a trap, chains slowing my ascent.

Hex set me free. I was on top of the pyramid, self-actualized.

And then I ran out of pills, again. I'd stretched out my intake as long as I could, knowing Hungarian's murder would make things tense with Egbert.

Anxiety forced me to procrastinate, pushing out a meet as late as I could. Hoping to have some small talk options on deck, I watched the most recent episode of *The League of Zeroes*. Alex Aurora's chest-boxed light display and projector eye made a big splash with the audience, but as with prior challengers, no one was able to unseat Buddy the Brain. There was something fundamentally unsettling about seeing his brain in a box outside his body. The risk involved was unparalleled, the technology—cables running from brain box to a spinal column interface at the base of his skull—was borderline mystical. Most doctors interviewed confessed to ignorance of the mechanics. They said Buddy should be dead. Buddy said they should work harder, and refused to reveal the name of his surgeon, who he could now afford to keep on confidential contract.

The guest musician that week was Robbie Dawn, pushing his creepy smarm and blue-eyed retro-soul. His cover of Marvin Gaye's "You Sure Love to Ball" had become an internet sensation and scored him a cross-generational hit that funded his independent label SonsJeunes. He'd had twelve number ones since his crossover, and you couldn't hit a club night in town without hearing one of his songs, or at least a remix. Most news stories focused on his business acumen and quick rise to fame, but everybody knew what really made all Robbie Dawn songs work: the drums. Those fucking drums, popping, exploding, insisting on their place at the center of your skull. The rhythms and tones swirled in a way that sunk right into your guts. You were nodding your head three seconds before one of those songs even started. Robbie refused to allow tours of his studio. When asked about his signature sound he played cavalier. "I like a certain tone, always have since I was young. But nobody was making the music I wanted to hear, so I had to innovate. I will say that I have a private database of drum sounds, and that the odds of anyone successfully copying what I do are one in a million. Now can we talk about my kids' charity?"

I felt better after the show. Buddy the Brain and Robbie Dawn both had secrets, sources of their power in the game. My run on Hex would be my secret, and take me exactly where I needed to go. No risk, no reward, right?

I waved my hand in front of my face and it was just my hand. The Hex was wearing off and reality had an ugly edge I wasn't excited about. Beautiful silver trails had been replaced by frailty, my hand vibrating with each beat of my heart. I became acutely aware of how thin the skin on my fingers was, how fast all of me could be rendered meat if inserted into the right kind of grinder.

I'd managed to steal a hard copy of Delta MedWorks' transaction records for the prior quarter. It weighed down my couch, an Oxford English Dictionary-dwarfing accumulation of data my sober brain would not be able to translate into meaning.

I pocketed my Hi-Pepper Bear Spray for the first time in too many Hex runs.

I put a little extra food in Deckard's tank, just in case. When our relationship went sideways, Hungarian had only stabbed me. I imagined Egbert and Port to be more matter-of-fact about putting an end to things.

"Fuck it, Deck. I'm going out."

And the vibe on 45th was way more warzone. Kept Squad had extra crew on the streets, flexing, emboldened by the appearance of an anti-Hex ally. But they had their guns showing, which played as alarm. They knew this disappearing brain gambit wasn't theirs, and the presence of a new force had them on alert. Their eyes were on me. Their safeties were off.

Beyond the Kept blocks, the aegis of fear had changed things less than I expected. Hex heads still darted from building to building or screamed at nothing anyone else could see. Shit—I was still out here too. Living inside the preternatural paranoia of the drug had rendered us immune to even rational fears. All stimulus was suspect and constant action was the order of the day.

But Port and Egbert were businessmen, not users, and they didn't have time to play conspiracy games. I was relieved to find they'd retained their post, less comforted by the fact that they now stood side by side. Port's gun remained holstered, but Egbert had one of his Viking-sized mitts wrapped around a machete handle.

I approached slowly. They tensed, shoulders up. Port's arm inched further into his jacket.

"What's up, Crooked D?" His tone was flat. There were no fatuous smiles or denigrating dick jokes forthcoming.

"Nothing much, fellas. How about…"

Egbert jumped in. "We're not your 'fellas.' In fact, we're nothing to you right now. See this?"

He lifted his machete into the streetlight so I could see it better. Written along the blade in black Sharpy: NOPE.

I nodded, eyes wide, glad my last Hex rush was running thin enough that I wasn't speaking before I could think.

Egbert brought the machete to rest, flat side of the blade across his shoulder. "This is what I like to call my Right of Refusal. We're in business now, understand? And if you make any offers that I'm not feeling, I'm comfortable exercising my rights. Say you understand."

"I understand."

"Okay, great. Now I'm betting you'll offer me some information."

I nodded, imagining the single swing of Egbert's arm that could send my head toppling to the street, wondering how long the remaining blood in my brain would allow me to witness my mistake.

"What was your connection to Hungarian Minor?"

"Just buying, I swear. Same as with you guys."

"See, I'm not okay with that answer. Because somebody ripped off the top of Hungo's head and disappeared with his brain. And that happened the same night you came to us and said you were looking for him. So I don't want anything in my life to be the same as Hungo's. Plus we've done some asking and it sounds like you might have had some reason to come at the guy."

"That was some old bullshit. I was young. I'd been jacked up for weeks. I was being ridiculous, and I overstepped my bounds. I pushed him as a joke, but he lost his balance and almost got clipped by a cab."

"Wait…a cab?"

"Yeah, that was before they restructured their service areas to exclude 45th."

"Those motherfuckers."

"Yeah."

A moment of silence passed, the briefest unity.

"So, Hungarian decided I couldn't buy anymore. And he gave me this."

I reached to pull down my pants and reveal the scar from the stabbing.

Port stepped in. "Hold it, D! We've seen enough of you already. Stand still."

I hadn't even thought about what else I was revealing. Port took my Hi-Pepper Bear Spray from my back pocket.

Egbert was nonplussed. "And why the fuck do you need that? Maybe to knock somebody out so you can get at their brain?"

"What?" I made a split-second decision not to argue about how many better ways you could incapacitate someone for brain removal. "No. No. I don't own a gun, that's all. I've been rolled out here before."

They nodded and let the logic of my explanation stand. But I could tell both of them also pictured me getting robbed and then coated in bear spray just for kicks.

"So Hungo cuts you off, stabs you, then later he takes to hiding in the sewers, and shows up dead the same night you come looking for him. And all I know about you for sure is that you're a square peg motherfucker who's buying too much and working on a 'project.'"

"And his dick looks like a hot dog that got hit with a sledgehammer and sewn back together by a blind lady."

"Thanks, Port."

"You're welcome, D."

"Shit ain't funny anymore." Egbert was not letting go. His Right of Refusal was hovering an inch off his shoulder now, locked at the ready. Hell, he could probably broker influence with the Kept Squad by feeding them a dead tweeker for another cautionary art installation. "Listen…it's not like you're the only guy who ever had beef with Hungo. And I know by the smell of you that you've been using most of what we sold you. But you're a risk, man. So, let's open things up. What's your project?"

My eyes locked on Egbert's machete, my legs ready to run if I detected the slightest downward swing. But bailing now was admitting guilt I didn't have, and my comedown loomed with equal threat. The only option was confession under duress, all Hail Marys and crossed fingers and please don't let me die on this street.

The project spilled out in a fear-fueled gush—the fucking bank, the cowboys, the bullshit, Delta MedWorks and their local affiliates, my plan to shut it all down.

It was my first time saying the plan out loud to someone other than Deckard, and it felt good, at first. But the longer I spoke, the more I felt like I was a distant entity listening to the ranting of a pants-shitting street prophet on his rickety milk carton pulpit. Even with the Right of Refusal looming, I did my best to avoid mention of "Martin S. Peppermill" or the name of the bank—I wasn't one hundred percent sure that Port and Egbert could be trusted with the whole picture.

Were they wired and feeding audio to federal drones? Were they part of the Blue Whale data retrieval system? Had I fallen for an undercover subterfuge?

The Fear rolled in faster, nearly paralyzing me. The Hex had taken me so far. Or had it? My mind was pulling in too much stimulus, none of it properly filtered for survival. All data was given significance. If everything was possible then anything could be. Uncertainty reigned as the lifeblood of conspiracy.

*What was I doing?*

I'd drifted off mid-sentence. Egbert's face had changed to a kind of laissez-faire sadness—he'd written me off as having premature dementia, more "sick old dog" than "rabid and dangerous."

But Port's face had lit up, clearly anxious to say something.

*What did he know? Or had he thought of another joke at the expense of my junk?*

"D, this is mad weird…probably just a coincidence."

"Probably just some bullshit." Egbert was *way* over this situation. "This guy is fucking fried."

Port remained excited. "Yeah, he's fried, no doubt. No doubt. But here's the thing—I talked to Sammy Felton,

Hungo's buddy. He's the guy who found the body. And he told me that before Hungo got snuffed he was running special jobs for a guy named Dr. T. I tried to get him to tell me more, but talking about it shook him up. Still, he dry snitched something about 'bodies being supplied.'"

"So?"

"Crooked D, what was the name of the doctor's office getting all that cash here in town?"

"Tikoshi Maxillofacial Surgery."

Port clapped once and nodded. "See. Tikoshi. Dr. T. That's what I'm saying. It's fucking weird, right? Just…who knows?"

Uncertainty engines were in overdrive. Conspiracy contagion thrived on possibility and coincidence as vectors.

My faith was restored. Some divine providence had brought me to this moment.

Could I find ties between Delta and the Hex trade? They had a massive pharma division, didn't they? What if the new restrictions on their overseas testing had caused them to shift to covert research right here in town? Why had Hungarian taken to hiding in the sewers? And where the fuck was his brain?

I wasn't crazy. I was on fire. If I could find a link between Hungarian's death and Delta MedWorks, then surely I could find a way in which our bank was complicit.

The Hex had led me here, and it would keep me on the path. I had to secure more.

I was dealing with businessmen who'd decided I was a liability. I realized the only move was to make the risk worth their while.

"I'll pay you triple for every pill you sell me, and I'll give each of you ten thousand dollars once my project is complete."

Egbert picked up on my newfound confidence and took it for a ride.

"If you can get us that kind of money, we want it as a down payment before your crazy ass gets killed."

Scared money don't make money, right? I could feel the truth—this was the only window I would get before the Right of Refusal closed the deal and severed all ties.

"Sure. I can get the cash. But I'm going to need your help with something."

Cue incredulity and a hand tightening around the grip of a machete.

"No! It's okay. Listen. Listen. Please. There's a man named Martin S. Peppermill..."

Then I sold them the beautiful idea of me not being me anymore, and we all agreed this was a step in the right direction.

# CHAPTER 5

# Black Hole/Brain Loss

There is no such thing as "all the money and drugs you could ever need." That's because of the need part, and how that only disappears once life is extinguished. The money buys the drugs, the drugs work harder and harder to trick your blackened dopamine receptors into giving a damn about living. At some point you make a choice: fight your need the rest of your goddamned long-suffering life, or fill your need until it disappears into the grave with you.

What I had for those last three blasted-out weeks was a more logical variation: More money and drugs than I ever should have had.

Some part of me knew better. But that part didn't understand the thrill of the game; it couldn't grasp how amazing it felt to walk into a bank as "Martin S. Peppermill" and withdraw so much cash they had to count out the stacks in a secured office.

Martin S. Peppermill was still a figment of my imagination, of course, but he now had an ATM card tied to his MK-

Oil account and a very official looking passport and driver's license courtesy of a friend of Port and Egbert. It had taken a series of multi-city ATM runs to put together the document acquisition cash, but I was able to perform much larger transactions with the I.D. I researched MK-Oil's files and knew enough about the business and its higher-ups to run a B.S. session with a bank manager if they came over for a chat. I had one suit nice enough to sell the role.

Port and Egbert got their twenty large. They used some of that cash to grease their superiors and allow greater Hex flow in my direction. And they even gave me back my bear spray, which I decided to carry at all times.

I knew my clock was ticking—quarter end at the bank was approaching and now I'd made dents in the Foreign Transit Comp GL which couldn't be ignored at reconciliation. The only choice at this point was to go balls out. If I slowed down I might start thinking about the choices I'd made and face the deep panic that was surely waiting for me. No, my mission timer was a fast-burning fuse and sleep was a luxury I'd have to trade for glory.

Two pills at a time now, too many times a day to track. I imagined my cognitive function running like a supercomputer. I pretended that this reallocation of mental prowess was where the blackouts were coming from. If brilliantly mapping the collusion between my bank and Delta meant that I periodically lost things like, say, conscious perception and memory, then that was just the cost of my newfound nobility.

Pain and gain. Guts and glory. Balancing the scales of justice. Icarus flew too close to the sun, but at least he flew. It became easier to think in loops of cliché than acknowledge the reality I'd created. Doom isn't really something you want to focus on.

I guess I should have paid more attention to the persistent dreams (which came during the day, and from which I have no recollection of waking): A black wolf watches me in the deep woods, waits for me to collapse, and doesn't even tear out my throat before he starts to gnaw on my skull.

I guess I should have spent less time worrying about invisible data receptors, and instead watched for the man in the green car who'd been paid to solve a problem.

I guess I should have realized that no matter what kind of conspiracy I could dream up for Delta MedWorks, the truth would be far worse. My mind was simply too moral to invent what they were capable of doing.

I did none of those things, not that I can remember. I'm not sure exactly what happened in my final days as a banker. It was definitely when I discovered how easy it is to end up with blood on your hands.

Even Hindsight looks back at this stretch of my life as a black hole, a spinning tangle of "What the fuck?" collapse which began the end of our world.

Here's what I remember…

The bleach on the kitchen linoleum turned my hair yellow green on the left side. I'd passed out in a puddle, my body honoring the periodic rest demands I tried to refuse. Clorox was the only product I used for my daily housecleaning anymore. I vented via my windows, to ensure the fumes weren't too much for Deckard, but I must have gassed myself beyond brain function. The skin on that side of my scalp blistered; the yellow green hair wouldn't be attached to my head for long. My Martin S. Peppermill runs now required a gauze patch and a fedora.

I was snarling in my office. Was it the wolf dream again? How long had I been snarling? Delores, sitting in the cubicle closest to my office, was speaking to a man I didn't recognize. Pointing. Whispering. The man nodded in a comforting way. "Yes, ma'am. We're aware of the problem. It will be dealt with." I didn't come out of my office for free pizza that day. I didn't want to accidentally hear what I was sure was being said.

I was no longer just Martin S. Peppermill. I was also Trevor Bainbridge, auto body and paint professional. A new batch of I.D., three accounts at separate banks, cash deposits daily, structured slightly below Fed reporting requirements.

I was also Maria Scharf, at only one bank, very far away. Lipstick, a wig, a lovely chartreuse scarf. I couldn't bring myself to do much mirror time that day—every glance made me feel like my mother was in the room with me, and that simply couldn't be—so I'm sure it played tranny. Bank anti-discrimination laws and a serious depository balance boost before quarter end made my appearance a non-issue to the branch. They took my money. I'd sat in the car for ten minutes before attempting the deposit, sweating, whispering the words, "Secret squirrel, secret squirrel."

Delta MedWorks: those motherfuckers. Melted dead jerks. Welted head burns. The enemy. The key. All day. All night. They were a scourge, a bank-backed monster, and I would prove it. I pulled a cliff-jump and requisitioned wire archives for a ten year stretch. I knew the request would find its way into an email to management, and had an explanation pre-fabricated. I'd claim a friend at the Fed had tipped me off to a retrospective review of dual signature docs and approval levels. I would make certain our files were clean, especially for our biggest client. Protect the bank. Protect our customer. Wink.

My Crooked D was despondent, barely functional. I researched Peyronie's disease, the scarring of the carpora cavernosa. I set up a multi-screen jack-off overture, all of my favorite scenes on loop. Nothing. Sitting in the desert in a car with no gas, pumping the accelerator. Tripled my Hex dose and forced the issue. Pain as I came, molten lead in my urethra. One testicle nearly sucked back up into my body, to escape the atrocity.

Mom called. I let it go to voice mail.

"It's broken, Deckard. It's just broken."

His shell took on a golden aura, shimmering through my tears. He hissed. I realized I was still naked and wearing Maria Scharf's lipstick. I dressed and cleaned my face, never looking at the mirror.

"I'm sorry. How about some extra worms tonight?" I fed him. Set him on the floor for a walkabout and cleaned his enclosure.

"I love you. Deck."

I thought the sound of thoughtless, whooping grief was coming from a neighbor's apartment, but the wailing disappeared when I stopped to catch my breath.

The Delta wire files arrived. I shuttled them from my office to the trunk of my car via briefcase. It took forty-two laps. I sent a mass email thanking my fellow employees for tolerating my unorthodox run/walk training. Marathon coming up. When I shut down my laptop for the day I saw a reflection in the black screen. That was me, wasn't it? How long had my nose been bleeding?

"Sir, I'm afraid we'll need a valid I.D. to accompany your initial deposit."

"Come again?"

"Well, sir, the I.D. provided isn't matching your new account documentation."

Shit. I was slipping. Who opened the New Era Credit Union account? Martin? Trevor? *Maria?* Was I supposed to be wearing a dress? No. No. Think fast. I knew the girl working new accounts was a trainee. I'd made sure. I had to act before she called over the Operations Supervisor.

"Sir, if you could…"

"Oh, dear, I'm so sorry." Big grin. *Sell it with everything you've got, damn it. Does MK-Oil have credit union accounts? Am I Trevor? I'm probably Trevor. Take the gamble.* "I must have given you my brother Martin's I.D. This is so embarrassing. We had poker night last week and, you know, boys being boys, we ended up at a strip club and my brother got tipsy and lost his I.D. there. Then he has the audacity to ask *me* to get it back for him the next day. I must have grabbed it by mistake."

Her suspicious squint opened up, her eyebrows raised. *Sell it. Grab that I.D. before she can scrutinize the photo a moment longer. You're sweating now. Not good. Shit, I should have visually differentiated Martin and Trevor with more than hairstyles. Glasses, maybe? An eye patch?*

"I'll be right back, sir."

"Oh, that's not necessary—I've got *my* I.D. right here." Shaking fingers, scrambling my wallet as fast as I could. "I… gosh, I'm kind of mortified…it's been such a long day already and we've had a lot of tension in our family and this isn't helping things and I…oh, okay, here it is."

I reached out my hand with Trevor's I.D., the other hand outstretched for reciprocal pass off, engulfed by a new sheet of cold sweat as I realized I'm trying to sell this brother story when the I.D.'s have different last names. *Maintain eye contact. Don't let her look at the license again. Try to pop some tears. Everybody has family strife.* And, despite the Hex-issue ocular dryness, I managed a lower lip quiver and the slightest of well-ups and this girl was just green enough to make a banking decision with her heart. The I.D.'s were exchanged, Martin's license back in my pocket so fast a tiny sonic boom should have issued.

"It's alright." She leaned forward, confiding, the smell of her sweet and light, her voice filled with the kind of innocence that the bank would systematically remove (if her job survived her issuing my fraudulent account). "I've got a teenage sister who's taking my mom and dad for a ride right now, and I'll tell you, I barely recognize her sometimes."

I nodded. "Those are tough years for any parent. Shoot, my parents ended up divorcing and sending my brother to military school. It got so ugly later that Martin stopped speaking to my dad and took my mom's last name." *Too much? Am I overselling it? Damn it. Shut up and get out.*

But her face relaxed further, my retro-fitted reality erasing her last doubt, creating false trust. And my head was already tilted down to avoid the scrutiny of electric eyes, so I didn't have to adjust to account for shame.

My bed was wherever my body just gave up. Waking on the bathroom floor was less of a surprise than the pain behind my left eye. Pressure, distension, some kind of fluid built up behind the optic nerve, sloshing like tiny razors. Popped a triple dose of dot-cons, shifted my head to the position which triggered the lowest agony. Smelled the smoke of an extinguished wooden match. The pain passed, but the ghost of it sat in my chest making accusations: *This is killing you.*

I arrived at work earlier and earlier, relieved that my I.D. card didn't seem to have any time restrictions, but still knowing that this deviation from pattern popped as anomaly. Late night cleaning staff gave me friendly greeting waves and then set to talking shit in a language I couldn't identify. No need for the overhead fluorescents, face warmed by coffee steam, monitor light falling across my eyes like recognition mapping grids. Tikoshi Maxillofacial Surgery in high focus. Was Dr. T. copping bodies from Hungarian Minor before somebody decided that Hungo was better off minus one brain? I found a three month pattern, disguised Delta shell funds moving to Dr. T., followed within days by a transfer of similar amount to Anson BioMed, further followed by a series of structured cash withdrawals.

Anson BioMed barely registered as a business. Just a PO Box, state registry as an LLC, and a tiny strip mall storefront with a few diabetes kits in the windows and some canes on the wall. The sign on the front door read, "Nature Calls—Be Back Soon!" but I had my sincere doubts that this place would exist once the lease was up. My fraud antennae—attuned by my own recent work in the art—called Anson BioMed for what it was: a Delta MedWorks filter and front for local business beneath the radar of acceptability. Anson's accounts were held outside of my purview, but I knew that if I could access the other bank's security footage I'd have some nice shots of Hungo, or maybe his crony Felton, putting their mitts on Delta's dirty money.

*But why?*

It was a question I couldn't answer from the safety of my apartment and the digital corridors of my undernet system. Which meant it was time to pay a down low visit to Dr. T.'s office and find out what kind of man would want bodies in secret supply.

Drive time killed my inertia and allowed thought: *A stakeout? Seriously—where's your Honorary Hardy Boy's Detective Club badge? When's the last time you ate? You really think a global medical company would leave a fraud trail so blatant that some Hex-head could expose the thing? Are you breathing enough? Can you take five sustained breaths? If you die, Deckard will starve. You think anyone will come and care for him? Does your mom deserve to bury you? Do you want to bequeath your porn collection to anyone? If you're right about Delta, what on Earth would stop them from crushing you? How many days left until the bank checks the Foreign Transit Comp GL? Haven't you seen that green car in your rearview before? How many times? Why did you give up the violin? Why won't anyone ever love...* and so I turned up the stereo to distortion-level and took to gumming powdered Hex from a tiny plastic baggy in my shirt pocket. I put the A/C on max hoping an ice age would slow my mind.

"Honey bear, I know you're always busy with your new job, but I feel like we haven't talked in forever and you know how I worry. Anyway, I'm probably being silly, but give me a call when you can. If I don't hear from you soon I'm just going to make the drive. I'll bring you some iced brownies. So call me. Love you."

The screen changed during my morning wire review. I was tracking the flow of funds, blackheart Delta pumping out millions to its tributaries, when a deposit far above the standard amount jumped from Anson to Dr. Tikoshi. But the funds *never* moved that direction. So I checked who'd sent the money to Anson BioMed and saw a name: ROBERT LINSON.

*What? Who? Okay, this needs a screen print and then...* And then the screen refreshed and ROBERT LINSON was long gone, replaced by the name of another Delta arterial, Selpak Transfers Inc.

I grabbed my private notebook (now number thirteen in a series, the prior twelve sitting at home, the canon of conspiracy) and wrote ROBERT LINSON as fast as I could, before I lost the thought to a random blackout or some fresh panic. Our wire system was live, but not malleable from my office. There had to be a user code tied to the change, some way of identifying who had altered the sender data, but I didn't know how to access that information. *Call the proof office? Talk to someone in I.T.? Wouldn't I send up another red flag? And if the system was live, did the person on the other end know who had accessed the record? Was I meant to see this name, a way of throwing me off the trail? Or did I happen to catch the alteration by being here so early? Am I the early bird or the early worm? No, this means something. They're getting sloppy. I'll be the king soon.* I made it three hours into the standard workday before bailing for an imaginary dental appointment. As I backed out of the parking lot I spotted three cowboys watching me from a second floor window.

None smiled, none waved.

You type something like "government collusion in corporate pharmaceutical testing" into a standard search engine, you almost expect the screen to go blank followed by "PLEASE WAIT, SIR" flashing in bold, followed by a pinch on the neck as the needle goes in, followed by everyone wondering how you could have died so suddenly. So, even when using my undernet connection I hesitated while typing in the admittedly-less-ominous search term "Robert Linson." Still, I pressed Enter, then took a break to scrub the mildew smell from Deckard's tank. I'd added so many layers of encryption and established a multi-national path so convoluted that the response would take more than a few seconds to ping back. When my results finally arrived I first heard the sound of Deck splashing around in the fresh water end of his tank, followed by the high pressure wash of my heartbeat filling my ears, an insistent double-bass pedal flutter thump. Because the first result returned made everything make even less sense:

"Robert Matthew Linson, better known by the stage name Robbie Dawn, is an American musician, singer-songwriter, multi-instrumentalist, activist, and philanthropist. Although initially popular for his early work with boy band Mode 5, he is best known for his solo career, pioneering production methods, and his innovative music label SonsJeunes." Three pages of scrolling, and every linked result was Robbie Dawn, until I reached a smattering of Bob Linson pro-fishing videos, obituaries, social profiles, and corrupted partials.

"Fuck me, Deck—I've finally lost it. I've really lost it." *But what other Robert Linson would have six hundred thousand dollars to send to a physician? The pro-fishing guy wore the same pants in every video—it ain't him. No—"Robbie Dawn" has the stadium-filler money. This is real. It can't be, it makes no fucking sense...but it feels real, doesn't it? Are you sure you saw his name on that screen? Yesterday you tried to eat a granola bar with the wrapper still on. You're losing it. This is your brain on Hex. You saw Robbie Dawn on* The League of Zeroes *and now he's part of the puzzle. How convenient. Are you sure your mom isn't the secret head of Delta MedWorks? How long until Deckard is part of the conspiracy? You are fabricating false twists to cover the truth: This was the wrong path, you've reached the end, and there's nowhere else to go.*

But as long as there was more Hex, more action, there was always somewhere else to go. I would keep trickling down this hill until I joined the larger river. A vast power was waiting for me to join its forward surge.

The new rabbit hole was a blur of band bios, big booty back-up dancers, and progressively more absurd/expensive music videos. Chronological clips charting a young man's growth from a gangly pop pawn to a self-styled Svengali who felt comfortable saying things like, "The real key to the mastery of my art has been staying humble and staying hungry." I watched everything in order, looking for a reason, a way in—I hoped to witness his face changing shape, taking on a leonine tightness, some way to explain his payment to Dr. Tikoshi. It had to be reconstructive surgery on the sly. But no—all this motherfucker did was age natural (and I'll be damned if his wrinkles didn't add charm), make hits, buy custom cars, and date starlets. I mapped his touring and studio sessions and there were no large gaps or extended stays when he came through town. Watched some of his videos twice, partially hoping his back-up dancers could stir Crooked D from his damaged slumber and partially because these songs were produced in the way that makes you shell out for serious headphones or a twelve point surround. I turned the music up—the swirling drums took on new resonance. Turned it up again and my bones shook. The gray tendrils of Hex-vision swirled in the periphery. The upstairs neighbor expressed his dissenting opinion with a double stomp on his floor and a muffled but still audible, "Turn it down, motherfucker." I dropped the volume and smiled. Popped another Hex off the coffee table and drowned it with a mug of cold coffee. Something had changed. I could feel it. There was *something* here. Streetlight through the window called me delusional, forced its outside perspective. I closed the blinds.

You can tell when they're coming for you if you study their faces. They smile more than they used to. They agree emphatically with casual statements and laugh longer than they should. It's a hood made from synthetic interactions, and you'll belong right up until the noose is snugged into place. I knew that, and things *were* too goddamned jovial that Friday morning. I even received a pat on the back and a "Doyle, howyabeen?" from a cowboy I hadn't spoken to in months. That was a clear enough sign, but the Robbie Dawn/Tikoshi link had me in blinders and I was on the hunt for other entities which might front funds for the pop star. Then I received the email. The subject line was: "Quick Meeting in Conf. Room B?" The light tone and question mark—as if the meeting was just another fun choice I could make—said one thing:

I was fucked.

I hustled over to an empty office on the fourth floor and scanned the parking lot—two vehicles I hadn't seen before near the entrance, both shiny black with deep window tints and incongruously colored plates. Government vehicles? Local cops? Whose jurisdiction was I even under anymore? Could be the FBI, FDIC, Secret Service, DEA, hell, maybe even the Postal Inspector. Whoever they were with, I knew I was facing thirty years minimum. They could bury me deeper—it all depended on the breadth of their knowledge. With the volume of Hex stashed at my place, I could even envision a trafficking arrest. No reasonable jury would believe all of those pills were for me. I'd almost feel too embarrassed to convince them otherwise. My stomach pinged acid pain like a whole field of bleeding ulcers had erupted. I could hear my teeth grinding as my panicked breath fogged my view of the offending new vehicles. *You knew this was coming. Maybe they only want to ask you about the Foreign Transit Comp GL? Can you spin it? Say the funds were being moved to test security levels for our Bruxton 505 compliance? But where did that money go, Doyle? How will you explain the missing funds?*

Nope—FUCKED. On my way to a pig-roasting bunk party at maximum security overflow, teeth punched out, Aryan rape squads trying to see who can prolapse my colon first.

*What have I done?*

My peripheral vision shrunk to pinpoint, and I couldn't tell if it was a Hex fluctuation or consciousness fading fast. Then the low growl of a wolf came from behind me, a full-body electric shiver, the closest thing I had to the holy guidance of cherubim. The sound vibrated in my bones and cleared my vision, filling me with new purpose and animal exigency:

I was surrounded by hunters, and I would escape at any cost.

I moved through the building with a new kind of confidence. Having left myself without any acceptable choices, I decided to embrace the unacceptable and go all in. FUCK IT! WHY NOT?

That meant lighting a trash fire in the fourth floor bathroom, knowing that the sprinklers would kick in shortly and the full-building evacuation would override whatever today's proceedings were to have been.

That meant a final jaunt to my office, head down, walking fast—I copped my last private, hand-written notebook and connected a nasty, virus-riddled USB stick to my laptop.

Granted permission for baboon-fucker.exe to run and hoped
to scorch enough of my trail to slow their realizations.

That meant throwing open the door to Conference Room B
and only hearing, "Hello, Mr. Doyle. Thank you..." before
my thumb depressed the trigger on my canister of Hi-Pepper
Bear Spray, coating the tiny room in blinding, breath-sucking
mist. Four occupants instantly dropped: my boss, his boss,
and two younger men in cheap suits. I caught a glimpse of
handcuffs flopping from the jacket of Cheap Suit #1, figured
that meant pistols within reach. I didn't wait to find out why
they wanted to thank me.

My final Fire-Day Friday—flashing red lights and an alarm
system blaring at Attention Must Be Paid decibel levels. I
had reached the lobby by the time the expando-foam started
slushing from suppression sprinklers. I regretted that they
weren't still on a water system, as that would have destroyed
more of my office contents. I hit the parking lot, squinted,
saw Delores getting out of her car, her arms full of pizza boxes.
She saw me and flinched. I realized I was smiling, then, a
full cat-got-the-canary grin, but I didn't know I was bleeding
from both nostrils until I reached my car. The Hex-speed was
saving my life/the Hex-speed was killing me. I checked the
rearview—my eyes were sparkling.

The key, I knew, was to maintain momentum. Powder to the gums. A fist full of lemony chemical dash wipes to staunch the nose bleed. A final stash run before the bank found the wherewithal to freeze funds across my network. Five hours before the branches closed for the weekend. Car engine humming in sync with the growls of my cherubim wolf. Killed the air-conditioning because it sounded like helicopter traffic. Stay ahead. Stay ahead. Shut down the crazy eyes. Come into each branch reserved, confident. Maybe smelling a little like pepper spray and flame retardant, but not in a way they can pin down. Cash withdrawal for Martin S. Peppermill/Trevor Bainbridge please. Apologize to the manager for requesting such a large amount without advance notice. A mix of hundreds and twenties would be fine. Thank you so much! Have a wonderful weekend! It's supposed to be sunny, you know? About time, right? Thanks again. Thanks so much.

Green car was in the rearview again, and then it was gone. Pulled a Robert Linson on me. *Were they waiting for this? They want the full case. All the money. The whole stash. They've got a device reading my cash—RFID's, security strips, radioactive paints…something.* I decided to leave two pick-up runs off my route: a few grand in Trevor Bainbridge's name at Community Central, and the entire Maria Scharf account. Besides, the latter was too far away and my lipstick and scarf were at home. Maybe they'd wait until I'd collected all their money before they tried to arrest me. Could I buy time by keeping the Scharf money buried? Green car re-appeared in the rearview, a hazy oasis shimmer on vibrating glass. Green car disappeared again. A drop of blood fell from my nose to my pants. Good. I fucking hated khakis anyway.

The briefest moment of reflection: *Are you sure they were there to arrest you today? What if the Feds were on the Delta MedWorks case too and looking for you to collude? Did you just commit arson, destroy bank property, and assault two bank officers and two agents under false pretense? If they weren't on to you before, that was a grand way to announce your suspect status. And how did that even work, anyway? You think your magic pills turned you into fucking James Bond? Did that even happen? How do you know you're not passed out somewhere, overdosing?*

No answers. The injection of reason was quickly replaced by two more questions:

*Are they already at my apartment?*

And

*What about Deckard?*

I convinced myself it had to be done, hoping that I'd thrown things into such chaos back at the bank that they were still reeling. There was no option but to raid my house on a rescue mission: grab Deckard/grab the Hex stash/grab the data drive containing the distillation of my hard copy conspiracy maps. Use part of my ill-gotten gains to buy my way underground via Port and Egbert. Finalize the Delta case and find the right buyer for the information. *That was always the plan, right? Wait, was that really my plan?* Sirens wailed in the distance, which was always the case as I approached home and the glories of 45th. But the day possessed an awful new possibility—those sirens could be for me. I parked on a side street to avoid being trapped in my parking garage. Grabbed the black plastic garbage bag of stolen cash from my trunk and flung it over my shoulder like Sketchy Santa. Took two of the deepest breaths I could, slammed shut the trunk, and decided the rescue mission was a Go.

I only used Deckard's travel enclosure for trips to visit my mom, and it was tight quarters. I was sure he hated it. I apologized, kissed the back of his head, and placed him inside. "Sorry. I'll grab you some water and an extra worm." Pocketed his dry food. Shifted my garbage bag funds over to a new tan sports duffel, packed to brimming. Filled a backpack with my Hex bundle, a fist-sized hard drive containing the core of my Delta findings, two pairs of boxer shorts, and a couple of t-shirts. Ditched the chemical-doused, blood-spattered work shirt for a gray tee and a black hoodie, replaced the khakis with jeans. Snugged a baseball cap low on my head and caught a vision of myself in the mirror: I'd expected Mission Impossible but was instead startled to see an emaciated tweeker was robbing my place. I waved. He waved back. Christ. I remembered the green car on my trail, hit the kitchen and rifled my utensil drawer for the biggest knife I owned. Ice-hardened eight inch blade. Worked great on lettuce—as long as I was only attacked by salads I'd be fine. Tucked it into the side pocket of my backpack and a cardboard sheath kept it from cutting through. One more frantic scan of the place. Half second's consideration: *Do I grab Big Booty Vol. 3?* Wolf at low growl, warm breath on my left ear. Odd confidence fighting confusion for mental space.

*How was I still free?*

"Cover your ears, Deck. Tuck in." I grabbed a hammer from the top of the fridge and did my best to decimate the undernet system in the living room. Grabbed a few pieces of the main drive to throw in the sewer. They'd find some of what I was working on, but not the whole picture. I contemplated lighting a fire for a moment, but this building was so old and under-maintained—I couldn't stomach the idea of all those low income families and worker drones gone barbecue. My hammer job would have to suffice. Felt fresh blood pool at the base of my nose. Tightened my backpack straps, grabbed the cash duffel and Deckard, and waved a final goodbye to the place where I'd pretended to live.

The car died two blocks after my turn onto 45th. Maybe my cash-grab speed run had finally broken the engine. Maybe a man in a green car had decided I'd be easier to track on foot and cut the fuel line. I wouldn't have smelled the gasoline through the blood and thick new coat of powdered Hex. Regardless, I had suddenly become a worldly possession-toting refugee—still in Kept Squad territory with enough pills to guarantee my immediate murder if caught—and there was no choice but to keep moving forward. The momentum had brought me this far. The Hex refresher had reset my system to one hundred percent confidence. And I hoped maybe the turtle would give me an extra crazy sheen: *Oh, man…Don't fuck with that turtle guy! He's out of his mind!* Confidence was not the same thing as reason.

I can't emphasize enough the sensation of being propelled forward by some benevolent force, that my righteousness had created a shining path. Perhaps that's how a pawn feels when moved forward by a self-assured chess player.

I cleared the Kept Squad blocks at a near jog, my left shoulder stressed from trying to keep Deckard's travel case steady. Regretted not having purchased a gun—*What has two thumbs and throws itself headfirst into corporate conspiracy without first buying a single firearm? This fucking guy. But I'm packing a red-eared slider turtle with a vicious hiss and a kitchen knife which struggles to slice steak fat…*Contemplated a way to brandish the knife without looking like a guy running down the street with a knife, a turtle, a duffel on my chest, and a backpack on my back. Nope—that was the best of my bad options. I stopped to reconfigure my travel set-up and the world pretty much exploded.

First: A shot to the kidneys and I dropped. Then I was dragged back up to my feet and pulled into an alley to my right. I heard my knife fall to the street. Saw Deckard and the duffel sitting exposed. Fists the size of my head wrapped around my backpack straps and hoodie, dragging me upright. I brought my hands up to protect my face from the pummeling that was about to commence. *This is how it all ends—everything you worked for stolen by some tweeker in a back alley. They'll probably turn Deck into soup or use him for a baseball. Will anyone even find your body?*

The grip on my shirt tightened. Hot, sour breath rolled across my face. Then a familiar voice, tainted by fear, shaking, "Is it still out there?"

"Egbert?"

"Shhh. Shhh. Quiet, motherfucker. It's out there."

"What's…"

"The thing, D. The thing got Port. Took a bullet and still got him."

"Wait, what?"

"Same thing that got Hungo. *Has to be.* Cracked Port's head open on the sidewalk and hunched over and started… just…slurping."

"You're not making any sense. Listen, I need to grab those bags…"

"You don't need shit, motherfucker. You brought this down on us. I told Port from the beginning—bad news."

Egbert's left fist tightened its grip and he slammed me against the bricks to ensure compliance. Whatever air I was holding rushed from my chest, left me straining to breathe. Egbert's right hand reached for the machete sheathed on his back. His all-black eyes fixed on mine for a moment and then his gaze went beyond and I realized he'd decided I was a plague rat to be destroyed.

"You must have brought this thing. *It said your fucking*

*name.* So I'm going to give it what it wants."

Egbert raised his Right of Refusal to the sky.

Then: Three loud cracks in sequence, and Egbert's machete-wielding hand disappeared, followed in short order by the front of his face, followed by a final blast which took off the back of his head. All that remained of Egbert's once sizeable skull was a fractured protrusion—one ear still attached, a cross-section of tattered brain exposed—and his considerable jaw. His beard was a mop of blood, his barely tethered tongue lolling above. His left hand hadn't forfeited its grip on me and the mass of his collapsing body dragged us down. My body landed on top of his and I watched his tongue flop back into the cavern where his face had been, and then, I swear, the force of my weight on his chest pushed a final breath from his lungs and his tongue flapped and flailed like a goddamn blowout noisemaker at a kid's party.

Then: I laughed. Because how else do you process something like that?

Then: "Alright, Doyle, on your feet."

And the man approached me and I heard the growl of a wolf grow louder and then I saw my savior. He looked like any other cowboy from my bank—pricey dress shirt, black slacks, slight paunch, gray at the temples. He had some kind of gun in his right hand, made from a burnished yellow plastic, blue smoke still oozing from the barrel. From the way Egbert's head had segmented I guessed this was not standard ordnance. I knew better than to question the man. The response would be a variation on their central theme—"Who are you to ask?" I felt certain that this man had been the one following me, that his purposefully nondescript green car was parked somewhere very near to my abandoned vehicle. He raised his gun and pointed it at me as I exited the alley, approaching my duffel and Deckard's enclosure.

"Leave the turtle, shitbird. Grab the bag." He glanced down quickly, referencing something on his phone. "Looks like there are still about eighty-two thousand in funds that we need to recover. You're going to help me with that before we deal with your corollary accountabilities."

He sounded like a banker, burying murder under jargon. I hoped I could appeal to his inherent greed.

"There's way more than eighty-two in that bag. Maybe you grab the duffel and I grab the turtle and you tell the boys back home that I've been dealt with. I'll hide deep. I swear. I'll leave the country and…"

"Kill it, Doyle. You shut your fucking mouth. You think it's just about the money? No way, pal, not anymore. We know about the research. Your attempts to inhibit our business relationships. And beyond that, there are four deaths which must be accounted for."

"Deaths? What deaths?"

Standing still, spinning.

"You didn't hear the news? Two prominent bankers and two federal agents died today. Some kind of chemical attack floored them and they didn't escape the fire which claimed the building. Agent Torres had asthma, so they're guessing he died before the fire even reached him. The rest probably burned alive. It's all over the news—you're a domestic terrorist. The media might be outside of your apartment by now. Do you wonder what they'll find? I don't. You come with me, we set things straight, maybe we can cut them off before your poor mother turns on the TV and finds out her son is a cross-dressing, porn-addicted, pill-popping terrorist."

"You're bluffing. I saw the sprinkler system turn on. I only started a tiny fire."

"Do you remember who financed our corporate center?"

Shit. Our own commercial division. They hired shifty, itinerant contractors, pocketed nebulous supply costs, and ran every project as cheap as they could. That sprinkler system could have been pumping out Mr. Bubbles for all I knew.

"I'm growing impatient. I've been authorized to close out this endeavor as I see fit. You can come with me now, or I can leave by myself. But think of your mother—the media circus, all those unanswered questions, nothing left of you to place in a coffin…"

My head swirled. I snorted back fresh blood and crusted Hex. I believed the man was willing to call it a day and vaporize me like Egbert's head—eighty-two grand was a pittance as a write off, and even if I'd really murdered those people, there's no way they actually wanted to take me to trial and risk my ideas entering the public record.

I raised my hands and stepped slowly toward the bag of cash.

Part of me—some selfish bastard part that didn't mind dying—always knew this was a potential endgame. But I pictured Deck starving without me, waiting in his enclosure for someone to come along and smash his shell out of dull curiosity. And I thought of my mother, the sad monologue she'd left on my voicemail as our final interaction, the way the stress of the media coverage would speed her decline from Pelton-Reyes and leave her ostracized in her conservative community, the way the vultures would perch in her yard and speculate and ensure they found the worst archival photo of me to let their viewers know I was a batshit crazy threat from birth and that my mother had failed in her duty to create a good citizen and…

Then: The sound of a starving animal attacking a carcass came from the alley behind me, low grunts and deep inhales and crunching bone.

*"You brought this thing."*

I twisted enough to catch the alley in my peripheral: a massive shape was hunched over Egbert's blasted leftovers, its face nuzzled deep into what remained of the dead dealer's head.

"Enough stalling, Doyle. Grab the goddamned bag."

"I'm not stalling. There's…"

The thing heard us; its head snapped to attention, and just as quickly it was running toward me.

*"Doyle!"* Its voice was so low it approached subsonic—I felt the rumble of my name in my chest.

It turns out that the body can automatically recalibrate to a new threat response. Mine instantly decided that Being Shot in the Face was a far better death than Being Eaten Alive by a Creature Which Knows My Name. I bolted in the direction of my bank's hired gun and the only real thought in my head was, "NO!"

I made it three strides before the thing had me in its hands. Too fast. Too strong. Its grip like a steel clamp on each side of my ribs until I heard a snap and felt something give on the right side of my chest. I was lifted off my feet. I felt the heat of the thing's breath ruffle my hair and the smell of decayed meat engulfed me. Then the sound of more bones popping, but no new pain bloomed in my ribs and I realized the sound was coming from the thing's mouth. I pictured the jaws of the creature unlocking, extending out to strip away the candy coating of my scalp.

I felt a massive row of flat teeth latching in above the base of my neck and the warmth of a tongue against my head like a pulsing microwaved steak and then—barely perceptible over the interior static of my mind being aware it was about to be eaten and swallowed—there was the sound of gunfire. The thing spun and threw my body to the street and everything was meat/electricity/smoke and bellowing and the wet sensation of the thing's saliva soaking my scalp.

Then: A vision. Couldn't be real. Had to be the combination of Hex and exhaustion and the raw pain of my cracked rib. Because the thing I'd been certain was a massive beast was wearing sweatpants and an oversized hoodie and a pair of tan work boots, and he was staring in shock at the stump of his left arm, missing from the elbow down. I rolled further away, certain with each rotation that something in my chest was about to puncture and deflate my lungs. When I looked again the thing was in mid-air, its overlong remaining arm outstretched, its power pole legs extended for first impact with his assailant's torso. Then the thud of bodies colliding, the cracking/clacking sound of the bank's assassin dropping his weapon as the thing snapped his wrist, the sound of joints popping as the thing's lower jaw opened to engulf the man's head. The thing pushed its brick-sized chin into the man's mouth, splitting my would-be-murderer's face open with crowbar efficiency, then it locked in its upper row of teeth along the man's forehead. The creature's maw was huge and thick and gleaming wet in the streetlight, and with one straining bite, jaw muscles pulsing like knotted rope, it collapsed the front of the man's face.

This did not stop the man from screaming through the final vestiges of his mouth. That sound was mercifully cut short as the thing crunched its fist into its prey's trachea.

I turned to crawl toward my bags, but the sensation of taking my eyes off the thing was repellent, like turning your back on a suddenly visible great white shark while out swimming. I pushed my body backwards with my arms and stayed low and tried to keep from crying out when my busted rib cage told me to stop and wait for the ambulance.

But this was 45th. Zero ambulances were forthcoming, and I didn't know how long this thing would be preoccupied with its smashed cowboy leftovers.

The thing lifted the man's head from the asphalt and then slammed it back down with two hard, sharp blows. It was clear from the sound that the man's skull had gone shattered eggshell. The thing laughed, pleased by the ease of access, and bent to eat.

Then: I reverse belly-crawled to my gear with all the grace and speed of a crushed armadillo, wondering at how death had come for me in the guise of some jacked-up mutant-mouthed Popeye-jawed gorilla-armed man-thing.

Honestly, part of me was really glad I wouldn't have to go to jail.

My right foot landed on something—the duffel. I chanced a quick look back and found my backpack and Deck's carrier. But that's it. *Where was my supposedly lethal Hi-Pepper Bear Spray now? Wasted in my fuck-it-up frenzy at the bank. My knife? Nowhere, flung to the street when Egbert grabbed me. No, it couldn't have gone too far...*

I rolled to my right to check my radius for the knife, and despite bracing myself with my arm, my chest lit up like wildfire.

If you've ever felt a pain like that then you know holding in a yell isn't some macho choice you can make. My scream was an autonomic pain vent, a short but very loud, "AAAAH!" that exploded from my mouth, followed by a wave of instant regret as I saw the thing across the street snap-to from its mind-munching reverie.

It rose from its hunched position over the corpse, standing about seven feet tall. Nowhere near the size of the Sasquatch I'd imagined when it had first grabbed me, but its frame was thick and over-muscled. Its neck and jaw pulsed and shifted in the streetlight in ways I told myself were only imagined, but even twenty feet away I could hear bones moving and locking in to place, the synovial pops of a structure under duress.

The thing walked toward me. I hoped that it was slow and sated, but also guessed it had assessed me as a limited flight risk. I rotated my head to the left and scanned for my knife to no avail other than the added benefit of sending another pain-shock through my chest.

*Was this all a dream? The bank assassin killed Egbert, this thing killed the assassin, and maybe a T-Rex was about to stomp down 45th and make a snack out of the brain-eater...*

"*Doyle, you dumb motherfucker.*" Oh, god, that voice. Distorted and low from moving through a wind-tunnel of a voice box. And happy. The thing was happy. I wouldn't lift my face to see its smile, that joyful blasted planet of a face with blood on its chin.

*It's talking. Maybe you can reason with it. Maybe it wants the money.*

"You're looking at our bag of money? We'll be taking that. You have nothing for us. *You bent-dick cocksucker!*" The thing gave an Etch A Sketch shake to its head, disturbed by its own outburst. "Some of us don't know we're dead yet. The anger stays at the surface."

What? The thing's inflections had changed with each sentence, its voice shifting oddly, at first malevolent and then too bright and lucid for the monstrous shape from which it emerged. I imagined producing any speech from that contorting cavern of a mouth to require deep focus.

"Your files are of use. The banker thinks you knew more than they could extrapolate from the security footage. *You pushed me, faggot! I'm going to slice off your turtle's legs and slap him around with a hockey...*QUIET." It took a deep breath. "You're not a popular guy around here."

I looked up at the thing. Its meaty forehead was scrunched with effort over its too-close eyes. Most of its face was mouth, and it barely had enough skin to cover the tips of its huge, thick teeth. It took another breath and the exhale brought waves of dumpster meat heat. It raised its left arm and surprised itself when no soothing hand landed on its forehead. The stump of its blasted limb was sealed with a gray/black crust.

"Oh. Shit." It waved the stump in the air while shaking its head. "Doc's gonna have to fix this up. But first things first: Does anyone else have a copy of your files? Have you been in contact with the media?"

Damn—I'd approached this whole debacle in Lone Wolf terms. *Note to Self: If ever again embroiled in conspiracy, please buy a gun and establish life-sustaining fail-safes.* For now all I had were more lies.

"Of course. The moment my name hits the obituaries my contact at the Post will be releasing a copy of my files to a number of interested parties. And there's a safe deposit box accessible only to my lawyer."

"*Bullshit. If you'd done any of that they'd have had me solve this problem at the first hint of an outside leak...* QUIET!" The thing's eyes rolled back in its head and it took two more breaths of deep exertion. The "QUIET" had the distinct sound of a stern schoolteacher silencing a room of rowdies. The thing continued. "We don't care anymore. We believe the only people who'd heard your story are within us now."

Who had heard my story? Port and Egbert? And I'd only told them parts.

The thing's eyes rolled back in its head for a moment. Then it smiled again, lips curling back off blood-stained enamel. "No. You are lying. The time for formalities is over. We will know the truth once you have joined us. There's room now." The thing's remaining hand absentmindedly rubbed its belly. A rivulet of red-tainted drool ran from the corner of its mouth.

I backed away. The thing walked toward me, one long arm swinging in its lope. A smile broke across its semi-simian face. This thing loved feeding time.

I wanted to say goodbye to Deckard but my tongue was frozen by my mind's thrumming NONONONONO and I realized that the paralysis felt in nightmares is a premonition of how you feel the moment you're about to die and then the thing was hunched with its good arm to the ground like a gorilla before leaping and I slid back and my fingers found something cold and metal behind me and then the thing was on me, so heavy, so strong, and without a thought outside dumb animal survival I was closing my eyes and swinging whatever I'd found toward the beast, and then my chest was pelted with wetness and warmth and I opened my eyes and saw the hilt of my steel kitchen knife twitching with each pulse of black blood that coursed around the blade in the creature's neck.

And at last, somehow: The sound of a wounded beast's bellowing filled the night, soon joined by the sound of my voice crying out as I willed my broken body—to roll away from the infuriated creature, to find all I had left in the world, to gather it and to escape. After that all I can remember is the sound of footfalls echoing through the cold tenement night, each one falling faster and faster, as if, through sheer exertion, they could catch up to my mind, long gone.

# ACT II
# ATTACHMENT

# CHAPTER 6

# Gullet Amplifiers

The day had started with a barrel of coffee, ritual pill popping, and bone-deep anxiety. The day ended in a terror-induced sprint away from the street where death tried to claim me three times over.

I mistakenly believed that my life had finally reached the peak of Crazy Bullshit Mountain.

Hindsight would indicate I'd only just made it to base camp.

I finally stopped running when the pain managed to override the fear and adrenaline. Whatever I had left in my gut made its splashing exit, a puddle of bile on cold concrete. I gingerly touched my busted torso with my free hand and wondered if all the running had allowed my smashed rib to saw open something inside.

Deckard hissed from his enclosure and I couldn't find the breath to apologize. Instead I kept walking.

*Toward where?*

I was certain I'd be jumped for my loot until I caught my reflection in a window: shell-shocked, blood-spattered, hair matted by a crust of dried spittle, my backpack and duffel and plastic carrying case as seemingly random accessories.

*You look homeless.*

I am.

*You look crazy.*

I am.

I'd become an invisible, too low for the lowest to rob, too crazy for the crazies to bother, a shambling object lesson response to all those "FUCK IT! WHY NOT?'s."

I limped down back streets just north of 45th, staying to the dark, thin membrane of territory which separated our workaday citizens from the scrappers on the other side of the tracks. Dawn approached. The harsh morning light brought three realizations:

1. Having my paranoia confirmed delivered not comfort, but the deeper terror of knowing that most things would remain beyond my understanding right up until the moment they killed me.

2. I was probably dying. Everything hurt. I couldn't remember what I'd last eaten or when I'd had water. I might be bleeding inside.

3. It was morbidly depressing to realize I was already jonesing for more Hex—even imminent death by machete/yellow pistol/brain-eating would not scare me straight.

At the merest thought of the pills, the chorus of justification began their sweet song: *Even if you wanted to detox, in this state the withdrawals would probably kill you. No, better to ride this out. Besides, the Hex only did what you wanted. Made you sharper. Put you on the trail. You found something real, something they're willing to kill you to hide. You can collate your evidence and sell it. Just a few more pills to get you through to shelter. Might be the only thing to keep you from going into shock. Might make the pain fade.*

And with that, the volume of the chorus clouded the last remnants of reason and doubt, and I was alley-bound. Then I was hunched, groaning, hiding, ignoring the drip of dark blood which fell from my nose and spattered on the pavement, ignoring the ever-ripening smell of my spit-soaked cranium, hoping that this could be a right thing, and my hands found the stash and there were four pills and that was a good start and the morning light shone bright silver.

This would save me.

I waited for the moaning audio vortex of the come-up, the confidence and propulsion, a return to the profligate power which had carried me through the storm of the last twenty-four hours, but instead I found only PAIN, sudden and crushing. A vice grip to the temples, my eyes being pushed out from behind, my chest a foundry fire, my buck eighty machine gun pulse wracking my ribs. Too many pills. *Fuck.*

And then the sounds came, as a flood, from behind my left shoulder—The black wolf's growl, never closer than that moment, furious but changing, rolling suddenly into a pained bark, a drowning cough, a wet splash, and then something massive was screaming, the sound like piston pressure knocking me flat, driving me blind, pulling me from my body in the alley to a tiny space somewhere inside my mind. There I was surrounded by a seething black ocean of consumption, only and always hunger, and I curled further into the shell of my consciousness, wanting, somehow, to pull the pills from my stomach and wake, to escape the rushing fluid around me as it wailed and surged and ruined all it touched. This place was worse than a vacuum or any simple absence. It was atrocity on loop, a space outside the laws of light and the time it brings, and whatever I was diminished until I only knew I existed because I could feel myself falling backwards, and the further I fell, the smaller I became, and the last vestiges of protection shattered and washed away, replaced by the dead black weight of that place, reason lost to the pain of being crushed into always-less and before thought disappeared beneath a squall of suffering I realized this would be all I'd ever know, and that I was being swallowed whole, forever.

# CHAPTER 7

# Signal Attenuation

"You shouldn't have brought him here."

"Really? Wait till you see what he's got with him. Trust me—we're lucky I grabbed this guy before the ambulances got there."

"I don't care. Look at his nose. He's still bleeding. He's connected. *They can hear...*"

"Nope. C'mon. Check out his eyes."

"Oh...Jesus! They're gonna jelly if he stays hooked in much longer."

"Yeah. I mean, he could be all the way subsumed, but I thought it was worth a shot. Besides, check this out."

"A turtle? You brought his pet turtle. That's really fucking helpful."

"No, not that case. Give me a sec...Okay, look in *this* bag."

"Is that for real?"

"Does that even matter? If it's counterfeit we can sell it to..."

"Kill it! Let me put some earplugs on this guy."

"Don't worry. I'm telling you, he's fried past the point of

transmitting. He's in their realm right now, the poor fuck. Besides, how do you know they couldn't still hear us through the vibrations on the hairs on the back of his hand, or his skin or something? We've been making assumptions."

"Can I assume you already ran a blocker?"

"Hundred fifty milligrams, right when I found him. He's so speedy I could barely get a vein to pop. I was thinking I'd have to resort to a rectal dose right before I got a thirty-one gauge to slide in by his clavicle."

"Rectal dose would have been a waste with him this far gone, anyways."

"I know…if I wasn't trying to save him then I would have felt weird grabbing all his stuff. I'm not a vulture."

"If he dies here, though, you'll keep his shit?"

"I mean, that's enough money to keep us going for a *long* time."

"And the turtle?"

"I don't know. Penance? Always wanted a pet."

"Sure. But how about instead of penance, we just pull this guy through? We bring him back from their side, he might not even care about that money anymore."

"Right?"

"Right."

"You think it's too soon for more perphenadol?"

"Not if we slow drip it and give him an ice bath."

"Sounds good. After that?"

"Maybe we scan the other bag, count that money, and wait to see if this guy is ever coming back from the big black."

"Hey!"

"What'd you find?"

"Check it."

"Damn. That's just... that's officially too much Hex."

"More at the bottom of the backpack, too. Looks like he ripped the bag open to get at his last fix. Who knows how many he took?"

"Maybe he's a dealer who didn't pay attention at orientation?"

"Can't be. Check his hands—that's a full set of fingers. None of the other marks, either, and I think our dealer database is current. Besides, habit like this, they would have culled him a long time ago."

"Then how the hell did he get that kind of supply?"

"Well, bags of money have certain capabilities."

"No. I mean, they'd give it away free if it weren't for the connection rites. There's got to be something else. Whatever this guy was doing, they needed him in their sphere of influence. They wanted a non-stop feed."

"Speaking of, he started showing signs of regular REM like ten minutes ago."

"Told you. One more round of perphenadol, a fluid push, and if he's still breathing tomorrow morning we bring in Ms. A. and cut those fuckers off."

"You think he's still in there?"

"I hope. I don't think they could send a mimic signal with this much blocker in his system. Besides, if they were running the body, why would they force it into an O.D.?"

"Shit. Well...would it be paranoia to say maybe they wanted us to take him in? Like they're on to us..."

"No, if they were on to us they'd send some Vakhtang goon. Or maybe they'd rig him or his turtle with a cell bomb, in which case we'd both be mushed, because they'd blow *that* before the perphenadol kicked in."

"Right?"

"Right. So, we'll keep pulling for this guy and maybe tomorrow he can answer some questions. Did you crack his hard drive yet?"

"Maybe twenty more minutes and I think we'll have something."

"Alright. That's enough time to take care of *this* shit."

"Okay. I'm with you. I'll grab the rest of the pills from his bag and meet you out at the barrel."

"No!"

"Whoa."

"I'm sorry. I didn't mean to yell. I just…No, we need to stay dual custody with the stash until it's gone. It's kind of talking to me right now."

"Goddamn. Okay, I'm glad you said it. I was thinking about pocketing one from his bag. Seriously. After everything else, still…"

"It's not your fault. Shit's persuasive. Must be some part of the connection rites hanging on. We'll have Ms. A. check us out tomorrow, make sure we're at full break."

"Okay."

"Right now, let's burn this batch before we convince each other to make an awful mistake."

"Agreed. We should drag the burn barrel to the back of the building first, run it through the exhaust fan filters. That much Hex smoke might send out a creeper signal if we take it to the alley."

"Let's do it."

"That's the last handful."

"You're sure."

"One hundred percent. I can already feel the itch disappearing from my shoulder."

"Shit. I can smell it through the mask."

"Yeah. I can smell it too. Filters should be working, though."

"What's it smell like to you?"

"The crash. Hot metal, gasoline…Marco…"

"Burning?"

"Yeah…Yup…"

"…"

"What do you smell?"

"My sister's campfire accident, when we were kids. We were twenty miles out from the hospital. That's how she lost her arm."

"Christ."

"Weird thing is, it doesn't smell like the fire, or her arm. It smells like her breath, when she was crying, before she went into shock. My mom held her in the back seat and they had her arm wrapped in a wet towel. I sat next to them, tried to help hold her still so she wouldn't hurt herself any worse, and she kept crying and yelling with this big open mouth and I remember her breath had this warm electric smell, like she was screaming the life out of her body."

"I don't want to stand here anymore."

"Me either. You want to risk leaving before it's all ash?"

"Nope."

"Me either."

"You notice the smoke, too?"

"The spiral? Yeah. Trying to ignore it, though."

"But you can't ignore it, and they know that."

"Right?"

"Right. Those fuckers."

"They ruin everything."

"BP and respiration are borderline normal. Pulse is *way* lower. He's definitely hanging in there."

"I guess next thing we have to address is that smell."

"Ladies love my natural musk."

"Yeah, yeah, cute. But you know what I mean. Ms. A.'s going to want him clean for the sacraments anyway."

"I'll help you rotate and lift him, but I'm not doing the sponge part."

"Tell you what—you wash his hair and I'll cover the rest."

"I don't know. His head smells like a fucking slaughterhouse mop, and I'll probably have to clean it three or four times to get that crust out. How about you do the whole guy and I'll take care of his turtle?"

"What?"

"Turtle needs some fresh water and I have to figure out how to get it to eat those weird little food flakes. And then I can take a look at what's on his hard drive."

"That seems comparable to a Hex coma sponge bath to you?"

"Are you forgetting I cleaned up the last rescue? And that she was a repeat voider?"

"Okay. No. That's true."

"Plus, when I clean the guys, sometimes they pop a flagpole."

"Must be your natural musk."

"Haha. I mean, I know it's autonomic or whatever, but it just makes me feel like I'm up to something with their body."

"But you're not. You're helping them. It's a loving act."

"Turtle needs a loving act, too, and I won't feel like a creepy orderly."

"This is your issue, much more than it is anyone else's. Unless, you know, you're secretly sitting on those flagpoles, wearing an adult diaper on your head, and posting pictures of that to the internet."

"That's a negative, and fuck you, asshole."

"What?"

"…"

"That was really abrupt."

"Yeah. I…uh…sorry. I feel off. I don't think those gas masks are quite equipped to deal with Hex smoke."

"Okay, let's chill out, then. I'll make some tea. We'll say nothing for the next hour, just in case we inhaled something."

"Tea it is. And we feed the turtle."

"Alright, I'm done reading it."

"And? He's crazy, right?"

"I don't know. It's hard for me to discount anything as crazy anymore…"

"But?"

"But this guy seems fucking bonkers. The state we found him in, I'm seeing this more as mental illness. Too much Hex for too long. Some of their chaos slipped right through."

"What about the bruising on his chest? That's starting to look like a handprint to me."

"Really? And exactly who would have a hand that size? You think this guy found some bank secrets and they decided to have a Kodiak bear take him out? Come on."

"All I'm saying is, it could be the bruising is deepest where his ribs were compressed. Could be the bank has a couple of giant motherfuckers on staff."

"What about all the medical stuff in there?"

"There's never been any link between Delta and the Hex trade. MyGenix, sure. Abett, probably. But they're both Canadian. Delta's Canadian arm doesn't have any tie to them."

"Yeah, but Hungarian Minor *was* a 5th Shelter Vakhtang. And he was on the Delta payroll."

"Only according to Captain Overdose over there."

"Sure, the source is questionable, but those transfer records are pretty clear, and Hungo was about as squirrely as any Vakhtang out there. If they needed bodies…"

"True. He might have done it for kicks."

"Plus, the missing brain thing never sat right with me. If Hungo violated Vakhtang code they would have spilled his guts and read his secrets. *And* they left his tongue. *It didn't match up.*"

"Shit."

"Exactly—something is off here. Then there's the weird bruising at the base of this guy's skull, and the fact that he appears to have his possessions with him, including all that money."

"Yeah, the money kind of kills the roaming homeless madman theory. He was so close to 45th when I found him, it was a miracle he had anything."

"So maybe he's not crazy."

"Oh, I'm not saying that. I mean, the Robbie Dawn stuff… *come fucking on.*"

"Late-stage Hex dementia?"

"You add up the mess of a man, his turtle, and the massive quantities of Hex and money and there's only one thing you've got for sure—deep fucking trouble."

"Right?"

"Right."

"Christ…I don't know. I'm exhausted. Let's get a couple of hours' sleep before Ms. A. arrives."

"Should we put sleeping beauty in restraints?"

"Yeah. Post-haste."

"Sister. Brother. We must begin immediately. His connection to their realm is so strong I could see its haze above your building. And if I could see it…"

"Yes, Ms. A. We understand."

"Thank you for cleaning the body. I see the first sacrament has been applied."

"Speaking of which, Ms. A., we're running fucking scary low on perphenado—OW!"

"What he means to say is that this man required most of our supply of the first sacrament, and we will need more if we are to continue our rescues."

"Thank you, sister—I will see to it that your outpost receives a package."

"Thank you. And I'm sorry to interrupt the proceedings, but we also had another concern. Since this man arrived, and since we destroyed his supply of the dark signal, we've noticed certain urges and feelings, and we're concerned that our own lights have suffered some corruption."

"Hold still for a moment and I will put hands to each of you."

"…"

"…"

"Sister and Brother, I am afraid that particular darkness is your own. Now, we must begin. Please remove your robes and stand at the head of the table."

"Yes, Ms. A."

"Now, each of you open your boxes, breathe light into your scarabs, and set them upon our brother's eyes."

"BY SMOKE FROM LIPS BY LIGHT FROM BLOOD BY THOUGHT FROM THOUGHT ALONE WE CALL YOU BACK. BY SMOKE FROM LIPS BY LIGHT FROM BLOOD BY THOUGHT FROM THOUGHT ALONE WE CLOSE THIS GATE AS STONE. BY SMOKE FROM LIPS BY LIGHT FROM BLOOD BY THOUGHT FROM THOUGHT ALONE WE CALL YOU BACK."

"Do you believe he'll return to his body, Ms. A.?"

"What I believe makes no difference. We've done what can be done. Their signal was as strong as I've seen it since the camp collapse ten years back."

"There's something else?"

"You can see it in my face, I suppose. You've always been the most attuned at this outpost."

"Thank you."

"You'd thank me for your burden? Haven't you found that

your perceptiveness makes all suffering seem more awful?"

"Well…I…yes, I suppose you're right. I just want to do well by our mission."

"You have, sister. You have."

"Will you tell me what is troubling you?"

"Yes. I think I recognize that man on the table, that he is a thief and a junkie and a murderer with close ties to the Vakhtang, that his name is S.P. Doyle, and that his presence here may bring great danger."

"You saw all this in his connection to their realm?"

"No—I saw this on last night's news. Based on that report, I would recommend that you keep him in those restraints until we know the rites were successful. Beyond that, if you confirm that this is indeed Mr. Doyle, you may want to ask him how he managed to crush the heads of four men, and what he might have done with their brains."

"You should be more formal with Ms. A."

"Like wear a tux and speak only in high elvish or something?"

"You know what I'm saying. We're supposed to speak to her with reverence, not act casual and drop f-bombs."

"Why? So she can have power over us? I thought power was off the worship list. Aren't we all light here?"

"No, it's not for power. She says language is a reflection of order from the chaos of thought."

"Hey, I was super tired. And you'll notice I had no trouble stripping naked and blowing on beetles and chanting and doing all the rites. I *believe*, you know. I've seen enough. Sometimes I just get weary of all the mystic jibber jabber."

"You want to join the Vakhtang, then? You can dodge the 'jibber jabber' while they feed you to the grinder."

"Come on, you know that's not what I'm saying. But I think we could, within reason, be a little more modern. Seems like everything we do has some kind of scientific analog and… wait a minute…did you hear that?"

"Is it him?"

"This soon after the rites? No way. Probably noise from the pipes. You finish putting away the ceremony bundle and I'll go check it out."

"Dearest, most formal sister of the light, I requesteth thine olde tymey presence over here right now!"

"He's back?"

"Yeah, bring some water. He can barely talk. Hold on… what…hold on, my partner here is bringing you something to drink."

"Here you go. I put a straw in it."

"Okay, pal, here's some water. Don't drink too fast or you'll end up horking it back up."

"There you go."

"…"

"What's that? You're too croaky, pal. I'm going to lean in so you can whisper. First, you gotta promise no biting or spitting or anything. You promise? Shake your head 'yes.' Okay, I'm listening."

"What's he saying?"

"Be quiet. I can barely hear him."

"…"

"Shit, he passed out. We pushed him too fast. What did he say?"

"I couldn't quite tell. Something about 'black wolf ate me,' which, you know, we could have expected. After that, I swear he said, 'I love you, angels.' So maybe that's about us. And then after that he said something about 'Deckert' or 'deck hard' or something."

"Maybe he was saying 'Deckard' like the name in those poems we found on his hard drive."

"A boyfriend?"

"I don't know. I got a weird feeling that the poems were about his turtle."

"Yeah, maybe. Who knows? This fucking guy, right?"

"Right."

"I'm cooked. Let's let him sleep and then we can find out if this guy still thinks we're angels in the morning."

"That sounds perfect. Can you look up that article Ms. A. told me about? I'll be with you in a sec."

"I don't know if you can hear me, Mr. Doyle, or if you really are Mr. Doyle at all, but I know one thing for sure: you have been to a terrible and hopeless place, far, far from the light. That place will never leave you. I wish I could tell you it would, but…it won't. And for that, I'm sorry. But at least you're here now, you're home, and that's mostly a good thing, I hope. We'll see. But I guess I just really wanted to be the first person to hold your hand and say, 'Welcome back.' So there it is, Mr. Doyle…welcome back."

# CHAPTER 8

# Recalibration

At first I'd believed the sound I heard was a new cruelty, a trick in the darkness to remind me of the world from which I'd been torn. The noise was barely human, a contorted, warbling static phantom which made me feel all the more alone in my suffering. I wished, as I had so many times before, that I could simply die and be free of that place.

But then, through the empty space, I heard a man's voice, distinct and clear. Angry.

"Listen, buddy. You've got to give me a vein to work with or I'm going to have to pump this shit up your ass. You don't want that. I don't want that. C'mon, motherfucker."

After that, I felt my body again, my real body for a wisp of a moment, as something sharp slid into my neck and sent a sweet sensation through my nerves, what I used to call pain before I fell into the throat of the black wolf.

Beyond that moment, I existed in two spaces: one which allowed me nothing, and another which allowed me the sound of two voices. One male, one female, both an almost unbearable kindness in contrast to the crushing abyss.

I was never religious, but given my new reality, I was converting. So as I was torn between the two worlds, as I understood that they were talking about some real, half-remembered version of myself, I came to believe that they were angels.

It was only after I woke in our world, naked and cold and strapped to a stretcher inside a dimly lit warehouse, that I began to have my doubts.

It was only after I looked down and saw two dead obsidian-black beetles on my broken chest—their mandibles latched into the thin skin above my heart—that I started to scream.

"Hey, sleeping beauty, hey, hey. You've got to calm down. Okay? We don't have an x-ray machine here but your chest is looking pretty roughed up. You keep hollering like that, it's only gonna get worse." It was the man who'd saved me. He wore khaki pants and a frayed blue t-shirt which barely concealed a paunch. The text on his shirt read "I HAD A BLAST AT COCONUTS!" Beneath the slogan was a cartoon drawing of an unconscious goat next to an empty beer mug. The man's fingers were dusted with bright orange Snak-Ums cheese.

I was not in any kind of sanctioned medical facility.

"He's up?" The woman's voice came from behind a curtain partition across the warehouse.

"Oh, yeah. He's wide awake now. We might need some codeine for his chest. I think his ribs are killing him."

"Not…my ribs…it's those bugs…they…"

"I know. It's kind of nasty. But those guys are why you're here now—they're the ones who clipped the signal. If you want I can pull off the thorax and abdomen, but Ms. A. says we have to leave the jaws in until they naturally unlock."

It seemed like madness. But then I thought of where I'd been, and I realized that they could coat my whole body in bullet ants if it kept me from going back to that place.

"It's okay," I said, "You can leave them. You...they saved me...I was in the throat..."

"Save it, buddy. You're here right now because we know all about that place. Trust me. Don't try to describe it—you'll just sound like you're spouting bad heavy metal lyrics, and the feeling might come back to you. It's best not to give it any energy at all."

"The Hex..."

"Is gone, buddy. It's all gone."

I was surprised to find, for the first time in months, that the absence of Hex was no longer terrifying. What had they done to me?

Her voice again. "I checked. We don't have any codeine. Tons of acetaminophen, but I'm guessing his liver is maxed out. Ask him if he can take a full breath."

"You heard her, buddy. Can you give us a big inhale?"

I tried. My right side set fire. The jaws of the beetles tore deeper. I cried out, which only made it worse. I tried to calm down before this turned into some new pain loop.

"He's pretty rough, Dara."

"Maybe put a topical by the scarabs, ice his ribs, and ask him to calm the fuck down? His body is still processing the perphenadol. I don't think more drugs is what this guy needs right now."

Amen. I thought of where I'd been, gave perspective to this pain, and took a few slow, measured breaths short of what shifted my busted chest.

The man leaned in close and studied my face. He had Snak-Um breath slightly underscored by the smell of sour lager.

"He sure looks like the picture in the article."

*Article?* Shit. The roasted bankers. The massacre on 45th. Who knew what the media was saying about me? Between the bank and Delta, there were billions of dollars available to make sure people heard the approved message. And mom. What about mom?

Panic again. Straining not to hyperventilate.

"Listen. Whatever they're saying about me, they're lying. You've got…"

"First things first, buddy. My name is Tim. My pal over in the kitchen is Dara. Now who exactly are you?"

They'd saved me. They had my things. They might already know the truth. The pain in my ribs and the restraints stripped me of my will to create any more fake realities.

"My name is S.P. Doyle. And I didn't…"

"Sorry to interrupt again, but do you have, um, any proof of that? We couldn't find identification in your bags."

"It's in my pants."

"Nope. We checked there too."

"There's a secret pocket near the crotch. Thin Velcro seam. It's hard to see but you can feel the cards."

"Okay…aaaand…got it."

He had the whole batch of I.D.'s: the Unsustainable Fraud Scheme Card Series. Collect 'em all, kids, and you too can live a lie.

"Dara, you've got to come see this."

She rounded the partition with a frustrated sigh. What kind of life was she living, that she could feel weary about paying attention to a suddenly conscious man she'd strapped to a table and saved from oblivion.

*You're here right now because we know all about that place.*

She had a large mug of steaming tea in her hands. I can't quite remember what she was wearing, probably just blue jeans and a white tee, pure utility. Short black hair against olive skin, both oily from staying awake for days saving my ass. I mainly remember the way she walked. It wasn't a show, some calculated sway of the hips, but rather a kind of gentleness that made me think it would be beautiful to watch her swim in a still pond, to see the way the water would move around her. It was grace.

The other thing I noticed, right away, was that she had only her right eye, the left covered by a patch. She passed her partner and leaned close to look at me, chamomile on her breath as a nice contrast to Mr. Snak-Um's. After a second's confusion, I figured out how to focus solely on her remaining eye, the green iris flecked with tiny hints of yellow. The beauty of it stood out in isolation.

Her gaze stayed on me. "Let me guess—He has a bunch of fake I.D.'s?"

"Well, a few. So the bank fraud part of his story, especially when you add in that big old sack of cash, that's probably legit. It's not so much that, as it is…well, check out *this* license."

Waking naked and strapped to a table after an overdose should have been awkward, but I'd heard their voices and knew that this situation was somehow par for their course. I was so grateful to be back in my body that I was barely conscious of my nudity, of the way my Crooked D was probably shriveled from the cold, of the fact that they must've attended to my other functions over the last few days. No, it was only when Dara turned to look at my fake I.D. as Maria Scharf that I felt my skin flush with embarrassment.

Part of this feeling came from knowing that I'd made such an ugly woman. My DMV yellow-neon-lit drag photo was some hellish mockery of the beauty that this woman effortlessly radiated.

Part of this feeling came from a sudden realization: From the very first moment Dara had looked into my eyes, I was falling for her.

Doom isn't something you want to focus on, but when you unexpectedly find yourself wanting someone who is literally surrounded by the truth of who you really are, it feels like disaster. This would not be my meet cute overdose or some story Dara and I would tell to our kids. I knew this would be another stillborn dream to file away.

But when she looked at the incriminating I.D., she smiled and nudged Tim. "Wow. Do you think he even checked the mirror? Yeesh. He's much more handsome as a man."

And then she winked at me and laughed, and hope returned as quickly as it had fled.

# CHAPTER 9

# Crackpots

If there were an audio recording of my first day in Tim and Dara's warehouse hideout it would reveal that I was attempting to spin my story into one of charming haplessness, to find some way to de-creep my path to their sanctuary.

I answered enough basic questions—Who are you? Which bank did you work for? Who was your Hex supplier? Does anyone else know about your plan?—to earn my way out of restraints and into a warm blanket on their couch. Dara handed me my own mug of hot tea and a towel-covered ice pack for my chest and gave me a warning.

"You're still in the early stages of separation from their signal. We got you this far. It would be *very* unwise for you to try to run. It's clear the officials are looking for you, but after what's happened to Mr. Port and Mr. Egbert, the authorities are the least of your concerns. I can tell you we've reviewed your hard drive, and read a very unflattering portrait of you in the Post, but I'm hoping you can give us a fuller picture."

I'd heard her, somewhere in the midst of my fugue

state, speaking with the one they called Ms. A. It was my involvement in the death of the Hex dealers that they were truly intrigued by. I'd give them all the info I had on that subject, but I knew I'd be remiss if I passed up this shot at revising the whole of my history.

So I tried to paint myself as an anti-corporate crusader, some Robin Hood trapped in the grip in a very bad drug habit, but my bag of cash (clearly never distributed to any poor souls) and the profound size of my Hex stash had already told them deeper truths.

I left out the unholy amount of masturbation, but they'd already seen Crooked D in all his punch drunk glory.

I tried to sell the idea that I had some agency in my escape from danger, but they'd found me broken and rag-dolled. Hell, beautiful dumb luck and their rescue efforts were the only reason I was speaking to them at all.

Every time I veered from the ugly truth into a version of the story more amenable to the survival of my ego, I noticed their eyes squinting, their lips tightening. Tim and Dara were ace lie detectors. I was mostly untrained at selling my delusions to anyone other than myself. It was frustrating.

When it came time to tell them about the thing that attacked me on 45$^{th}$, I figured their bullshit detectors would swing way into the red, but during that part they quietly listened and nodded. There is no feasible way to describe being mauled by a near-invincible brain-eating man-gorilla with multiple voices and an extendable jaw without sounding like you should be committed. But then I remembered what Tim had said:

*You're here right now because we know all about that place.*

If he was telling the truth—and the fact that I was back

among the living with two beetle heads sticking out of my chest gave me cause to believe he was—then they had seen weirder.

They had seen worse.

When I started to tell them about the overdose, they both held up their hands to cut me off.

Tim spoke first, "You don't need to talk about that place. There are...um...this is hard to explain, but there are reverberations of that place inside of you, in ways you can't remove. In ways we don't really understand. But we know that the more you talk about them, about that place, the stronger those vibrations become. It brings you back into their interest. They'll start to use you again, and..."

Dara raised another hand to silence Tim. She came over to the couch and sat beside me. I spilled a splash of scalding tea on my leg but pretended not to feel it. She was so close.

She made eye contact with me again, and said, "Don't look away, okay?"

Then she reached up and lifted the patch that covered her left eye.

Except it wasn't her eye in that orbit anymore. It was a jet-black glass stone.

"The longer you're there," she said, "the more you become their instrument, the more your body becomes part of their signal. Eventually your matter softens as they pull you across. The eyes go first—they become a kind of jelly. This almost happened to you."

"But you saved me."

"Tim and I saved you, just as he and Ms. A. saved me years ago...The sacraments...the medicines we use...were not as strong back when I had fallen into their realm. Ms. A. was unable to save this eye. The jelly hardened like glass."

"You couldn't remove it?"

"Ms. A. believed it might explode in my skull if we tried. Besides that, it serves as a reminder of why I have to live like this." She gestured to the expanse of the creaking, mostly abandoned warehouse with its ad hoc rescue room, metal tubs, extension cord networks, and cots for beds. She flipped the patch back down over the orb. "It reminds me of our sacred mission."

I'd never been close to someone who spoke like she did, with a clarity of purpose and resolve. It was intoxicating. I hoped neither she nor Tim could read that feeling on my face. I hoped she'd never get off the couch.

*I'm staring at her. I'm sitting here staring at her. Am I smiling? Should I be smiling? She just showed me some hardened black jelly eye and told me she's on a sacred mission. I should have something to say. Her hair looks so soft. I wonder what it smells like.*

"Mr. Doyle?"

"Oh, I'm sorry. I'm drifting. Not feeling one hundred percent yet. I mean, I've still got this beetle-heart thing going on." I tapped the dried insect heads latched on to my chest and cringed at the pain. She leaned back.

*I'm fucking this up. How do I fix this? Try to engage her.*

"So you guys are like an anti-Hex rescue or something?"

"Or something. It's not just Hex we're fighting, but that's their strongest instrument right now."

"And when you say 'them' you're talking about the dealers."

"No, the dealers are only part of their forces. But they're the part that you managed to gain some influence with before they were killed."

*This isn't about me. Shit. She's being friendly to get information about Port and Egbert. Maybe Hungo, too. And I don't really know anything about them outside of the fact that they're dead and something gigantic ate their brains. But she's intrigued. Keep her going.*

"What's the name of their group? You said they were part of some gang. 'Walk-Gang' or 'Wu-Tang' or something."

*Not even a smile from her. Fucking this up again. Why would she want a cutesy joke? You want to be irreverent about some part of her sacred mission. There's such a thing as being dumb and clever at the same time. Slow down. Think, damn it.*

"They are called the Vakhtang. And no, it's not quite a gang, though portions of their group function using similar hierarchies. They tend to steal the most effective parts of other organizations' methods."

"Like the Yakuza finger thing?" Her face brightened at the observation.

"Yes! Exactly like that. They've been honing methods of fear and control for centuries."

"Centuries?" It was my turn to lean back. "This is some Mason or Illuminati thing?"

"Really? You want us to believe your story about brain-gobbling man-monsters and international pop stars feeding money to a massive bank and biomed conspiracy, but you're incredulous when it comes to this?"

She had a point.

Tim spoke up, reminding me that he, you know, existed.

"He's been to their realm. And Ms. A. probably won't let us release him until we figure out what happened with Hungo, or Egbert and his buddy. Plus, everybody already thinks he's a nut. Let's just tell him what we know. At least enough to get him to stop asking dumb questions. Maybe if he knows about them it will spark some memory to help us."

*Thank you, Tim. I don't even mind your little dig, so long as I can keep her sitting here, talking to me.*

"Fair enough. Can you grab the teapot? I think there are a couple of cups left in there."

*Yeah, Tim—Go get us something to drink.*

"Alright," she said to me, "it's my turn to sound like a lunatic, but I swear that everything I'm going to tell you is true."

I tried to turn my body toward hers on the couch, to show her I was really listening, but my ribs lit up again like I was kicked by a spooked horse. I let loose a high-pitched yelp and popped tears before I had a chance to exercise the kind of restraint I thought she might find attractive. I collapsed back to my slouched position on the couch and felt a sheen of sweat bloom across my face.

My dance of seduction continued as my blanket flopped open, leaving me exposed, cringing, bruised and dead-bugged next to Dara.

"Don't move. Just...stop. I can help you."

She repositioned my ice pack. "Do you think you can sit up a little bit without making any of those sad animal noises?" She didn't wink this time, but the kindness in her voice still came through. Was she the type who liked damaged goods, or was I confusing her bedside manner for something more?

She moved to wrap the blanket back around me, but halted. "That ice seems to have calmed your bruising a bit. Look at *that*."

The bruise, clear as day now, showed the shape of the massive hand which had so easily fractured my frame. Dara and I looked at each other with wide eyes. Sure, this was good for proving out my batshit story, but this also meant

I hadn't suffered some feverish Hex hallucination that night, which further meant that we had to adjust our reality to fit in fucking brain-munching mutants.

Dara put it into words. "Oh dear. That is one hundred percent no good." She yelled across the warehouse, "Tim, you've got to see something." Then she turned back to me. "You say this thing knows who you are?"

I nodded.

"You killed it though, right?"

"I think so. I mean, I stabbed it in the neck. I don't think it could have survived that."

*Yeah, but it also shrugged off having an arm blasted clean away.*

Tim had returned with the teapot. "What's up?"

She gingerly peeled back my ice pack to reveal the outline of the beast's hand.

Tim's eyebrows raised. "Oh."

Dara was shaking her head from side to side, the way you have to when a new burden is thrust into a life that's already reached its bullshit threshold. "Yeah. It's a problem, right?"

And I knew Tim would say "Right" without even thinking, the ingrained call and response they'd developed while fighting in solidarity for so long, but instead of his voice there was a sharp cracking sound from the other side of the warehouse and Tim said nothing at all because the teapot in his hands had somehow exploded, and the look on his face told me that didn't make any sense to him until he looked down to see the smoking, heart-sized hole in his chest.

Dara was closer to Tim when the shot hit and she caught the worst of the blowout, a mist of scalding water, blackened blood, and porcelain shrapnel. I expected her to look back to me, the shock on her face confirming that this had really happened, but she had already dropped from the couch and was moving in a crouch toward a small wooden cabinet in the corner. Only once she reached the cover of the case did she look back to see if I was alive.

And there I was, still half-slumped on the couch, holding my mug like I was waiting for Dara to come back and finish her story, frozen in some old reality that had been blasted in half.

She yelled, "Get down!" and the sound of her voice pulled me into the now. I rolled from the couch to my knees and tried to flatten out. My ribs popped in protest and the pain must have overridden whatever adrenaline was supposed to send me running to safety, because my next step as a man of action was to pass the fuck out.

I came to just moments later, static haze on my vision making everything seem like a broadcast floating somewhere behind my head. Some kind of warrior woman was across the room, tucked down low, searching desperately through a wooden cabinet. Someone was coming after her, I could tell. She ran her hands through her hair and it stayed slicked back. A sheen of sweat coated her, the light from the lamps far overhead shone on the muscles of her arms as they tensed.

The woman had found something. She pulled what looked to be a bright silver surgical steel slingshot from the cabinet. She turned to me and yelled, "Close your eyes, Doyle."

Man, she was beautiful. This was a great show.

*Wait.*

*Doyle?*

*That's.*

*ME.*

And the show was over and now we were about to die

again, and I tried to process her command but I also thought that whatever was coming to kill me would have a way easier time if I was lying prone with my eyes closed, so instead I pushed up on my arms and tried to crawl toward her and I saw everything.

Dara rose up from behind her cover with the slingshot pulled back. A man in a brown suit was running toward her, his outstretched arm holding a plastic yellow gun still discharging blue smoke.

*My enemies. My fault. And he's got the drop.*

I yelled, "Over here!" as loud as my chest would allow.

The man turned his head for the slightest moment.

Dara released the band of the slingshot.

The man dropped. Dara closed her eye and ducked back behind the cabinet.

Something was stuck to the man's chest.

At first my brain processed the object as a rotten mandarin, and I thought Dara had made a real desperation move, flinging old fruit from their pantry at our would-be assassin.

But then the thing started to move, flattening to the shape of a shimmering oil puddle over the man's heart. Tendrils spread out from the center, swimming over and under his skin, knitting itself across the surface of him.

It didn't think to fill his mouth, so we could still hear him screaming.

As quickly as the fluid web had spread across the surface of his body, it hardened, and there was a shifting, clicking sound, the chitinous crunch of insect jaws.

The man turned to look at me, both of us flat on the cold concrete.

*"Please. No."*

His eyes, black jelly now, oozed to the ground.

The web in his skin compacted toward an invisible center near the man's back, bending and rolling his limbs and neck beneath his torso.

The skyscraper-drop sound of all of his bones breaking at once echoed through the warehouse.

Whatever had tried to stay inside the man found the pressure too great as the tendrils knitted themselves, smaller and smaller, into a shrinking black mass. A rupture of organs fell wet to the floor.

The clicking, fist-sized tumor spun a few feet from the floor, gaining speed until a cold black shimmer came from its center and pulled at my chest.

*That place. He's going to that place.*

Then, without a sound, the dark light disappeared, spun into nothing, and even though this man had tried to kill me, the only thing I could think was, *"Please. No."*

# CHAPTER 10

# Externalities

She was the one who placed the weight of the dead on my chest. There'd been no mirrors or moments to reflect for so long, but the shock in her face made everything real. Tim had saved my life, and because of that, he was gone.

"We have to move. See if you can get yourself dressed while I call Ms. A." Sharp, direct, the softness and compassion in her voice departed. Zero eye contact. What was I to her? Maybe an asset. Definitely a problem. Toxic cargo she was forced to carry.

*Make yourself useful. Get off this floor. Find your clothes. Grit your fucking teeth against the pain and don't let her hear a word out of you unless she asks for something. She just lost her friend. She killed the man who came for you. Find some way to make this right.*

*But how can any of this ever be right? That man…*

"Ms. A.? We've lost Tim…No, I don't sense they were involved in this…I think this is related to Mr. Doyle's other activities…That's a strong possibility…We'll await transport…

I've secured the interior…There's something else…I…I used one of their recovered armaments…The cell bomb…I swear to you, there was no other choice. You know…Yes…I believe he watched…Oh, no, I can take care of it."

I forced myself to my feet, pushing off the couch with wet spaghetti arms and waiting for my head to stop swimming. My blanket fell to the ground and I didn't retrieve it. What was modesty after what I'd just seen? Besides, I couldn't take another ass-over-teakettle tumble without something finally shattering in my chest.

I stumbled toward the table where I'd been restrained, figuring my clothes had to be close by. Nothing. I leaned against the table to take a series of short, cautious breaths.

"Doyle!"

I turned. Dara approached, her earlier grace turned to panicked swiftness.

"Look down, and do not look up again."

*What? Why…*

The heads of the scarabs had returned to life, their jaws pulsing and clamping in the paper-thin skin over my heart. Twin rivulets came from each puncture: thin blood, black jelly.

Dara said, "You should have listened to me. You should have trusted me."

I started to look up, to tell her I was sorry, that it would never happen again, but she slapped her hand across the top of my head.

"Jesus! Simple fucking instructions. Keep your head down."

I heard her walk behind me, then the tiny sound of a plastic cap dropping to the floor.

"You looked, right? That was all they needed to tune in, and now you're transmitting again. Those beetles won't muddy their signal much longer. We have to get you back to Ms. A. before they know where we are."

"I could wear a blindfold. Maybe some earplugs, too."

"Where we're going we can't risk any kind of information being sent through."

She stepped closer, the smell of her still sweet through stress sweat and gun smoke. I could already feel the pressure of that place gnawing at the back of my eyes.

"This is the only way."

Her hand touched the left side of my neck, pressing in, and I felt goosebumps spread across my skin before she pushed in the needle. Then my vision swirled and I felt her arms tucking in under my shoulders as I dropped.

I returned to the same strange haze I'd escaped a day prior, before Tim's heart was turned to ashes and I saw a man pulled into nothing.

The first time you go through a mystical cleansing of otherworldly forces and subsequent resurrection into the human world, it feels like a miracle. The second time less so. It feels like a procedure, another thing to endure to survive. My new context gave their chanting a veneer of reason, turned magic scarabs to detox medicine. The biggest difference this time was that I understood enough about the world, and the forces in it, that remaining in the ether seemed preferable.

Alas, consciousness found me and kicked my ass back into the world of the hated, hunted, and haunted.

And, yeah, I was strapped to a table. Again.

C'est la vie.

"Forgive us the blindfold. We've decided to increase our security given recent events. I'm sure you understand."

Ms. A. was near me. I recognized the mix of caring, light condescension, and weariness in her voice. I could smell sandalwood. Maybe a hint of pastrami. I pictured her as some kind of furry, dwarven woman with one cyclopean eye and fingernails like claws. Perhaps she ran a new age bookstore. Perhaps she slept on a bed of writhing snakes or made love to a minotaur each night to reset the heavens. Who knew? It was tough to get a proper assessment given the whole bound and blindfolded thing.

I was happy, though, to realize that they'd at least clothed me after this last procedure. The fabric was thin and papery, maybe some kind of post-surgical garb, but I felt less like a cosmetic company's test monkey.

I heard Ms. A. move closer, then felt her warm hand lightly caress the right side of my chest.

"Can you please take a deep breath for me?"

I knew I couldn't, but she'd saved my life twice by my count, and I wasn't really in a bargaining position, so I gave it my best, braced for the sharp shock, inhaled and...nothing.

"You...you fixed the break. How?"

"Your feelings about the answer to that question would be directly affected by how you feel about having ground sea slug eggs injected into your bone marrow. Would you still like to know?"

I couldn't tell if she was messing with me, but I remembered the scarabs and decided it was best to shake my head No.

"Fair enough. Questions tend to prompt more questions anyway, and it's best we keep things moving. I think we can both agree that there have been some unfortunate losses of late."

I shook my head Yes. She continued.

"These kinds of losses shift a balance which is very important to us and to our mission. Losing Tim, in particular, comes at a great cost. He had a knack for finding those who've fallen into the realm, some kind of perception which guided him to the lost. He found you just moments after you'd collapsed, and I have no doubt he saved you. I also have no doubt that he'd do it again, given the chance.

"But he won't have any more chances, and that saddens and worries me greatly. Which brings us to you, our catalyst. You caused this imbalance—though I have no doubt *their* influence was upon you—and now you must set it right."

The idea of Right, of anything being right again, almost made me laugh. I couldn't fix Tim's death. I couldn't undo any of the bullshit which had brought me into Ms. A.'s world. And I couldn't fathom a world where Right mattered when monsters were allowed to exist and our reality sat on the narrowest precipice above an endless void. We were meat to the grinder, fucked beyond unfuckability.

Ms. A. said, "I can see the doubt on your face, but you'll move past it. You'll find it's of no value to you once you have purpose."

"You want me to replace Tim or something? I don't have any kind of special perception."

"No, you could never replace Tim, just as he could never replace you."

"You want my money?"

I heard a metal folding chair smash against a wall, then

footsteps rushing toward me.

"*Fuck your money, Doyle!* Tim's fucking dead and I sent someone into the realm just to keep us alive and you think we want your goddamned *money*?" Hot, angry breath. Jasmine tea.

*Shit. Dara's been in here the whole time.*

Ms. A.'s soothing voice stepped in. "Dara, I must ask you to go. Please. Give him a chance to understand." Then whispers, a disagreement in which Dara eventually acquiesced.

"Yes, Ms. A. Let me know if you need anything."

A door closed.

"I'm sorry. She's grieving."

"Tim meant a lot to her. I could tell."

"It's not only that. She and Tim understood the perils of our occupation, and I would hope they'd been wise enough to mourn each other while they were still alive. I believe she's suffering because she knows what a terrible thing she did to save your life."

*Please. No.*

That place…I felt a twinge in my chest—the scarabs working overtime to purge me of…what?

"Your brow is sweating at the thought of them."

Her hand was on my chest again, but this time she grabbed the flesh of my belly and gave it a hard, fast twist.

"Aaaaah!"

"Apologies, but I had to clear your head. Every moment you think of them, their path to you becomes clearer. Dara will need to teach you meditations which can be of assistance. I don't know that you'd survive a third ceremony without your insides melting."

"But you're speaking about them now. Aren't you creating a connection to them?"

"That's part of the mystery. Speaking of *them* doesn't have much of an effect, but triggered memories of their realm in specific seem to do something in the visual cortex which allows them to transmit."

And she tweaked my belly a second time to clear her mention of that place, just to make me feel a little bit more like maybe I'd died during my Hex overdose and slipped into some kind of mystical dipshit purgatory where nobody would ever give me a straight answer and I'd spend eternity strapped to a variety of tables in a miasma of confusion and disbelief.

I shook my head from left to right, an uncontrollable physical manifestation of the shitshow my existence had become. How was this my reality?

"I know this is a difficult adjustment."

And the award for Understatement of the Year goes to: The Magical Ms. A.!

I said, "I can't take this shit anymore. I can't. Please. Let me go. I'll run far and fast, and I'll never think about any un-named forces or anything, and I'll see how long I can go before some bank goon blows my head off and that'll be just fine."

I almost expected another slap to come swooping down on my still-tingling cheek. Instead, I felt her hand against my brow, pushing down, like she was shutting off some third eye that wouldn't stop staring straight into the madness.

Then her voice—stripped of its prior placations and kindly seductions—was in my head. "You will listen to me and you will take this to heart. Let it sink in deep as unassailable truth, and hold it there as you would the last flicker of flame on a black forest night. There is a force which wishes to imbalance and consume our existence. You have perceived the nature of this energy, as much as any human mind can. If we allow this force into our world, it will unravel all order and swallow all light. Time and matter and creation and destruction will all be undone, and there will be no cycles, no new light born, and anything that was ever capable of perceiving its existence will instead know only pain, everlasting.

"And you, with your self-pity and your poison ego, have unwittingly become an agent of this force. You have survived this long because they wanted to use you. Whatever you have revealed in your ridiculous quest for money and revenge is of concern to the Vakhtang and the power they foolishly serve. They knew who you worked for. They wanted you in their sphere of influence and they needed your information. You are only alive because you have served as an instrument for something worse than death.

"So, we're going to offer you the opportunity to make things right, as much as any one person can.

"You can choose to work for us, to help us discover whatever it is in your files that caused the Vakhtang to take such an interest in you.

"Or, you can choose escape. We know you'd never willingly serve the Vakhtang, but without our protection they might ensnare you again. The business you used to work for also seems determined to end your life. And given how much you know about us and the importance of our mission, we'd be hesitant to see you fall into the wrong hands. Considering all those facts, the only reasonable escape for you is sitting on an end table near the door to this room."

Her hand lifted from my forehead. She unlatched my restraints and walked across the room. I heard the door open, and then she spoke, her voice returned to its maternal gentility. "And should you choose escape, Mr. Doyle, please be considerate and make certain you're in the corner with the plastic sheeting."

*Tonight's very special episode of Point/Counterpoint comes to you live from a crinkled plastic tarp in the corner of a dimly lit room. In a very rare moment of thoughtful introspection and analysis, both Points and Counterpoints will be delivered by Former Banker/Hex Junky & Current Cult Compound Prisoner S.P. Doyle.*

*Moderating tonight's event will be the often-silent-but-period-ically-explosive-final-say-on-all-matters known as Shotgun.*

P: You saw what happened to the man Dara hit with the cell bomb. Why go on in a world where that could happen?

CP: Because that's the same fate Tim and Dara and Ms. A. saved you from suffering. You owe them. What if you can stop that from happening again? And what's the point in dying? I doubt your remains would leave this building. People will just think you've disappeared. And if the bank, or Delta, or the Vakhtang, or anybody else who wants you dead still thinks you're alive, what will stop them from finding your mom?

P: How do you know they haven't already found her?

CP: I don't. But if you're alive then maybe there's a chance to protect her.

P: Right. Instead of "maybes," let's talk facts. Nine, possibly ten people are dead, and at least a few of those are my fault. Tim for certain.

CP: Most of those deaths stemmed from occupational hazards. You get paid to murder, don't act surprised when it's your turn for a dirt nap. Or if you sell fucked-up drugs and make tweekers show you their junk, sometimes a giant mutant eats your brains. That's the streets. But Tim?...Yeah. Poor Tim. Could be the only way to reconcile that is to put the screws to the fuckers who killed him. You could take down the bank and expose Delta MedWorks, and then devote the rest of your life to fighting Tim's fight. But you have to go on.

P: Why?

CP: Because of the worst-case scenario: These wingnuts are telling the truth, and that terrible place you went to wasn't a nasty O.D. hallucination, but really and verifiably was some kind of realm ruled by an unmerciful destructive force which, due to the absence of anybody giving a damn about fighting it, makes its way into our world and tears everything woefully fucking asunder. And I'm not just talking about all those shitty adults being sucked into the realm, the murderers and rapists and CEO's. Nope. Everyone. Everything. Baby humans, baby pandas, little kids who still high five and hug and mean it, wise old ladies, monks, turtles. It's like the whole universe getting cancer. Everything is death. Worse, everything is nothing at all.

P: ...

CP: *Nobody* deserves that.

P: But I'm useless.

CP: Stop living in the past. If you're worried about accomplishing something, walk out of this room right now and tell Ms. A. that you're ready for duty. Find a way to protect your mom. Take care of Deckard. Make things right with Dara.

P: Dara hates me.

CP: Dara is grieving. Remember how sweet she was before Tim got killed? Remember the way she touched you, the way she smelled, the way she moved?

P: She hates me. I'm useless. Mom's probably dead.

CP: Hey, buddy, focus here.

P: Tim's dead. My fault. Dara hates me. Mom's dead. I ruined everything. Everyone is suffering. It's all my fault.

CP: No. No. You have to stop.

P: I should be dead. I can't be loved. There's no hope. We're all dead already. I'll make it stop.

CP: Shit. You're not listening. Slow it down. Breathe. You're on loop. Put the shotgun down. If you do this, you'll prove every bad thing you've ever thought about yourself.

P: Please. Let me die.

CP: No.

P: Why go on?

It was a loop, a sickening circuit, the taste of shotgun oil and salty crocodile tears, the human mind as a trap, cruel in its self-sustaining tyranny.

The circle was finally severed, after hours spent inside that place, by a small sound.

Someone was crying outside my door. It was soft but certain, muffled by hands or the crook of an arm. Somehow, from the reservation and control in the sound, I knew it was Dara.

I placed the shotgun on the floor and crossed the room. I reached the door and put my ear to it. She stopped crying for a moment. She said, "I can't keep going like this."

It sounded like the truth.

She kept crying there, in the chair outside my room, and then I opened the door and walked out and crouched in front of her.

She said it again. "I'm sorry. I can't keep living like this."

I put my hand on her knee, looked her in the eye, and said, "Me either."

# CHAPTER 11

# Enrollment Drive

Whatever dream we'd sold ourselves in that moment, wishing for each other's suffering to finally cease, we still had to see Ms. A.

We walked down a long concrete hall, a corridor of low light and echoing feet. My surgical scrubs made papery brushing sounds with each step. The coolness of the air and prominent venting told me we were probably underground. We passed what felt like thirty doors, some of them dead-bolted from the exterior. There was a steel door near the end, no window, no slots, an arcane symbol in white paint on the surface. A strong, low voice came from inside, its timbre a brew of anger and batshit confidence.

"They're coming! Sooner than you think, pallies! Sooner than you think!"

Dara shook her head and rolled her eyes. She slapped her palm against the door twice and yelled back, "Shut the fuck up, Clarence." She turned to me. "Supposedly he's been saying that since 1918. You have to give him points for persistence."

"But how…"

"Don't ask. Half these doors behind you, you'd have some question like that. We used to have more of these guys in containment, but they executed a lot of their own in the Brubaker raid."

"Wait…Brubaker? That was that tenement fire about five years ago, right? I thought that was gang retaliation."

"It was, kind of. Just not involving the gangs that were in the news. And it was more extermination than retaliation. We've barely recovered since. Ms. A. was ahead of it though— she already had this place locked down. Only a few of us knew this existed and we started the transport one night before they hit Brubaker. Fucking Matthew…"

"Somebody sold you guys out?"

"Which time? I mean, look at this place. We live like this. Always afraid. Always on the move. Life with the Vakhtang starts to look a lot prettier after a while. The control, the money, the longevity, that illusion of power. They've got it good so long as you don't consider the trade-off."

*Please. No.*

"But how do they not understand what they're feeding into? Or where they're headed?"

"You worked for the bank, right? You must understand the immense power of self-serving delusion."

I much preferred this new round of Point/Counterpoint. The playful lilt in her voice was far more charming than the dull weight of the shotgun.

I don't know what we thought Ms. A. was going to tell us.

Part of me hoped that she'd take one look at Dara, give us some kind of blessing, and send us on our way. *Sure, listen, kids—I get it. This is a grind. Life is short and the weight of what I'm asking you to do and to know is too much to bear. You've fought long and hard enough. So head out that door and lay low and try to find some way back to blissful ignorance for your remaining years.*

At the end of another long corridor we reached Ms. A.'s command center, which turned out to be a La-Z-Boy recliner, abutted by a small end table holding a lamp, a remote control, and much to my relief, Deckard in his travel case. A massive flat screen TV hung from the concrete wall. A screensaver of slowly drifting clouds served faux-window duty.

Already disappointed by the lack of candles, occult books, and cauldrons, I was doubly let down when Ms. A. rose from her chair and revealed herself. Two sleepy hazel eyes behind wireframe rims, bright white teeth, gray and blonde hair in a bob cut. Light blue sweater. Khaki capris. Flip-flops. A total absence of bushy hair, shrunken heads, snakes, crystal jewelry, or sassy talking animal sidekicks. She reminded me of a demure bank teller, the kind who quietly took their breaks with a crossword puzzle and had husbands named Vern and got really excited about baking for company picnics. Totally not mystical, which was weird because earlier I think she might have spoken to me telepathically or through her hand or…something. She had been so close in that room, and I realized I hadn't felt her breath.

She approached me, arms out. "Mr. Doyle! I wasn't sure you'd be joining us."

I was still so wrapped up in the dissonance of her appearance that I didn't even lift my arms when she came to hug me. She insisted, locking her small frame against mine and putting her head against my chest for far longer than socially reasonable. She sighed with relief, but I filled with anxiety at the sensation—the feeling of her reminded me of my mother.

*Mom.*

*Was she even still alive?*

Ms. A. said, "You have made a brave choice. I was not certain, after all you've seen, that you would choose to remain."

"Well, you put a gun to my head."

"No. I put a suggestion in your mind and a gun in your hands."

I wanted to argue with her, to let her know that playing Zen master now didn't strip the past of its more Jim Jonesian bent, and that I knew the gun in my room wasn't the only one she had trained on me, but then I looked at her face, at the wrinkles deepened by the strain of always living under the rules of war, and at the ways her eyes had misted over, and I realized she was both relieved and happy that I wasn't another casualty.

I think she really softened me up with that hug.

Ms. A. turned away from me and approached Dara.

"I can see you're distressed, dear. I can imagine how trying the last few days must have been for you. You've been stronger than anyone should have to be. I *know* Cassandra would be so proud of you."

At that—the mention of Cassandra—I saw Dara's face tighten. Her hands clenched. She stood up and widened her shoulders.

*Oh, Ms. A., you are fucking GOOD. Whatever you just did, you put the fight back in your soldier.*

It was then that I realized we would never escape.

Ms. A. walked over to the end table in the center of the room and picked up a remote control.

"I'm so grateful that you're both here now, because there's something that's been troubling me this morning, and I think Mr. Doyle may be able to shed further light on this problem."

The televised image shifted, blue sky and clouds replaced by the paused image of a peroxide-blonde reporter chomping at the bit to deliver what the bright red on-screen graphic promised would be BREAKING NEWS.

"And now a K-10 exclusive. Our own Mitch Cardell is live on the scene of a triple homicide just reported in the NoBu financial district. Mitch, what can you tell us about the scene there?"

"Thanks, Melody. Information is scarce so far. As you can see, police vehicles are still arriving and the crime scene is being contained as we speak. We know that there have been three deaths, and that the bodies were found in the alley behind me, adjacent to high-end restaurant Au Vin. Though police are not yet releasing any details, we were able to interview a local resident who agreed to speak with us on a condition of anonymity."

They cut to a close-up swarm of pixels, the "anonymity" angle clearly being played by the news station to obscure the fact that their credible witness was, in actuality, a pickled stew-bum, his slurred speech apparent even when it was pitch-shifted to a lower resonance. I swore that the batch of yellow pixels on the screen had to be a piece of corn in the guy's beard.

"They came into my home. So rude, man, you know nobody cares, but they woke me up anyway, and I thought somebody was digging into my buffet, but the moon was barely up, so the restaurant ain't closed yet. You know. So I go around the corner of the trash bin to see what the noise is about and that's when I saw it. This gorilla, I swear, biggest damn one I ever saw, and he's got a guy pinned to the ground, squirming, one hand holding the guy's wrists and the other smashing down on his face. I spot two other guys, but they're already dead. You can tell. So, you know me, I'm not letting some monkey make me the next meal, so I tuck back until the slurping sound is over and then the thing jumped right up to the fire escape and disappeared. All I know is, Metro Zoo better send out some folks with elephant guns."

A voice from offscreen. "Can you tell us anything about the condition of the bodies?"

"Bodies? Shoot, bodies was fine. Nice suits, all of 'em." The stew-bum itched his beard, displaying what could have been a pixelated Rolex on his wrist. "It's their heads that wasn't. [Beep]ing monkey popped their heads open like some kind of nutcracker. Or skullcracker, I guess. Ha! Kind of thing, might drive a man to drink. By the way, you think I could…"

The station was wise enough to cut before The Dread Alley Pirate Cornbeard finished asking for his booze payout.

Melody from K-10 was back onscreen. "We promise to stay with this story as…"

Ms. A. had paused the broadcast and pulled up another show from her recorder.

"I believe it's worth noting that this next report aired at the same time last night."

Another talking head was on-screen, the man's blinding porcelain veneers competing for info-space amid tickers, trackers, corner grabs, and a graphic reading HOSPITAL IN CRISIS.

"...while officials have not released information about the nature of the homicides, we can confirm that three patients in the St. Mercy intensive care unit were killed. Early reports also indicate that two hospital pharmacists were assaulted and the hospital's entire supply of an atypical antipsychotic known as perphenadol was stolen."

Dara gave Ms. A. a confused look.

"The hospital's media liaison will be issuing a statement regarding the tragedy once the victims' families have been notified. Stay tuned..."

Ms. A. paused the footage again and pulled up a third file. "This aired half an hour later."

"Police are asking for assistance in identifying the man seen here, from closed circuit camera footage provided by St. Mercy Hospital. Though the man's face is not visible in this footage, police say that the man's missing left arm and substantial size—he's estimated to be around seven feet tall and weigh about four hundred pounds—may be enough to aid in identification. Viewers with any information about this man are asked to call..."

Ms. A. flipped the screen back to the idyllic drifting cloud setting and turned to look me in the eyes. "I think now you can understand why I've been troubled."

*Because you live in some underground tunnel prison system packed full of undying agents of the Vakhtang? Because you look like you're supposed to be dropping little kids off at lacrosse, not threatening the life of one of your very confused captives? Or is it the thing with the corn in the guy's beard? Because I agree, it's gross.*

I said none of that, of course, only raised my eyebrows inquisitively and hoped she'd continue.

"Dara related your story to me during your last period of recovery, and I think there was more veracity to it than we'd originally suspected."

There's a feeling you get when the death of others makes people believe what you're saying is true, and it is far from vindication. I nodded my head, then asked, "So what are we supposed to do now?"

"Well, we have to follow our assumptions. So, assuming that you're right, and Delta MedWorks has been funneling massive amounts of money to Dr. Tikoshi for the work that resulted in the creation of these things…"

"Wait. *Things*?"

"Yes. You saw the reports. They were both live on the scene within minutes of each other. St. Mercy and Au Vin are miles apart. And only in the latter report was the assailant said to be missing an arm. So we must assume that the thing which launched the assault on the hospital and stole the sacrament was the same which attacked you and the other men on 45th."

"But I stabbed that thing in the neck. It had collapsed."

"Something that large, something with that kind of appetite…perhaps its neck is not so densely packed with vital elements. I could show you a man in room twenty-eight who has thick parallel scars running across his throat, and he's still very much alive."

Initially I wanted to grab Ms. A. and shake her and say, "I know. I get it. You guys are living in bizarre, cryptic world of opposing mystical forces and everything I believed has been a lie, but please, can we focus on the problem at hand without any more asides reminding me of how little I know." But then I realized I was just kind of embarrassed about not having killed the thing which attacked me. I wanted Dara to think of me as a capable, "Can Totally Kill An Enemy With A Knife To The Neck" kind of guy. The new truth—I dumb luck pig stuck the thing hard enough to allow me to run away—played a lot less macho. And the fact that it went on to slaughter a batch of feeble hospital patients was beyond insult to injury.

It was damning.

Could I have stopped that from happening? Could I have saved those poor people?

"I can see this is disturbing you. But you are neither responsible for this thing's existence or its actions. All you can be responsible for is what happens next. In order to stop this we need to know why these things have been created, and why the Vakhtang were so intrigued by Delta MedWorks and Dr. Tikoshi that they kept you alive and gave you access to so much of the dark signal."

Dara spoke. "The quantity of Hex we found in your bag was greater an amount than even Hex dealers are allowed to carry. With that level of dosage provided, we suspect they were periodically operating you as a mimic. Did you have frequent nosebleeds, or extended black-out periods during which you still appeared to have done research?"

I got the inference—my own paranoid research was of such scattershot quality that every once in a while the Vakhtang had to hijack my consciousness to get some real work done.

"That happened pretty much every day, for weeks."

"If you were on that level of dosage, you could have been subsumed into their realm at any time. The fact that they kept you alive and working means your investigation was of great interest. They only abandoned you once it appeared that your physical vessel had been wrecked."

Ms. A. jumped in. "Or maybe they believed, as we do,

that the creature you described was eating people's brains for purposes other than nutrition."

All of those voices coming out of the thing's massive mouth.

*We will know the truth once you have joined us. There's room now.*

I'd barely had time to process that night, to even believe it had really happened.

"So maybe they shut down my body in the hopes that the thing would survive, come back, and get a second chance at cracking my skull?"

Dara and Ms. A. nodded, both watching my face to see how a man might respond to the news that his brain was offered up as bait.

I pictured my body collapsed in the alley, my mind raw meat hiding the egg of some parasitic dark force hoping to be consumed by a massive mutant man-gorilla. I saw my masticated gray matter sliding down a gullet, merging with whatever nasty network of nerves would allow a man's consciousness to be stolen within the belly of a beast.

In retrospect, I should have understood that this was exactly what Ms. A. wanted me to see.

At the time, all I could feel were waves of violation, and in their passing, rage. The kind of anger which good leaders know well enough to harness.

Ms. A. said, "The forces which compel the Vakhtang are most concerned with access to human consciousness. Something in our minds—maybe some subatomic vestige of their darkness which slipped into our universe eons ago— vibrates at the exact frequency which allows them access to our world. Their goal, since the dawn of our existence, has been to attune enough human minds to their signal to allow our world to be pulled into theirs.

"They have used many tools to access our minds throughout history—religions, rituals, hive dynamics, and most recently, pharmaceuticals."

"And you think they want this creature as some kind of new tool?"

"Either that, or they view it as competition."

"Hearts and minds, huh?"

"Just minds."

"Those motherfuckers."

"Please calm down."

And Ms. A. must have known that the best way to keep a person angry is to tell them to calm down.

"No. We've got to find some way to stop this."

"I agree. What would you suggest?"

"You've got to have some kind of crack team, right? People trained like Dara who could launch a raid on Dr. Tikoshi's office."

"Would you be surprised to hear that Tikoshi Maxillofacial Surgery has been closed for the last two months? His voice mail says he's in the Bahamas. We hope otherwise. And no, we don't have a special team dedicated to situations like this. Tim and Dara's primary mission was rescue, reducing the number of minds held by the dark signal. Our other two local operatives are currently on loan to Los Angeles, investigating a new kind of film projector which causes us great concern. I'm afraid that Dara is our only resource right now."

Dara looked down and sighed. Missing Tim? Something else? I was only beginning to understand her existence in this pressure cooker.

I said, "She shouldn't have to face this alone." Dara's

head lifted in my periphery. "I know a lot about this case, or whatever it is. I'm joining your mission."

"Very good. Very good."

"Is there some kind of ritual I need to go through, or a secret training camp or something?"

"No, Mr. Doyle. I only need you to answer a question."

"Okay, shoot."

"Do you pledge to give all you have, including your life, to defend our world from the scourge of the Vakhtang?"

I thought, "What life?"

I said, "Sure."

And Ms. A. was hugging me again, and Dara placed her hand on the center of my back, and I'll be damned if I didn't feel a big, crazy smile spread across my face.

# CHAPTER 12

# Networking

Before Dara and I hit the streets, I asked Ms. A. if she could do four things:

1. Acquire my clothes—The feeling of being fully dressed in my own attire was almost foreign at first, and my hoodie and thick denim jeans felt like combination cloak/armor. I'd really always taken clothing for granted.

2. Remove the bugs—The scarabs on my chest appeared to be well and fully dead. Ms. A. swept her hand over my chest. The beetles unclenched their jaws and fell to the floor. My heart fluttered and then resumed its regularly scheduled beat. I filed the whole experience under the tab "Magic Shit I Must Compartmentalize and Ignore So I Can Keep Functioning."

3. Feed my turtle while we were out—It was tough to tell if Deck had lost weight, but I imagined this must all

have been very stressful for him, and I wasn't sure he'd been properly tended. I made sure his case had fresh water and I promised him I'd grab him a fat batch of feeder worms at the next opportunity. I almost picked him up to kiss his shell, but Dara was watching.

4. Offer sanctuary to my mother—I told Ms. A. that I would make contact with my mother while we were out, and she swore to ready a safe room near the entrance to their compound where things were more homey and less underground jail-y.

And because my brain believed in nothing so much as deceiving itself, I emerged onto the streets of my city feeling like things, in whatever weird way, were finally looking up.

Dara said she thought she knew someone—a low level Vakhtang Hex dealer named Toro—who could help us find Dr. Tikoshi.

She had a busted-up blue sedan parked three blocks from the compound. I wondered whether the massive dents and whole body scratches were an artifice or relics of past conflicts, but decided it was cooler to not ask. I was doing a good job playing detached until I hopped in and Dara told me to reach under the seat.

The pistol felt cold and heavy in my hands as I pulled it loose from a mounted holster beneath the bucket seat.

Dara said, "You have any experience with those?"

"No."

"That's right—you're more of a pepper spray kind of guy."
She smiled.

I tried to smile back, but when someone puts a gun in your
hands, whatever you've just agreed to do gains a little more
gravity.

"Safety's on the side there. I recommend you leave that
on until we get to Toro's place. At that point, I'd definitely
suggest you turn it off."

Toro's place was outside the city in a commuter burb called
Hilston Heights. We parked a block from his house and got
out. I knew the streetlights were rigged and the drones were
on their circuit, but I always felt less watched in the outskirts:
the sound of crickets at early dusk, the smell of barbecue and
fresh cut grass (for those who could afford to pay the water
premiums). It was deceptive.

Dara handed me a face mask with a plastic strap on the
back. Every inch of the face was beige and polygon-warbled.

I knew about these from our bank's security bulletins—
the masks were the last volley against facial recognition
technology, but you had to have a 3D printer to make them,
and those had been outlawed long ago.

"They didn't get your printer with the identichip overrides?"

"No," said Dara, "they did, and we turned the husk over
to the government. But not before we 3D printed our own
knockoff printer. It doesn't work as well, but these masks
turned out great. I hope."

"Cool. What's the plan here?"

"Follow me. And Doyle?"

"Yeah."

"Safety off now. Aim at his chest, but don't pull the trigger unless it's the only choice."

I flipped the switch and looked at the pistol in my hand, knowing that the device was now officially set to Kill. A layer of slick sweat caused my mask to slip around on my face. I focused on Dara. Even in this situation, the way she moved was beautiful. She crossed the street with confidence. I moved behind her in what could only be called a scamper.

She ran around to the side of the house and quietly lifted the black metal latch on a gate to the backyard. I edged along with the gun pointed up, doing my best to remember how the fake police approached in movies. I was supposed to clear corners, right? Was I supposed to pull the trigger, or squeeze? Should I keep my elbows bent? The mask was blocking my view, giving me tunnel vision. Dara never stopped moving.

I rushed into the backyard with her, but she started running without warning, great gazelle leaps toward something I couldn't see, and then I heard a shot and felt wood shards pelt the right side of my face and I decided the best idea was to hit the fucking deck.

The grass was so green. Like they'd spray-painted it. The soil smelled fresh and wet.

My cheek was definitely bleeding. You can tell when it's blood moving across your skin because of the warmth.

"Doyle!"

I popped up and ran toward the voice. My mask was making it hard to tell where she was, but I heard a man say, "Goddamn, bitch! Easy, easy..." and then they were in my view.

At first it was really confusing, because the man had horns and I believed Dara had caught the devil, that she had his arm pinned behind his body at an angle that had to be just short of snapping the thing. Then I reached up under my mask and wiped away the blood in my right eye and that's when I realized the devil was wearing sandals and Bermuda shorts and sporting a much bigger beer belly than any metaphysical being would bother to have.

"Doyle! Coverage!"

She pushed Toro's body out further from hers but maintained the cruel angle of his arm between them. I pointed my gun at the man's torso and tried to stabilize my shakes so the guy wouldn't pick up the amateur hour vibes I must have been radiating.

Toro cringed. "Alright, cyclops. You got my gun. Your man's got me covered. Think you can ease up on that arm now?"

Dara pulled down on his wrist and he yelped at the shock. She pushed his body toward a red metal barbecue grill near the fence.

"Steaks, Toro? Doesn't that border on cannibalism?"

And then I realized I'd seen this man before, during the first season of *The League of Zeroes*, and back then he was known as The Bully. His modification scheme wasn't that inventive—a bovine imitation setup with the bull ring in the nose, horn implants in the forehead, bull tattoos galore, and a synthetic tail implant. He was voted out of the Big Top early in his season. If I remembered right, he was an asshole then. Apparently that wasn't an act.

Dara shifted closer to the barbecue and used her free hand to lift his tongs from the side of the cooker and bury them deep in the smoking coals.

Toro started to sweat. "You think this is the first time someone's tried to home vade me? C'mon, girl, I'm no dummy. Whatever you're looking for, it ain't here. You roll out now, maybe I don't have security gridtrack you. They're probably on their way for a 'shots fired' call anyway."

"I don't want your poison, and I don't want your money."

"Shoot, girl. You want an autograph? I don't even charge for that."

She pushed him closer to the grill. The treasure trail hair under his belly button curled away from the heat of the fire. Another inch and the suburban air would fill with the smell of Toro's sizzling yellow belly fat.

"Okay, okay. I'm listening."

"You answer straight the first time. I know how you make your money now that you're off the freak circuit. So does the Kept Squad. Any more bullshit and we rope you up and drop you on the wrong part of 45$^{th}$. I heard they're taking dealers' brains now."

"That's rumors. I watch the news. That brain thing don't discriminate. Dealers, NoBu bankers, sickies."

*Bankers? Shit. Our cowboys used to celebrate closed deals at Au Vin. The fire at the bank, maybe the guys outside Au Vin... were Delta and Dr. Tikoshi running clean-up operations? Was anybody knowing anything suddenly too much exposure?*

Dara gave Toro's wrist another rotation. He howled. I imagined Dara's face was as expressionless as her mask. How long had she been doing this kind of thing?

"So you want us to take you to Kept right now?"

"No. No games. Ask your questions."

"You ever work with Hungarian Minor?"

"I know him. Never ran deals with him though. Didn't like his vibe. Seemed like a guy who's more into, um, special privileges."

"Like what?"

"He ran with young punks. Always the *young* ones, you know. And I think he had some serious mileage on those knives he was packing."

"You hear anything about him working for a 'Dr. T.'?"

"No. Like I said, dude creeped me out. It was kind of a relief when he disappeared."

"You said 'no' but you shook your head up and down. Do you know Dr. T.?"

"No. Is that like some dude's street name or…"

"Dr. Tikoshi. Do you know him?" Dara reach over and pulled the glowing red tongs from the coals. "Your horns are too big to only be dermally secured, right? Or…no, look at that scar along the hairline. That's hack work, but I bet that means the plates aren't screwed in to your skull." She waved the tongs in front of his eyes. "Maybe I can use this to convert you to a fucking unicorn."

She raised the tongs to the horn on the left side of his head and hovered.

"Dr. Tikoshi."

He said, "I'm not afraid of those tongs, bitch. Back when I was The Bully I was branded five times."

So she broke his wrist.

I flinched when it crunched, but I kept my gun trained on Toro. Dara abandoned the snapped arm and grabbed his remaining healthy limb. He curled his damaged wrist toward his body, but not before I saw the missing fingers on his hand.

"Dr. Tikoshi."

"Alright. Easy. Listen." Toro looked around, scanning the sky and his house for something. "The bosses say we don't even talk about Dr. T. I think he used to work for us, but something went bad. Or maybe he's working for them again. I think they've tried to merc him a couple of times. It's confusing. So Hungarian definitely wasn't supposed to be working with him on some side job, and I sure as shit don't know what they were up to. I only know Dr. T. from the circuit. He did a lot of the more experimental modifications back in the day. He made everybody sign non-disclosure forms and refused to be filmed for *League* or *Oddfellas*. Lots of rumors about him, like he would do whatever you requested, even if he knew it would kill you. But I never met him. My guy was Dr. Shinori."

"Would Shinori know Dr. Tikoshi?"

"Yeah. I mean, that was one of the rumors—that they were old buddies. Like, *really* old."

The sound of sirens rang out in the distance. The audio sensors in the light poles would have triangulated the gunshot to this street by now.

"You still have contact with Shinori?"

"No, not for a few years at least. He used to do touch-up work for me when my shit got infected. But he's still in town, I think, doing plastic surgery out of the Brubaker East offices."

"Thank you, Toro. I'm going to let go of your wrist now, and if you try to turn and touch me, Mr. Doyle will unload his pistol, which happens to be packed with boiler rounds."

Toro's eyes went wide at that, the flesh of his forehead wrinkling against his surgical steel protrusions.

Dara continued. "And if we find ourselves being gridtracked, or discover that Dr. Shinori has been alerted to our interest, the Kept Squad will have your horns mounted over their mantle by midnight."

I wanted to say something cool, too, but it was my first

gunpoint interrogation and I'd just discovered I was packing some kind of jacked-up bullets so the nerves got to me and all I said was, "Enjoy your burnt steak, jerk-ass."

Dara was laughing as we sped across town to the Brubaker district. "What was that?"

"The 'jerk-ass' thing? Or the part where I crashed to the ground and left you without coverage because I got pegged by siding shrapnel?"

"The first one."

"I wanted to let him know we were serious."

"But I'd already delivered legitimate threats."

"Well, the guy shot at me. I figured I deserved to get a jab in."

"True. You know I broke his wrist though, right? It's not like the burnt steak was the worst of his problems."

"You've got a point. And why was he making so many steaks, anyway?"

"Probably has mimic whores to feed."

"What?"

"It's another Vakhtang 'benefit.' Some of these guys will grab a girl off the street and pump her with a super-dose of Hex. Puts her consciousness somewhere in their realm, but her body is still here, alive, and open to suggestion."

"Jesus."

"Sometimes we find them dumped after their eyes jelly. Sometimes they get pulled through. If Toro had one, she must have been chained up, or she would have jumped us."

"If he's that kind of guy, why didn't we just kill him?"

Dara's stern face and the expanding sound of the road rolling beneath us made me think this was the wrong question until she broke the silence.

"I used to think like that, too. But they always find new replacements, and the murder puts heat on us. We've found containment and conversion work better. Besides, killing is easy for them. It shouldn't be for us." She took a deep breath. "It isn't, for me."

Her brow furrowed. I could see her having memories she didn't want. I changed the subject.

"By the way, thanks for using my real name back there."

"What do you mean? I assumed S.P. Doyle was one of your false identities."

"No, that's my birth name."

"Not Maria Scharf?"

"You've seen me naked. Did I look like a Maria to you?"

She laughed and raised her eyebrows, and then her cheeks lit up bright red. The woman who had broken a bull-man's wrist blushed, and something about that brought me joy.

"So, what's the S.P. stand for? It wasn't on any of your I.D.s and Ms. A. didn't have time to pull your birth records."

"Not telling."

"I'll tell you mine if you tell me yours."

"Dara's not your real name."

"Well, that's my first name, but I try not to tell anybody my surname."

"Let me guess...Dara McBarfshit?"

"Close, but it's worse."

"Than McBarfshit? That's not even a real name. And it's got barf in it."

"And shit. But, no, it's worse, somehow."

"I don't buy it."

"Okay—Borkowski."

"Dara Borkowski? Wow. I don't...I mean...yeah, that's one to process. That's like the sound of an obese flightless bird falling down a flight of stairs into a bowl of porridge. That's really rough."

"It's really Polish."

"Okay, fine. That was a doozer. Mine's a lot more Irish, I think."

"Go ahead. Just say it."

"S.P. stands for Shenanigans Patrick."

Dara's jaw dropped. "No."

"Yup. Shenanigans, like some Irish-themed mall chain brewpub."

"So why don't you go by Patrick?"

"I don't know. Pat for short. Pat the Bunny. I was a chubby kid. I would have gotten a lot of Fatty Patty. It doesn't have the elegance of, say, Borkowski."

"Yeah. Borkowski is like the sound of a Polish guy projectile vomiting. Still, *Shenanigans*...Man, your parents..."

"They were young. I think they thought a name like that would give me character. My mom said they wanted to change it when I started kindergarten, but the paperwork was a bitch, so that's when I became S.P. And after a while everybody just called me Doyle."

My parents.

*Mom.*

"I need to pick up a phone. Now."

It turned out Ms. A. had decided that my cash was already property of the mission (for lifesaving services rendered, I guess). Dara peeled off eighty bucks from what looked to be a three or four grand stash under her seat, and I used the money to cop a prepaid phone.

The convenience store guy would think I was robbing the joint if I went in there wearing an anti-face rec mask, so I opted to keep my hoodie up and head tilted down, and hope that kept me off everyone's respective radars. I wondered what would happen if my face appeared on even one camera. Who would track me down first? The Feds? The cops? Delta MedWorks? The bank? Vakhtang goons carrying a cell bomb with my name on it? That fucking one-armed gorilla brain cruncher thing?

Hindsight stepped in to remind me that my mistakes seemed far more egregious now that I was sober and on the run.

The kid behind the counter handed me my change. I didn't make eye contact for fear of showing my full face, but I could tell he had a lower lip ring and long red hair and his skin had that yellow-white isolation tan you get from pointing device screens at your face all day. He smelled like he was sweating high fructose everything and having twenty smoke breaks a day. Still he was nice enough to take a moment from his grind to offer me some helpful advice.

"Lots of people open up their phones out front and start making calls, but if I was you I'd get to my car and lock the doors first. I was just listening to the news and they said more bodies were found down by the river. No brains. The skullcracker is still out there, man. Shit's crazy."

"Thanks, man. Good lookin' out."

Back in the car, I locked the door and ripped open the phone packaging.

Three calls in a row. No pick-ups. I finally decided to leave a message, even though I'd heard a strange click right after the beep.

"Hi, mom, it's me. I'm so sorry I didn't manage to call you earlier, and I can't imagine what you must be thinking, but I wanted you to know that I'm alive…and I…I need you to know that whatever you've heard, most of it's probably not true. I'm, uh, I'm in a safe place right now, kind of, but I won't be able to keep this phone for long, so I need you to call me back at this number as soon as you get this, because I think you need to…well, I don't want to say more right now, I can't but…listen, mom…I just love you so, so much, and I'm so sorry for whatever you're going through right now, but please, call me back. Love you. Bye."

I wanted to curl up and find some way to not be me and hide from the world I'd made, but I knew Dara was sitting right there. I looked over to her and saw she was the one crying, and that, somehow, was terrifying.

"What is it?"

"They ruin everything, Doyle. Everything."

She sniffled and rubbed the tears from her good eye with the back of her hand. She started the ignition and we drove through the night in heavy silence.

# CHAPTER 13

## Private Consultation

The thing Toro neglected to mention about Dr. Shinori was that he had a tenuous grip on the English language.

Picture a naked man coated in lard and trying to pull himself up a black silk rope. Now imagine that man has had all of his arm muscles replaced with pudding. And then cut off his lard-laced hands and grease the bloody stumps. Now you've arrived, metaphorically at least, at the idea of Dr. Shinori's English skills. (Which, still, by far, trumped my Japanese language skills, but that's beside the point.)

So even when Dara and I bum rushed Shinori's office at the tail end of clinic closing and applied our now classic wrist-leverage/gunpoint persuasion technique, the results were questionable.

"Dr. Tikoshi."

"No."

"No, you don't know him, or no, you won't talk to us?"

"Draw."

Shinori pointed with his free hand at a pad of paper on his

desk next to a long charcoal stick.

I said, "Maybe we should let him draw."

"No. He's smart enough to practice medicine here, he's probably got more English skills than he's letting on. This is a gambit."

I thought of Toro. "I don't know. It's not like he's had the most discerning clientele."

"You want me to let him loose so he can set off an alarm or grab a gun from his desk drawer? No. He'll talk. We just need to put on our best listening ears right now." She turned her attention back to Shinori, bending his wrist beyond ninety degrees. "Dr. Tikoshi."

"Brainy."

"He's smart?"

"No. Yes. No. He buddy."

"He's your buddy?"

"No. Long time. Seven three one buddy. Before deal."

"What deal?"

"No."

Dara looked at me, shaking her head. Never before had the threat of violence yielded less information. We were setting a new high score with no witnesses.

Dara said, "Give him the charcoal and hold the paper for him. And watch for groin kicks, or headbutts, or whatever he's thinking this might get him."

I handed Dr. Shinori the charcoal stick from as far away as I could and then held the pad of paper in front of him.

He said, "Buddy," and then drew.

He turned the drawing to me—a crude sketch of a man holding a box, with lines running from the box to the back of the man's head—and I let out a little fanboy noise that I would have found embarrassing if Dara didn't already know I was a guy with a crooked penis and a name like Shenanigans.

"He's talking about *The League of Zeroes*. Buddy the Brain. He's been the head of the League for two seasons now."

"The idiot who put his brain in a box?"

Dr. Shinori nodded Yes and pointed at his drawing.

"And Dr. Tikoshi is his doctor?"

Another nod. Then Dr. Shinori flipped the page on his art pad and drew a clock with an arrow outside of it pointing counter-clockwise, and after that, a small explosion coming out of the ground. I'd spent a good portion of my higher education experience watching game shows, so I got it right away.

"He used to be your patient?"

"What?" asked Dara.

"Look at his drawing—the past, the explosion."

"So?"

"Was, mine."

"That's ridiculous."

"Yeah, but it was right." Dr. Shinori was nodding and pointing his charcoal at the page excitedly as if to say, "You got it. You got it."

"Wait," Dara asked, "If he can conjugate English responses into these complex visual interpretations, why can't he just speak to us?"

Dr. Shinori said, "No."

Dara tweaked his wrist again.

Dr. Shinori drew. He turned the page to me, excited to see if I would nail it again.

On the far left there was a shoddy drawing of a man in a lab coat with swirling arrows above his head. In the middle there was a snare drum. On the far right there was a rudimentary sun cresting over a hill.

"Dr. Tikoshi is dizzy from drumming in the sunshine?"

"No."

"Dr. Tikoshi is spinning…um, he's dancing…no, he's crazy?"

Dr. Shinori pointed at his nose. I'd nailed it.

"So he's crazy from drums and sunshine."

"No." And Dr. Shinori had to be right, because "crazy from drums and sunshine" isn't a thing.

I stopped. I spun in place. I felt oddly guilty for holding this charming man under the threat of violence. And then the answer hit me.

"He's crazy, and he's working on something to do with drums. The last part is the dawn."

Another nose point. I was crushing this game.

Saying the answer out loud made me think of something, but Dara extrapolated faster than I did.

"Wait…what about *Robbie* Dawn? I mean, it still wouldn't make any sense to me, especially the drum part. That can't be right. I don't know. Maybe you did see something about him on your computer screen. But why would working for him make Dr. Tikoshi crazy?"

Dr. Shinori pointed to his drawing of the clock with the arrows pointing counter.

"No. He thinks Dr. Tikoshi has always been crazy."

"And why would he be working on drums for Robbie Dawn?"

"No." And Shinori added a negative head shake to let us know that there was no further info forthcoming on the topic.

"Okay, Dr. Shinori—I feel like you're being very honest with us, and I thank you for that. We're almost done here, and I'm going to release some of the pressure on your arm now." Dr. Shinori gave a relieved sigh. Dara continued. "Do you think Dr. Tikoshi could also be involved in some kind of genetic experimentation? The kind of thing that might create a new type of lifeform?"

He took to drawing again. He turned the art toward me.

Some kind of machine press was spewing out tiny coins.

I got it. Makes cents.

"He says that would track."

"Okay then, Dr. Shinori, it's time for the million dollar question. Where is Dr. Tikoshi?"

He said, "No." But he also reached over and pulled out his drawing of the man with lines running from a box to his head and handed it to me, and that was our first step on the path to abducting Buddy the Brain.

# CHAPTER 14

# Home

The phone was set to vibrate, and I hadn't felt it buzzing against my leg when we were playing our demented parlor game in Shinori's office.

One new message.

*Please let her be okay.*

My heart decided I was running a sprint, though I was sitting still in the passenger seat of the blue sedan. Dara activated the door locks and decided we should keep moving.

I played the message. A strange series of clicks, then her voice.

"Hi, honey. It's mom. I can't tell you how good it is to get a message from you. I'm so grateful to know you're alive. This last week…it's been really hard, and I don't want to believe anything they're telling me. I told them that you liked your job and that you'd just had a big promotion and you wouldn't even need to steal, but they showed me some footage, and…I know you. You wouldn't hurt a fly. Whatever has happened, you know I still love you, okay, and we'll meet up and figure things out and I think I can do one of those reverse mortgage things if we need to get you a lawyer. Your timing is great, anyway. I *had* to get out of the house. The cameras were driving me crazy, and I swear I heard someone on the roof. I've been having these weird pressure sensations in my head, and...well, you don't need to hear my problems right now. I'm in the car, headed your way. I'll probably stop for some tacos, so I'll be in town in about two hours. Call me when you get this, okay? We'll figure things out. Love you so much."

I dialed her three times. Nothing. Maybe her battery was dead. She always forgot her charger. Maybe she was eating tacos. She didn't like to talk when she was driving, especially in the evening.

*Maybe she's tied to a chair. Maybe someone working for Delta is speeding up her Pelton-Reyes with a riot-busting radiation rifle. Maybe someone is injecting a super-dose of Hex into her neck right now and waiting for her eyes to turn black.*

Dara looked over at me. "Nothing?"

"Nope." I kept it short. Saying any more would let the panic go full bloom.

"Best case scenario says they're tracking her to you. They'll want you to communicate. Between these two calls and your attempts to reach her, they've probably pinged your phone. If we get back to the compound we've got a short burst communicator that can reach her without trace once she's in a twenty mile radius. Maybe Ms. A. can think of a safe meeting spot, or at least some place we'd have the advantage."

Dara sounded confident, but I remembered what she'd said earlier: *They ruin everything.*

I cracked my phone in half, pulled the components, and flung them from the car window.

Dara's grip on the steering wheel was white knuckle, but

she drove slowly and came to a full stop at every signal. Even a cursory traffic violation at this point would billboard our faces across the tracking networks.

*And there are murderers watching my mom, right now. And it's my fault.*

I needed something to stop me from thinking.

"Who's Cassandra? Ms. A. mentioned her back at the compound."

Dara's jaw muscles clenched.

"Was she another partner of yours with the mission, or..."

"Cassie was my sister."

*"Was." Damn it. I should have figured.*

"I'm sorry. We don't have to talk about it."

"No, it's okay. I love Cassie. I'm not pretending she never existed to save myself from pain. That kind of thing kills you inside."

It sounded like something Ms. A. would have told her— Dara remembering her sister kept the fires stoked. It kept her on mission.

"You have any siblings?" Dara asked.

"No."

"Well, you might not completely understand what I tell you, but that's okay. The thing about a sibling is that you can hate them, and that comes and goes, mainly because of how much they're just like you, or because you think of all the love you have to share with them and what it might be like if you had it all. But no matter how you feel about them, the moment they're in pain, you hurt with them. You share their suffering because they're pretty much a variation on the theme of you, you know?"

I didn't, not really, and I knew better than to say, "Sure,

that's how I feel about Deckard," because I was just smart enough not to compare her dead sister to my turtle (and I simultaneously realized how sad it was that Deckard was my closest friend). Still, I nodded because the way she was speaking kept me from thinking about what was happening. It was selfish of me, but she could have stopped at any time. Maybe this was a ritual for her.

"So Cassie had an accident when we were kids. A freak thing, falling into a campfire, but the way she landed had destroyed one of her arms by the time we made it to the E.R."

"That's brutal."

"It was worse afterwards. We shared a bedroom, and she used to wake up screaming, thinking her arm was still on fire. None of the specialists could do anything for her. They said her brain would have to reorganize itself around the absence of her arm, and after that the phantom pains would disappear. But they didn't go away. They got worse."

We stopped at an overlong red light. Dara scanned our surroundings, since we were almost back to the compound. She grabbed a device from the back seat—something like a cop's speed detector—and held it against the roof of the car.

"There's no drone signal, for now."

The light turned green.

"So by the time we hit high school, Cassie's phantom pain was hitting her in broad daylight, and you can imagine how popular that made her with the student body. Some football guy…what was his name? Scotty Halstrom. He used to pull his arm into his sleeve and shake his elbow at her and say, "'Where'd my arm go, Cassie? I'm stumped!'"

"Christ."

"Yeah. So I broke his nose, got expelled. Zero tolerance

policy. I switch to a new school, leaving Cassie alone with those shitbricks, and the first kids I make friends with are, um, I think the friendly term was 'free spirits.'"

"Loadies?"

"Yup. And I was pissed, so I dug in deep, and fast. There's no gateway drug if you try all of them at once. And this was, how long ago now? Jesus, eighteen years ago. So Hex was landing, and it was my go to, my absolute favorite. You know how it pulls you in."

"Yeah."

"So I'm in love with Hex. I *live* in that world, all silver, all the time, zero problems. A little paranoia about the wolf I can feel over my left shoulder, but you know how quickly you get distracted. And I started to think I was an absolute genius, because I'd figured out how to help my sister."

"Shit."

"I know now that they'd probably planted the suggestion, because it wasn't rational. I mean, Hex didn't really even block the hurt so much as it kept all the signals so busy that pain became scattershot. Still, I thought it would help her. I truly did. She was barely sleeping by then, from the phantom pain. We were in separate rooms, but I'd hear her moaning. So I told her to trust me, that I had medicine that would really help her. I knew she wouldn't smoke it or snort it, so I told her to put it on her gums."

"But I thought it wasn't very effective as a sub-lingual."

"It still worked. Well enough at least. She didn't really sleep, but all that stimulus blocked the pain. She thought she was free. I thought I'd saved her from some curse. We sat on her bed all night, holding each other, talking…"

"Dara, you don't have to…"

"No, I really don't, do I? You know how it goes from there…Eight months later, Tim finds Cassie and I in a fucking dumpster. She'd been dating a Vakhtang who called himself Romulus, made sure she had a steady line on her medicine. He must have been bored that night, because he decided we'd be more fun as mimics. I remember being pinned down, then falling backwards into nothing.

*We know all about that place.*

"Cassie's dose pretty much melted her. Mine must have been lower, or my tolerance had built up, or Tim got the perphenadol into me first. I don't know. But Ms. A. took me in, and I never looked back. My parents know I'm alive, but I'll never see them again."

"You were just a kid."

"It doesn't matter. I did what I did. Ms. A. sent my parents an anonymous message to let them know where they could find Cassie. Supposedly Tim cleaned her up and put glass inserts in her eye sockets, for my parents' sake. I thought that was really kind. Ms. A. and her crew were my new family, and that was the only way I could stand to keep going."

"Dara, I'm so…"

"I know, but it doesn't change anything. And we're here."

She killed the engine, and we hopped out of the car. I set the safety on the pistol she'd given me and tucked it into the back of my pants. We were parked in a different spot than when we'd left, further from the compound. The sedan's engine ticked as it cooled. Fifty story towers loomed over the street, but if you tilted your head and looked straight up, you could still see the night sky.

# CHAPTER 15

# Orbital Broadcast

"Ms. A., I've got to get in contact with my mom right away. She's already headed into town."

"You spoke with her?"

"Just messages back and forth."

"And you're one hundred percent certain that the voice on the phone was hers?"

"Of course…wait…what are you saying?" *But I knew. My brain wouldn't let me think it any sooner. If the Vakhtang got to her, they could have turned her into a mimic. It would be a great way to gain access to me, maybe even to Ms. A.'s compound.* "It definitely sounded like my mom. The cadence, the inflections, everything. Nothing she said sounded suspect, but I think she's definitely being followed, and her phone is making a ton of clicking noises."

"That's understandable. That's good. I can tell I've upset you, but it's a necessity that we stay aware of all possibilities. Dara, did you have a clear path home?"

"Considering the nests we stirred up, surprisingly clear."

"Hmmm." Ms. A. turned and walked toward a thin unfinished hallway, pushing aside the beads strung across the entrance. "Let's grab the short burst radio and see if we can't guide mom to a safe zone."

"But won't her phone still be tapped?"

"Of course. She'll have to acquire an interim phone. And even if she makes it to a safe house without being tracked, we're going to have to cover her head and treat her with the sacrament."

"You're going to bag her and shoot her up with perphenadol?"

"We aren't protecting proprietary fast food recipes here. This compound is one of the last few American outposts working against the Vakhtang. We are admitting your mother as a great kindness, and with great risk."

We neared the end of the hallway and a single steel door with three locked deadbolts and a key code entry box.

"I meant to ask you, Ms. A. If their cult or gang or whatever is called the Vakhtang, what are we called?"

"We have no name. Something named is more easily defined, infiltrated, and broken. Our desire is to function outside of any rigid structure—to simply exist, in as low-profile a way as is possible, as a counterbalance, until the blessed day when we are no longer needed."

"So Lazer Crew is off the table?"

"I can hear the wavering in your voice, and I do not mind your humor. If it helps you survive, then it has value. But I need a moment to track down the radio, please."

She entered a long string of numbers and the steel door unlatched. Here, finally, were the accoutrements I'd expected in her office. Heads in jars (their all-black, unblinking eyes staring back at me), perfect steel cubes emanating a low red light, a six-legged rat in a wire cage, rows of hanging herbs, surgical supplies floating in a thin purple gel. A glass case filled with iridescent scarabs denuding a too-fresh lamb's head. An entire wall dedicated to guns, ammunition, scopes, and grenades. And to our right, a six-tiered rack of shiny silver devices, their metal carrying the same sheen I'd seen on the slingshot Dara had used to launch a cell bomb.

I looked over at Dara to find her quiet and distracted. I'd forced her to think about Cassie. Now she couldn't stop.

Ms. A. hunkered down by the second shelf from the floor and pushed aside an object which had altogether too many electric wires and elongated probes.

"Here we are." She pulled out a small rectangular receiver with two dials and a CB-style communicator hooked onto the side. She blew years of dust from the top and then nodded her head. "This old thing ought to work perfectly. We should be able to transmit from the main room. Shall we?"

She turned and headed out of the storage zone. I followed far enough behind to grab something which had caught my eye.

I'd always wanted brass knuckles. I'd never punched anyone, but they seemed like they were exactly what you'd need if you did have to go in swinging. The fact that this pair was bright silver and filed under a tag reading "Core Purge" made them even cooler.

They fit perfectly, and felt warm when I slid them into my back pocket.

Back through the rattling bead curtain, around a corner,

up a flight of stairs, and we'd made it to what Ms. A. was referring to as the main room. The coolness of the space told me we were still underground, but Ms. A. gestured toward a rectangular gap in the concrete at the center of the chamber. She set the radio beneath the gap, then hopped on a stool so she could reach a red button submerged into the concrete ceiling. Two steel grates separated and thin moonlight poured into the corridor above our heads, illuminating a fine lace of copper circuits covering the walls.

"We can amplify and reach out from here."

I looked back and noticed Dara hadn't entered the room. I walked back to where we'd come in and heard a quiet moaning at the base of the staircase. Dara was seated with her head in her hands. I hurried down to her.

"What is it?"

"Oh, nothing. Just a hell of a headache. Long day, you know?"

She tried to stand, but her legs buckled underneath her.

I yelled to Ms. A. "Something's wrong."

I heard her flip flops slapping the concrete as she rushed to us.

"Stand back. Give her some room."

Ms. A. lifted up Dara's head, barely kept it from lolling back down. She held a hand to Dara's forehead, then held that same hand a few inches from Dara's face and closed her eyes.

*What was this? How could I help?*

"What can I do?"

Ms. A.'s eyes opened and her face snapped to mine. "You can shut your goddamned mouth."

I'd never heard Ms. A. break from her Good Witch composure. Something was very wrong.

Ms. A. had her hand back in front of Dara's face, her own

eyes closed, sweat beading on her forehead from exertion.

"I can't close it down. She's looping. What happened out there? Why is she transmitting? She's been able to block them out for years."

"I don't know."

*Cassie. We'd talked about their realm. Her overdose. She couldn't stop thinking about it.*

Ms. A. lifted Dara's eye patch. Something swirled beneath the hardened black surface of her eye.

"Was anyone following you?"

"No. Dara said we were in the clear."

"Would anyone have known where you were going?"

"Toro. He knew we were headed to the clinic to see Shinori. Damn it. We should have found a way to intercept Shinori outside of his work."

"It's too late now. They could have set up there in advance. If they sent a full surge broadcast with a wave cannon it would have brought the fluid inside her jellied eye back into sync. And I believe she was thinking about Cassandra...We are left with only one choice, and we must move quickly."

I grabbed supplies, as best I could, from Ms. A.'s instructions, though the scarabs were far harder to round up than I'd anticipated. And when I secured the superior rectus forceps and what appeared to be a child-sized scalpel, I realized we were about to remove Dara's ruined eye.

You can feel scorching hot inside, and still find yourself coated in a cold sweat. I was no doctor. I didn't know any of Ms. A.'s rituals. How were the two of us going to pull this off without killing Dara?

*I was the one who asked her about Cassie. But I didn't shoot her with a wave cannon. I didn't even know what that was.*

I shook it off. There could be only purpose now. Dara was the only living person, other than my mother, who even knew my real name. She wasn't going to die like this.

I made my way back to the base of the stairs to see Ms. A. had dragged Dara's limp body ten yards down the hall. I caught up and set the supply bag on the ground and grabbed Dara's feet. We got her next to the cot in one of Ms. A.'s makeshift surgical spaces.

"On three. One, two, three!"

We lifted Dara beneath her hips and her shoulders and flopped her deadweight onto the stretcher. Ms. A. opened Dara's shirt. We felt a wave of heat lift from her torso.

"We don't have long. Grab the supply bag."

It was unsettling to notice that Ms. A.'s attention was constantly being drawn to the doorway of the O.R. I did my best to hand her the items she needed and to wipe the sweat from her forehead. I brushed Dara's matted hair back from her face and applied a cool washcloth to her brow and a wide blue ice pack to her chest.

Ms. A. cycled through the ritual, running a perphenadol spike, applying the scarabs, pushing her hands against some invisible resistance above Dara's eye. I joined Ms. A. in her ceremonial chanting, an incantation of light and blood that I found I'd memorized without trying.

We couldn't bring down Dara's temp. Her blood pressure soared, her vascular system a topographic map across her skin.

Ms. A. said, "I have no choice. We cannot wait any longer to perform the enucleation. Please bring me the satchel."

I brought her the closest thing I could find to what she'd requested, less a satchel than a marble bag made from bright silver chainmail with a fold-over steel latch on top.

Ms. A. opened the latch and sat the bag on the tray next to her. Then she grabbed the forceps and asked me to pick up a tiny scalpel.

"We've always been concerned that an x-ray might activate Dara's eye in some way we couldn't predict, so I'm not sure whether or not her optic nerve is still attached. If it is, I'll need you to sever it as quickly as you possibly can. But first, I need you to make an incision in my thumb."

"What? If you bleed on her that's an infection risk."

"No, it's our only chance of confusing the jelly into thinking it's still in contact with flesh while we move it."

I looked at Ms. A.'s near-panicked face, then down to the beetles latched in to Dara's chest. Ms. A. was right—this was neither the time nor place to enforce traditional medical standards.

Ms. A. pulled the latex covering from her left thumb and put it just above Dara's eye. I placed the scalpel against the pad of her finger, but hesitated.

"She's dying, Doyle. I don't know if we can stop her from being subsumed."

I pushed in, and after a second's resistance the scalpel slid right through to the bone. I pulled back from the shock of it and almost flayed Ms. A.'s thumb wide open. She inhaled sharply, but held her stand steady. Dark blood pooled over the obsidian surface of Dara's eye. Ms. A. pushed down with the forceps in her other hand, moving them past Dara's eyelids as delicately as she could. Once she had purchase on the underside of the eye, she looked to me.

"I'm going to pull up now. If anything at all is holding that eye to Dara's head, you slash right through it without pause. Can you do that?"

"Yes." Sweat dripped from my forehead to Dara's bare skin. My whole body shook with each heartbeat.

Ms. A. said, "And…pulling…now!"

The black eye held there for a moment, and then there was a burbling, sucking sound as the orb moved upward and Ms. A.'s pooled blood rushed down to fill Dara's eye socket. I did my best to watch the underside of the eye through the blood and when Ms. A. didn't seem to be able to lift any further I placed my face right down by Dara's and felt her shallow breath and slid the scalpel down into the thin space between the eye and the socket beneath, and I rotated my wrist to sever whatever held strong.

Lubricated by Ms. A.'s blood, the eye slid free of Dara's face without a sound. The thinnest vine of twitching blackness— like a severed spider's leg—clung to its base. A light drift of smoke rose from Dara's empty socket, something purified in blood.

Ms. A. reached over with her free hand and opened the small chain-mail bag on the surgical tray and gingerly placed the eye inside. She flipped the fold-over latch and secured the steel pins and only then did I see her stop to inhale.

Ms. A. and I worked to clean Dara's wound and be certain she was comfortable. The way her eyelids flopped inward was unsettling. She'd definitely want a glass eye, or maybe even a functional implant, once she was well. She wouldn't even have to wear the patch anymore. In the meantime, we taped sterile gauze over the socket.

"She's stabilizing, and I don't sense any further transmissions coming from this thing." She held the silver bag at arm's length like it was worm-riddled dog shit. "To be sure, I'd like to place this in another containment device for storage until we can be rid of it."

"'If thy right eye offend thee, pluck it out, and cast it away,' huh?"

"Christian?"

"No, but I tried to read the Bible in my early twenties. Too many pages of people begetting each other, so I skimmed for the trippy parts. Do you need me to join you?"

"No, you stay with Dara." And when she said it I realized that was exactly what I wanted to do, and I looked down to find I was already holding Dara's hand.

The explosion came from the hallway moments later.

Smoke and the smell of burning flesh rolled through the door in filthy plumes. Concrete chips skittered across the ground.

*Ms. A.*

I thought the eye had exploded as she'd feared it might, but then I heard men's voices.

"Clear?"

"Clear. Mostly. It's kind of a mess."

"Shit, man. Try to save a couple to take back to council and we won't get busted for jumping the gun."

"Agreed. Just remember, the one-eyed bitch is mine. I'm

not feeding her to the council."

The first I didn't recognize. The latter was Toro.

*Even with our scramblers on, they could have followed Dara's signal right to our doorstep. That's why Ms. A. kept checking the entrance during surgery.*

I remembered the pistol tucked into the back of my jeans, pulled it, flipped off the safety.

*Killing is easy for them. But it shouldn't be for us.*

Did I have any choice? I could hear their footsteps in the hall. I pushed Dara's stretcher across the room and tucked it into the corner closest to the entrance. She mumbled something at the disturbance.

"You hear that?" Toro said.

"Yeah. Third door on the left."

And now I knew they had their guns trained on our room. There had to be a way to regain the element of surprise. I scanned the space. There was some kind of gas tank in the corner, but I didn't know what I could do with that. Open the valve? Maybe that poisons everybody. Throw it into the hallway and hope I can pull off a trick shot? Even if I could, what's to say the explosion wouldn't engulf us all?

Then I saw the carrying case. I wasn't sure how Ms. A. selected which scarabs to use for her ritual, so I'd brought down a plastic box full of the things. I grabbed the case and crept closer to the door, pistol in my other hand. When it sounded like the men were about ten yards away, I flipped the lid to the container and slid it as hard as I could down the hall.

Gunshots erupted. Plastic shattered. A man screamed.

I rounded the corner as low as I could to see Toro collapsed on the ground, frantically trying to knock the beetles from his body.

"They're in my fucking pants, Pedro!"

Pedro looked up from his friend in time to see the man who'd beetle-bombed them, but I had the drop. I pointed in Pedro's direction and closed my eyes reflexively and squeezed off three shots. The first knocked me on my ass, and I heard the second ricocheting down the concrete corridor, but the third shot was accompanied by a grunt. Pedro was on the ground now, too. And he was smoking.

No, he was...steaming?

His skin bubbled bright red. Vapor rolled from his mouth, ears, and nose, and the hole in his abdomen. He looked up at me just as his eyes erupted outward and two puffs of steam floated from his face.

What had Dara called these? Boiler rounds? Why did something like this exist?

Toro was rising to his feet, pushing up with his good arm, covered in crushed Coleoptera fragments. I aimed at him, eyes open this time, but that seemed to throw me off. My three remaining shots went wild, embedding in concrete or flying off down the hall. Behind Toro I could see all that was left of Ms. A.: flesh-and-blood wallpaper showing the blast pattern of the detonated grenade.

Toro charged, firing his gun. I dove back through the doorway to Dara's room. Thudding to the concrete stole my breath. I couldn't reach the scalpel on the surgical tray.

Toro rushed through the entrance, shoulder-checking me so hard I flew against the back wall and slid down to the floor. He lifted his gun and aimed and pulled the trigger. It clicked on nothing because he'd wasted his bullets on beetle shelters and hallway concrete. Undeterred, he charged toward me and swung a boot into my ribs and I fell over and he brought his boot down on my chest again. I reached into my back pocket with the arm pinned underneath me, realizing my pilfered knucks were all I had, and held up my other arm to shield off his boot as he tried to stomp my head.

My fingers laced in through the silver knuckles and the thing felt warm and heavy in my hand. Toro lifted his leg again, swinging it back in a full pendulum arch, and I reached out and grabbed his other leg and pulled it toward me as hard as I could.

Toro dropped and let out a sincerely felt, "OOF!" and then I was above him on my knees and I aimed my heavy metal hand for his jaw, but he raised both his arms and my punch glanced downward and caught him right in the center of his chest.

Which, it turned out, was exactly what I was supposed to do with those things. But at the time, per my M.O., it was dumb luck.

Dara explained the Core Purge to me later: It was a Vakhtang weapon they'd secured, and it did something to bone and cartilage which caused it to vibrate at precisely the wrong frequency for the human body.

So at that moment, when my punch landed square in the middle of Toro's xyphoid process, it turned his rib cage into some kind of ungodly tuning fork. He vibrated on the floor and his eyes rolled back in his head. Having just seen what boiler rounds were capable of, I knew well enough to step back.

Toro reached out his arms to me, as if I could stabilize him, and then his back arched until his horns scraped on the floor beneath him, and there was a low rumbling from his mouth as the purge came: body-wracking spasms rolled through him and he flopped onto his side and there was a heaving sound and then a splash as he let loose the liquefied slurry that used to be his organs.

It only stopped once his esophagus prolapsed and hung from his mouth like a massive cow's tongue. All of this took about a minute, but time stretches out when you're witnessing an abomination.

My hands were shaking. I pulled the silver knuckles from my fist and threw them across the room.

*Those were in my back pocket. Jesus. What if I'd sat down too fast?*

I looked at Dara, sliding in and out of consciousness, stirring on the stretcher. We had to move. It was possible Toro and Pedro had launched their rogue assault on the fly, but what if they were always transmitting to the Vakhtang organization, sending their experiences to some kind of central hive? I understood nothing, truly, aside from the fact that people were trying to kill us, and they would not stop. And the compound, painted in a fresh coat of Ms. A., wasn't a safe place anymore.

I rolled Dara into another room, so if she woke she wouldn't find the puddled remains of Toro. I ran from room to room and gathered what I thought we might be able to fit in the blue sedan. Every little sound was Them, someone else who'd come to kill us. It was tough to focus through the fear, and I couldn't stand being away from Dara while I knew she was incapacitated.

I piled our gear by the front door—Ms. A.'s radio, Deckard in his enclosure, one suitcase filled with clothes and cash, our guns, my backpack. Was this all we had?

I found an old picture of Dara by her sleeping cot. She was much younger in the photo, her arm wrapped around another girl, both of them smiling on a picnic blanket. The younger girl was leaning to one side, doing her best to conceal a missing arm. I popped the picture out of the frame and slid it into my pocket.

I rushed back toward Dara's room, passing the steel door with the white symbol painted on the front. Clarence heard me walk by and called after. "They're here, pallies. I can feel them. All will be aligned at last! They're closer than ever!"

I yelled back, "Shut the fuck up, Clarence!" But he was right. They were closing in. I could feel it too.

I reached Dara and tried to wake her gently. I placed one hand against her cheek and brushed back her hair with the other.

"Dara?"

Her eye fluttered open briefly, then rolled back in her head. She moaned in complaint.

"You've got to wake up. We have to go. I think the Vakhtang know we're here."

Their name hit her like freezing water. She opened her eye and focused on me.

"I'm still alive?"

"Yeah."

"Fuck. My bad eye? They did something to it…"

"We got it out."

"Where's Ms. A.?"

"She's gone."

"She left ahead of us?"

"No."

"Oh…"

"I'm sorry."

"We're in real trouble."

"Yeah. I think so. We've got to go now."

"Where?"

"I don't know."

"That's a hell of a plan."

"I came up with it myself. I only know we need to go, and now. Do you think you can walk?"

She pushed herself upright on the stretcher. Dead scarabs fell from her chest, their signal-blocking services rendered as sacrifice. She swayed and held her head. Staying up was taking all her focus. "My balance is kind of a hot mess right now. Think you could button up my shirt?"

I could.

"That's better. Now you think you can put your arm under mine while we walk?"

I did.

There'd been no time to alter the hallway's abattoir status. Dara leaned on me and we walked softly through the remnants of what was left of her world, trailing bloody footprints on our way to a future that neither of us could any longer imagine.

# ACT III
## ALL THE THINGS YOU HOPE FOR WILL BE UTTERLY DESTROYED

# CHAPTER 16

# Any Port

If there was another compound set up and waiting somewhere in the city, the only woman who knew about it had been vaporized. As business resumption plans went, the mission's was far too dependent on key figures not being murdered.

Dara asked me to drive, slow and steady, while she combed her contacts for someone sympathetic to our cause. But it turned out that even people who'd contracted for Ms. A. in the past weren't too keen on the idea of taking in a one-eyed woman, a known fugitive, and his turtle.

Leon Spasky ran guns to the mission, but his industry demanded no ideological loyalties be shown. "I'm not snitching or anything, but I take you in and that goes public, maybe I lose a major client. Maybe worse. Sorry. Good luck, y'all."

Claire DuBois worked undercover for narcotics. She'd survived deep cover in a low level Hex distribution ring thanks to information fed to her by the mission. Ms. A. had literally saved this woman's life before, and yet: "There's too much heat on your pal. Rumor mill is saying he killed two of ours. They find you guys with me, that's a death sentence. I can't. I've got to go."

I realized I *had* killed two of theirs. Just not the two they knew about yet. Still, I riled at the scapegoat status I was catching from every side.

*Better call a press conference and clear things up.*

Dara turned to me. "Last chance. Here goes."

Huey Sheppard called himself a psychic energy adjustment agent, and saw himself as a healer, repairing chakras, auras, and like, freeing consciousness, man. Which was all semi-tolerable, considering he was also a hell of a drug dealer.

"You've reached Megaton Consulting. May I ask who's calling?"

I could hear the voice on the phone, clearly the kind of forced falsetto a man would put in place when trying to sound like a woman.

"Huey, it's Dara. You know voice rec software would still pick up your audio signature, right?"

Huey cleared his throat and came back with an even higher voice, some kind of chipmunk/dolphin hybrid. "My dear, I simply don't know what you're talking about."

"Wait, are you supposed to be southern now? Goddamn it, this is serious. How much longer do you need me to talk?"

"A moment more, dear."

"Alright. A moment's about all I have to…"

"Okay, okay. I've gotcha." Huey returned to what I assumed was his regular voice: low, male, scratchy and worn, the sound of a larynx run ragged by too many nights of shouting acid-head epiphanies.

"You know there's better software now. You could have picked up my voice in a couple of seconds."

"I know. My voice rec is fast. It's my new tracking system that takes a minute. You guys are near my hood. Why?"

"We need a favor."

"What? I just delivered Ms. A.'s dry cleaning last week. I told her the next round is going to take a while longer to tidy up. The amount of laundry she wants done, it'll take some effort."

He sounded exasperated. I knew we'd been running through the mission's perphenadol stash at top speed, and I guessed the theft at St. Mercy wasn't making it any easier to come by.

"That's not it, Huey. I'm up in the air right now, and I need an emergency landing."

"Any other passengers with you?"

"Only one. And a turtle."

"*Cool.* What kind?"

I spoke up. "He's a red-eared slider."

"Whoa. Who's that?"

"I told you, I've got another passenger."

"Put him on."

"Hello?"

"The alphabet, pal. Get going."

I made it to Q before he cut me off.

"Okay. Can you give the phone back to Dara please?" I passed it to her, my eyebrows raised, hoping I hadn't blown it.

"You trust this guy? News says he's involved in some serious shit."

"The news is lying. Come on. You know better than to buy their line."

"I know, I know. But it's the brain stuff. I like my brain. I'm fond of it, right where it is inside my head."

"That's not him. Trust me, it can't be. He's just a guy who got caught up in a bad habit and made a few mistakes at work."

"He's clean now? What am I saying? He's with you, he'd have to be. Any chance you guys are still in possession of some of his, uh, workplace mistakes?"

*We can buy this guy.*

I'd never felt that sensation before, the thrill of money turning into real power.

"We are, and we're in the mood to be rid of them."

"Then I think I can help you with your problem. The runway is clear for your emergency landing. Ring through when you're near the rear service elevator and I'll make sure Orwell takes a nap."

Dara hung up and set the phone in her lap. She smiled at me, but it was half-hearted and she quickly laid her head back on the seat. She shouldn't even have been out of bed. How was I going to care for her wounded socket? How did we know there wasn't some tiny shard of the bad eye retreating from the surgery and corkscrewing into her brain?

"I need some sleep. Once I introduce you to Huey, I'm crashing. You guys can work on setting up the radio and contacting your mom. I think the two of you will get along fine."

"Yeah, how's that?"

"He's fucking crazy, too. His paranoid fantasies have paranoid fantasies. Speaking of which, if he asks you if you can cross your eyes, say no. Otherwise, he'll think you're part of the Atlantean Underground, and you'll have to undergo electro-shock testing to prove you're not half-fish."

"Seriously?"

"He made Tim go through an hour of testing. He

threatened our connection if Tim didn't submit. Ms. A. asked him to bite the bullet for the sake of the mission. He took hundreds of shocks. It was brutal."

"How did it turn out?"

"At the end of the day it was decided that Tim was not a fish. We were all very relieved."

Dara pointed ahead. "Take that next left and park in the dirt lot behind the red building. And I have to warn you about one other thing."

It turned out that all first-time visitors to Huey's hyper-secure penthouse apartment had to undergo a full body scan in the dual-locking chamber he'd installed in his foyer.

Huey's full body scans were executed by a vintage CorTec Guardian Bot 3.0.

Yes, that's the version which requires you to strip naked.

Yes, that's the version which was reviled by human rights groups and ultimately recalled by the government for its faulty lubricant secretion valve.

No, I don't want to talk about my experience with the CorTec Guardian Bot 3.0.

# CHAPTER 17

## Huey's Cosmic Blessings

Ms. A.'s radio device did nothing for us. Maybe Ms. A. was supposed to charge some energy field inside of the thing. Maybe it needed the tower of copper circuits I'd seen back at the compound. Maybe I was supposed to fill the interior with magical beetles and jam the receiver down my throat. I had no idea how her gear worked.

Dara was finally passed out on the long side of a sectional couch in Huey's living room. She'd sipped on a cup of steaming chamomile tea, pulled a large gray and black afghan blanket over herself, and started snoring. Even in my panic, I couldn't bring myself to wake her. The sooner she recovered, the better. I was rudderless, veering wildly between angry and afraid. And Huey wasn't much help.

"How long has it been since she left that message?"

"More than a day now."

"You couldn't get through to her after that?"

"No. And we knew her line was tapped, but Ms. A. told me we could stay off-grid if we used this P.O.S. to contact her.

But then Dara got sick, and the Vakhtang attacked…"

"Wait, did you say Vakhtang?"

"Yeah."

"So they *are* real. I knew it. I fucking *knew* it. Ms. A. would never say what you guys were actually up to, but I had a funny feeling. Have you seen any of them transform into wolves? Or do that thing where they ride around on lions eating poor people?"

"Uh, no."

"What about their undertongues? Have you seen one of them use their undertongues to hypnotize somebody?"

"Where did you get this information about the Vakhtang?"

"Sources. I'm not going to tell you."

"The internet?"

"Maybe." Huey looked down, a slight frown on his face. "Yeah."

"I'll tell you what. You help me reach my mom, and I'll tell you all the real things I know about the Vakhtang."

"Nothing's *real*. It's just the things you think you know. Perception is a web of lies that helps our bodies float through space."

I think he was jockeying, trying to take back some kind of intellectual upper hand. It gave me a headache.

"Okay then. I'll tell you all the lies my brain thinks it knows then."

Somehow he viewed that as a win. His eyes brightened. "I have an idea. I could make you a poultice of lark root. If you dry it and then smoke it, that should put you in contact with your mom."

"What?"

"Sure—it's what the Ordu tribes used to speak to their ancestors."

"My mom's not some spiritual ancestor. She's here, in town, and someone else is tracking her, and it can't be anybody who means her well, and it's sure as shit not going to help her if I'm tripping balls on fucking lark root in your apartment."

"That's ethnocentricity, man. That's ugly. No bueno."

"I need to find my mom. I need a real, immediate solution."

"Oh…wait a minute. Wait a minute. I think I've got it."

Huey grabbed his laptop, executed three fingerprint scans, a retinal scan, and connected a device which unleashed a four hundred character password after he turned a small gold key in its side. Then he stared at the screen for a full three minutes without pressing a key and finally said, "There we go."

I tried to look over his shoulder and he rotated away. "I just met you. Back it up."

"Okay. Sorry."

"It's cool. Now I wouldn't say that I have access to the gridtracking system, but if I did, I might be able to tell you that there's a guy named Desmond three blocks from here, and he'd definitely be the go-to if you were looking for less than traditional communications."

"Can you tell me what he looks like?"

"Yup—about six feet tall, rocking a zebra head hoodie. Looks like he's drinking a bottle of Sternwheeler. Corner of Gatlin and Oates."

I jumped to my feet.

"If you use a phone to call your mom, it's tainted no matter what. You can't bring that shit back here. And it won't be cheap, Doyle. Tell him it's for Megaton Consulting and maybe you'll get an employee discount."

Five grand for a cracked phone. I don't think I got the discount.

I hopped in the blue sedan and drove around the city. If they did manage to trace my phone down through three satellite hook-ups and towers in Germany and Japan, at least they'd only capture me.

Each time I dialed mom's number there was an agonizing five minute pause before the ring.

Then four more rings.

Then voice mail.

Fuck.

I thought of all the times I'd dodged her calls, and how much I only wanted to hear her voice right now.

I turned on the A/C to kill the flop sweat.

There were no buttons on the dash which could help with overwhelming guilt.

I called again. Ten more times.

*Pick up, mom.*

Nothing.

I left a message: "Mom, if you get this, call back right away. I love you."

I scanned the streetlights and rounded the corners looking for blind angles. Found a small alley with thick awnings obscuring the entrance. Hopped out of the car, ducked into the side street, and looked skyward for roaming eyes. Buried my new phone under a pile of abandoned engine parts and prayed there'd be a message soon.

"You were gone for a long time. We're going to need to do a full body scan again."

I pressed the intercom button and leaned into the mic. "No fucking way. Fuck that. Tell Dara to grab our shit. We're out of here."

Suppressed laughter from the other end. "I'm kidding. Only joshing you. I'll beep you through."

Huey was waiting for me on the other side of the entrance. "Didn't know you were so el sensitivo. You have to laugh or they win, right? Anyway, even if you go now, I'm still getting paid for the heat you're putting on my place."

I pushed by him and ran to Dara on the couch. I grabbed her hand and rubbed her shoulder. She woke, just barely.

"Wha...."

"We have to go after them."

"Who?"

"The bank. Delta MedWorks. They've got my mom. I know it. She's not picking up."

"But if they had her, wouldn't they use her to draw you out?"

"Maybe that's their plan, but how would they know where I was? I barely know where I am, and I'm me."

"They'd pick up her phone calls, though. That's how they'd find you."

She was probably right, but I needed her to be wrong, because if my mom wasn't leverage she was something worse: a loose end. An externality. How would they know how little I'd told her? They might even think she was in on the bank fraud.

"Where do we start? If your hypothesis is right, Delta MedWorks has been eliminating the bankers who knew about the business with Dr. Tikoshi. Do you even know the name of anyone at Delta who would be involved in the cover-up?"

"No. I don't think any of the names in my bank's wire records were real."

"So do we start by shaking down the mostly dead batch of bankers, or do we go after the totally nebulous medical company hierarchy first?"

"I don't know. We have to do something." I looked over at Huey. He was rapt, taking notes, probably performing the mental gymnastics to fit everything we were saying into his pre-existing theories about the Reptilian Illuminati's plan to raise Atlantis and create a super-race of humanoid fish-snakes.

Dara raised her hand and placed her palm against my jawline. "We barely have any resources now. One side of my face feels like somebody smacked me with a brick, and my eyelids are doing something really weird and sticky under this bandage. When's the last time you slept? I don't know if we can make any good decisions right now."

It was the truth—I hadn't felt this exhausted since right before my Hex implosion—but it wasn't a truth I could accept. All I could think about was my mother: the way she'd held me and hummed lullabies, the way we survived the shock of my father's death together, and how she always meant it when she said she loved me, even when she could tell I was totally fucking up.

Then I realized what we needed to do.

"What if we find Dr. Tikoshi? We get him, we've got our own leverage. He knows exactly what Delta is doing. I can link him to them and the bank, and they know that. We have Tikoshi, we can negotiate."

"Tikoshi went underground. Or he might actually be in the Bahamas."

"No, I saw Shinori's face when we asked about Dr. T. He thinks Tikoshi is still in town."

"I don't know—that wasn't communication's finest hour. How do we know what he was saying?"

"He was adamant. He kept pointing at that picture of Buddy the Brain. That's the connection."

"So, that's our lead? You want to hop on a plane to L.A. so we can ask some reality show dimwit to help us find Dr. Tikoshi? Even if that would work, you're all over the news—they'd pop you in the airport."

"Guys!" Huey interrupted. He was excited, barely able to sit still. "Guys, you are not going to believe this. I mean, this is some serious cosmic serendipity manifested consciousness shit. We are literally making the world with our collective perceptions right now, I think."

"What?"

"Well, you're talking about Buddy the Brain, right? The *League of Zeroes* guy?"

"Yeah."

"Okay, so this might go outside of doctor/patient confidentiality laws…"

"You're not a doctor, Huey." Dara was sitting firmly at zero patience. "But please continue to your point."

"I beg to differ about the doctor thing, but my main point is, Buddy uses my services as a healer. He's had all kinds of problems since he put his brain in that box, and not all of them are conditions traditional western medicine is ready to deal with. Plus, he has to change out the cerebrospinal fluid in his box every couple of months. He says the stage lights thicken it, like old oil or something. And CSF isn't easy to come by, for most people. I have to work with the black market in China and let me tell you, those guys…"

"How does any of this help us?"

"Well, I don't know if Buddy's primary surgeon is really this Dr. Tikoshi you're talking about, but I can tell you that Buddy calls me all the time for supplies, and we deliver them locally. So my best guess is that Buddy flies into town each weekend to have his mods maintained." Huey grabbed his laptop and started pecking. "Here…let me check…my courier records…and…BINGO. There you go. It's what? Thursday? So by tomorrow, Buddy the Brain will be lounging in his luxury condo at the Haversham Towers. And…" Huey hesitated.

"What?"

"Well, Buddy is a good client. A *very* good client. And I know who you roll with. You guys can be kind of rough. I don't want to lose business. That being said…if you guys were to make me some sort of compensatory offer to brace against potential losses, I could probably make sure you were in the right place at the right time. You rough up my courier, unbeknownst to me of course, and then you make his delivery. Buddy the Brain opens the door for his medicine, and there you go."

I looked at Dara, "There you go."

We prepped.

Buddy's order came in close to midnight. We had until four the next afternoon to make our delivery—a concerning assortment of painkillers, one vial of powdered rhino horn, and twelve fluid ounces of somebody else's cerebrospinal fluid.

We crossed our fingers and hoped that Buddy's celebrity cash cow status and exclusive contract meant he'd still have a line on the location of the elusive Dr. T.

We sifted through the remaining loot I'd gathered when we abandoned the compound. Huey got his payment, nearly destroying our bankroll. I searched for extra cords that might make Ms. A.'s ancient radio work, but found none. Dara pulled the anti-face rec masks and two pistols from the car, cleaning both sets and reloading the guns.

While Dara was handling the tactical gear I let Deckard out for a constitutional and carrier cleaning. He clearly relished stretching his legs after so much time in his shitty transitory home. I watched him crawl across the floor for a moment but found myself suddenly overwhelmed and had to look away.

*Was he all I had left of my old life? Had I ruined everything else?*

I was relieved when Huey asked me questions about Deck. He even picked him up for a moment, surprisingly hiss-free, and looked him in the eyes and said, "What a good little guy." I realized that whenever I left Deck now, I was doing so believing I might die and leave him an orphan. Huey seemed like he'd be willing to bring an abandoned turtle into his life. Though I was also fairly certain Huey was the kind of guy who would let a turtle share his hallucinogens. Still, I felt like Deck had a place to land, and that gave me the oddest sense of courage.

Every few hours I broke from our prep routine and made the hike to my new phone.

Every few hours I checked for messages and came back with nothing aside from a heavier heart.

Huey performed some kind of herbal antiseptic lavage on

Dara's eye socket, sponging off Ms. A.'s crusted blood as it washed loose. After that Huey grabbed a scanner and held it over Dara's good eye, then the empty socket.

"What the fuck? Why are you scanning me again? You know who I am."

"This isn't for I.D."

He disappeared around the corner and came back in twenty minutes with his hands cupped around something.

"Check this out." Huey extended one arm, displaying something in his palm. "Here's looking at you, kid."

"It's beautiful."

I came over to see. The false eye was perfect, an almost exact replica of the real one already in her head.

"It's mapped to the empty socket, since they're never symmetrical. The material is designed for interior implant to prevent rejection. And here are some lubricating drops so your eyelids won't stick to it."

Dara pulled her lids back and pushed in the eye. She blinked a few times, walked to a mirror in the kitchen area to check herself out, and returned beaming.

"Okay—you're *kind of* a doctor. But how did you make this? You know 3D printers are illegal."

Huey smiled. "Any law which runs counter to the good of man is no law at all."

"You fucking hippy." She reached out and put a hand on his shoulder and whispered, "*Thank you.*"

"You're welcome. Maybe it will help you to evade the Vakhtang."

Dara turned on me, anger creeping into her face (though I was totally distracted by how beautiful she still looked with two eyes).

"He knows about the Vakhtang?"

"Oh yeah, he knows all about the shapeshifting and the lion attacks and the undertongues and everything." I smiled. Her shoulders dropped.

Huey chimed in. "He didn't tell me anything. I have my own sources."

The first rays of morning light fell through the window.

"Doyle, if we don't crash now, we're going to be a fucking shambles by this afternoon."

"I don't know if I can sleep. I need to keep checking my phone. I can't stop thinking about my mom."

"Well, you checked a minute ago. How about we rest for a few hours? You can set an alarm."

"Alright, but I'll probably just be laying there."

"I know."

She pulled her blanket from the couch and spread it out on the floor and put a few cushions down for pillows and waved to me to lay down by her, so I did, with my back to her, and I felt her fingers running through my hair and she said, "See if you can take ten deep breaths," and the first breath was shaky, but by the end of the second I knew that this was a good moment, and that I should try to stay here for as long as I could, and I wondered why life couldn't always be this, only this, and then sleep, long denied, finally came.

# CHAPTER 18

# Drunken Noodle

"We've got two hours until Buddy's expecting his delivery, and if we park the car early, in that part of town, it'll be noticed," she said. "Besides, I'm fucking starving and I can hear your stomach grumbling from over here."

She was right—Huey's fridge had been a condiment museum. Exotic jellies, hot sauces from around the globe, and one jar of pickled jalapenos. All we'd had since landing at his penthouse was a bowl of stale corn chips.

"I know a place. Low grid visibility and the owner is friendly to our cause."

Khao Tom's was a tiny hole-in-the-wall diner, but the cinder blocks were coated in bright orange paint and the host couldn't have smiled any bigger when he saw Dara.

He swept a hand across the room—probably a grander gesture than the four tiny, plastic-covered tables deserved—and said, "Any seat."

We picked a table near a bamboo-print folding screen, where we could both place our backs against the wall and watch the entrance. The smell of jasmine rice and fish sauce hit me and I realized I was about to drool.

The host walked over. "Dara, so good to see you."

"Thank you, Sunan. It's lovely to see you too."

"So you know, you're not paying today. Look at this." The host pulled a phone from his pocket and showed her something on the screen.

"Oh, that's wonderful. You must be so proud." Dara stood and hugged the man. His arms were stiff at first, but he returned the embrace. I caught a glimpse of his phone and saw a young man wearing a bright blue cap and gown. Dara sat back down.

Sunan said, "Kiet's studying engineering at university next year. We're nervous, but…" He raised his hands, palms open: What can you do?

"He'll be fine. I know it."

Sunan smiled and slid his phone back into his pocket. "Drinks?"

"Two iced teas, please. And actually, we could use a big plate of pad kee mao with chicken. And some salad rolls with peanut sauce." She looked to me. "Does that sound good to you?"

I trusted her. "Sure."

He took our menus and the tiny space filled with the scent of sweet oil and crushed peppers.

"You know their family?" I asked.

"Yeah, sort of. Tim and I rescued his son Kiet around four…no, wow…around five years ago. Kid thought Hex would work for a study aid."

"But he's fine now?"

"Looks like he's doing awesome. That can happen, you know? I think, maybe, sometimes things can go right."

Our drinks arrived. I took one sip of the sweet tea and my stomach flipped. I realized I might not be able to hold down my food. I was still so worried about my mom. I kept checking the entrance. Then I felt Dara's hand reach across the table and settle on top of mine.

"Hey. Hey. Be here for a moment, okay? Have some more of your tea."

"But I can't stop thinking…"

"Yes, you can. You have to, or what's the point? Look at me."

And I did, and I remembered how I felt when I first saw her, and I sensed the warmth of her hand, and I decided she was right. We needed this.

So we told jokes—hers about a penguin, mine about a squashed tomato—and we laughed and drained our teas and Sunan popped by with refills. Our plate arrived piled high with wide, spicy noodles and chicken and basil and pepper and onion, and we devoured it so fast we had to laugh again.

"Where'd you learn to eat?" I said. "The prison commissary? The African veldt? You think somebody was coming after your noodles?"

"You were. You looked like you were in a competitive eating tournament."

We leaned back in our chairs and sighed. Sunan brought us lemongrass waters with lime.

"This is good."

"Yeah."

We sat there quietly and listened to what might have been Thai covers of Beach Boys songs. After a while Dara checked her watch, and stood. She yelled to the kitchen, "Thank you, Sunan. Give my best to Kiet. Tell him congratulations for me."

I stood and followed her out into the sun. It was only when we got into the car and she handed me a pistol that I remembered everything was still wrong.

# CHAPTER 19

# Trunk People

I couldn't recall from the TV show if the box surrounding Buddy's brain was bulletproof or not, so I kept the pistol levelled at his torso. It's not like I wanted to kill him anyway—he was our ticket to see Dr. T. On top of that, I was kind of a fan.

Buddy was lounging on a leather couch, shirtless, clearly already loaded. He watched us with an odd smile on his face, like he was enjoying a passable, if not hilarious, sitcom. His fiber-optic-linked brain rested three feet to his left on a small Doric column, coils of connective line piled on the couch next to him.

Dara had Buddy's unarmed bodyguard covered. She demanded he place thick yellow plastic cuffs on himself.

"Fuck off, skeez."

"Aww, don't be mad at me. Maybe redirect that anger toward yourself. Take stock of your mistakes. Ask yourself, 'What kind of security agent would let their client answer the door?' or, 'Why didn't I take my service weapon into the bathroom?'"

"Not putting these on. That's a fact."

"Then there will be no next time for you to get things right. And I'll have to use this to ensure your compliance." Dara pulled what looked like a keyless entry remote from her left pocket and let her thumb hover over a bright silver button in its center.

The bodyguard tried to conceal a shiver, but it was clear he wanted no truck with whatever it was she was wielding. "Okay, okay. I'll put them on."

"Just a heads-up—more than ten pounds pressure in any direction and those cuffs activate. If that happens, there go your hands. So no wiggling. Now click 'em."

We heard the cuffs latch into place.

I've never seen three hundred pounds of angry muscle calm so quickly.

Some awful part of me wanted to rush over and start tickling the guy, to see what would happen, but Buddy pulled me from my weird flight of fantasy.

"This is real?" Buddy rose from the couch and stumbled toward me. The cord extending from the base of his skull uncoiled from the leather cushions as he approached. "I'm awake?"

Buddy reached out to touch me. Dara turned her pistol toward him and yelled, "Freeze."

Buddy stopped short of pinching me to verify I was flesh. He established eye contact and said, "That woman is very beautiful, but she is very serious. I have stopped trying to sleep with very serious women because they always want to pee on me when we're in the shower together. They think I need it, because of all of *this*." He gestured back at the vast hotel suite, the grand piano, the cityscape beyond the window.

I pictured a small bird flying through the noxious cloud of Buddy's breath and dropping straight to the ground, dead on impact. They played Buddy's indulgences for cheap thrills on *The League of Zeroes*, but in close proximity his life seemed much less a bacchanal and much more a toxic meltdown.

Buddy turned to face Dara. "Ma'am, you're not here to pee on me, are you?"

I'll be damned if he wasn't earnest. I started to laugh, but remembered how Port and Egbert had played my addled states for kicks, and refrained.

Buddy's bodyguard spoke, surely and softly. "Boss, this is real. You're awake. I need you to take this seriously."

"Oh, Boudreaux—you could be saying that in my dream. What's today's password?"

Boudreaux the bodyguard scrunched his brow, then the answer came to him. "Bluebird's egg."

Buddy raised a hand to me, dismissively. "Pardon me, exhausted phantom. I have to find an envelope." He started to walk away, but turned back suddenly and yelled, "EAT YOUR GUN, PHANTOM!"

And I jumped, but I didn't eat my gun, and that seemed to give the situation more gravity for Buddy. He returned to his hunt for an envelope.

"Here it is. Here it is!" Buddy lifted a small yellow envelope from an ottoman near the couch. He opened the flap and pulled a small white card from inside.

His eyebrows raised as he read. "*Bluebird's egg.*"

"Told you, boss."

"Well, then, I'm going to sit back down. Gun man, do you want me to be seated?"

"Uh, sure." I was kind of thrown off.

Buddy settled back into the couch, air puffing from the leather beneath him.

"So, gun man, how long have you known Boudreaux?"

"What?"

"I'm assuming this is for money, since I wouldn't grant Boudreaux's request for a raise…"

"Boss, no. I don't know these fuckers. I've never seen them before."

"I'm talking to gun man, Boudreaux. No need for your theatrics. How much do I have to pay you to discontinue this charade?"

Dara walked over and stood beside me, then let out a huff.

"She's relentlessly serious, isn't she?" I pictured the grim look on her face earlier as she'd placed an arm lock on Huey's courier and then swiftly choked him into unconsciousness. Serious, for her, was just the tip of a pyramid built on persistence and drive. It was why it felt special when she joked with me and let me see beyond her default settings. I looked over to see Dara sweating, arms tensed, her mouth compressed to a thin line. There was something stunning about the tautness of her body, and I wanted to make a statue in her honor, or kiss the side of her face, but then I saw the massive guy in handcuffs on the floor behind her and remembered this was a hostage situation and we were in negotiations with a man who wasn't quite sure if we existed.

Dara remained focused. "I am serious, and I need you to understand that this is very real, and that if you don't help us, you will find yourself disconnected from your fancy luggage over there." She pointed her pistol at his brain, still sitting on its stately column. It hadn't moved even as he'd fumbled around the room. I guessed the column was custom and had some kind of suction cups to keep the brain box steady. Did he fly with that thing, or have one fabricated for any place he was a frequent guest?

"Doyle! Gun!"

I'd let my arm drop, caught in the mental drift. The few hours of rest Dara and I had tucked away weren't enough to return me to proper function. I righted my pistol.

"Listen to your cruel mistress, gun man!" Buddy found us amusing. The expression on his face made me feel like a jester performing for a child king. "You two have a desperation in your faces which makes me like you. This isn't a money squeeze, is it? You'd already have a wrench to my brainjack like the ogres AsparaGus sent to extort me."

"No money, Buddy. We're looking for a friend of yours."

"Oh. I'm afraid you're far too early. Bobby won't be here for another week. He used to arrive day of show, but the Center fucked up his lighting last time, so he's running an extra rehearsal. Even so, we'll be waiting until next Thursday. Are we camping out? I'll need my supplies. You must be the couple from...just a moment." Buddy reached over and gave the top of his brain box two thumps with his fist. "I needed to jog my memory." He turned to us, gauged the reception to the gag. Dara was stone-faced. I did my best not to laugh. Buddy shrugged off the dead air. "That's right—the Stockholm couple. You guys really don't give up. Bobby must have woven quite a spell on you."

Dara walked around the ottoman, raised her foot, and brought her heel down on Buddy's instep.

Buddy yowled and clutched his foot close to his body. Then he closed his eyes and said, "Change to bird. Change to bird."

He opened his eyes, dismay apparent, the absence of avian transformation finally forcing him to accept that this was truly happening. "Alright, invaders. What do I have to do to make you leave?"

"All we really need is a medical referral." I wondered why she wasn't just saying Dr. Tikoshi's name, then realized she was leaving gaps to allow Huey plausible deniability. "Who does your work?"

"Oh, come on, you guys—you know I've got a private contract. I can't divulge my doctor's name or every two bit mutie on the circuit will be hitting him up for their mods." Dara pulled the Keyless Entry Fob of Doom from her pocket and showed it to Buddy. He was unimpressed.

"You're going to open your car from far away if I don't refer you to my doctor?"

"No, boss. Tell her what she wants." Boudreaux spoke as urgently as he could, doing his best to remain still and save his hands. "You could always go back to Dr. Shinori."

"Shinori never did a damn thing without consulting Tikoshi. Besides, he tried to bootleg my surgery videos. He's dead to me."

"I know, boss." Boudreaux sighed, clearly weary of having tended to this collapsing man's whims for so long. He addressed Dara. "Listen, lady—what you're doing now isn't right. Buddy isn't *here*, you know? He's had a hard road since he lost his mom and between all the surgeries and the meds he's…he's somewhere else and if you use that on him it's like kicking a coma patient in the teeth. So, please, put the SoniScrape back in your pocket and talk to me."

Buddy beamed. "Boudreaux loves me!"

Maybe Boudreaux did love Buddy. Maybe he loved his

paycheck. Regardless, he could form coherent ideas and never tried to turn into a bird, so he felt like a much stronger resource.

"Okay," she said to Boudreaux, "we need to meet Buddy's doctor, stat."

"I can make that happen. If we do that, you let Buddy and me go?"

"Yes. I promise."

"Even though we've seen your faces?"

He had a point. Dara had nixed the anti-rec masks, figuring five star hotel security wasn't going to let us stroll through the lobby looking like we fronted a bad heavy metal band.

"Yes. You know it doesn't really matter who we are. We're not here for your client, and we'll never trouble you again. You seem like a reasonable man, which means you'll be wise enough to know that's the truth. You'll move on after this is over. And *that guy*..."

Buddy had closed his eyes again, and it sounded like he was whispering, "Lift as vapor. Lift as vapor."

"That guy might not ever know this happened."


The rear storage space of Buddy's SUV was crowded. I guessed that the commercials for his rig never advertised, "The trunk area fits up to two full grown anti-Vakhtang missionaries and one man's disembodied brain."

Dara was spooned into my body with her arms wrapped around Buddy's box, her pistol aimed at the cable junction where the fiber optic lines ran into the container and transitioned to a baffling mix of wiring and human matter.

The cerebrospinal fluid definitely needed a refresher. I didn't know if Buddy's gray matter was shedding a soup of dead cells, or if some chemical was tainting the mix, but his brain looked like it was floating in an unfiltered, long forgotten fish tank. No wonder the guy had gone loop-de-loop.

Boudreaux drove and Buddy rode shotgun. I wasn't sure we could trust the bodyguard at the wheel, but Dara had figured this was the only way to make the approach without spooking Dr. Tikoshi. We had Boudreaux's primary source of income hostage. We had the SoniScrape, whatever the hell that was. Hopefully those things were enough to keep Boudreaux from driving us to some kind of safe house where other employees of Buddy's were waiting to gun us down.

I hadn't been so close to a woman in ages, and the heat from Dara's body slipped through my shirt and made me want to push closer to her, but I wasn't sure if that was where we were at, or if there was any "we" at all, so I read the room and realized that even if she was in love with me this was no time for a make-out session.

Plus, Buddy's brain box smelled weird. Where had this thing been? What secretions had coated its shining surface? I pictured labia sliding against the enclosure, the brain looking out and wondering why these fleshy flowers were so eager to break in.

It helped to crush the ardor.

The smell of Dara's skin brought it back. I hoped my erection would tuck down the left side of my boxers instead of probing outwards, searching for access. I looked to the sky outside the windows and saw high-rises rolling by. Clustered masses of neon bullshit, an unavoidable enfilade of advertisements. Money in constant motion. I thought of the bank. Ardor was again defeated.

Then, there *he* was, Robbie Dawn at billboard height. "ONE NIGHT ONLY AT THE FREEDOM FINANCE MUTUAL CENTER!" The show date was next Friday.

Three echoes:

*He's crazy, and he's working on something to do with drums. The last part is the dawn.*

And

*This is some serious cosmic serendipity manifested consciousness shit.*

And

*Bobby won't be here for another week.*

Bobby/Robbie/Robert Matthew Linson/Robbie Dawn.

Robbie Dawn/SelPak Transfers/Anson Biomed/Dr. T./ Delta MedWorks.

Poison money moving in all directions. Bad business. Further echoes from a distant reality, but they sounded so close now.

Even my new friends who fought drug-induced metaphysical vortexes and used bugs for medicine had thought my Robbie Dawn fixation was cuckoo bullshit, but I wasn't high now, and this wasn't some daffy hallucination. This confirmed Dr. Shinori's illustrated assertions. This was real. It had to be.

I yelled from my storage space at the back of the vehicle.

"Buddy, how did you meet Robbie Dawn?"

"Boudreaux, I think the truck is asking me questions."

"No, boss—there are two people with guns in the back. They're forcing us to take them to your doctor."

"Really? That's a problem. Why are they asking about Bobby?"

"I don't know, boss."

"Okay, well, I'll clear things up for them. HELLO,

TRUNK PEOPLE. MY FRIEND BOBBY IS NOT A
DOCTOR OR A PRODUCT NAMED ROBBIE. HE IS
A TIMELESS MAN WITH THE VOICE OF AN ANGEL.
Do you think that satisfied them?"

"I doubt it, boss."

I wasn't sure how to crack Buddy's code. I slapped the
top of his brain box twice, hoping that might shock him
into coherence. I wondered if we were causing a delay, by
dragging his brain all the way back here. Were we reducing
his bandwidth and waiting for thoughts to render? I decided
to take a "When in Rome" approach and speak to him in my
most addlepated Gibberese.

"Buddy, this is Trunk Man. You have become a future mist
and slipped forward in time to a false reality. This has never
happened, so you may speak your true heart and leave old
feelings trapped in another universe."

"That's wonderful, Trunk Man. Do you promise not to
breathe me in?"

"I'm not even here. I'm a broadcast bounced off a dying sun."

Dara shook her head as if this was a futile line of pursuit,
but I continued, thinking provocation might force his ego to
surface and keep him focused.

"Your friend Robbie…"

"It's Bobby."

I took a deep breath and remembered I had to adjust to
Buddy's boggled reality for this to work.

"Sorry. Your friend *Bobby* is much more famous than you,
and his talents are natural."

"Striving and changing are fundamental to nature, too.
Bobby was born with his talents, but I cultivated mine. The
butterfly is as natural as the praying mantis."

Dara slapped her forehead.

"You are wise. But what of Bobby's fame? You have sacrificed so much more to become what you are."

"Bobby has more abstractions to trade and more toys to play with. Neither of us can casually grab a cup of coffee without horrible consequences. Once you lose the coffee run, everything else is just details...Trunk Man, I am convinced I have legs. And if I know about the legs, that means I have eyes to see."

*Shit. Don't lose him.*

"Buddy, you're slipping out of the future mist. You'll be solid soon. Now's the time to purge yourself of ill will. Tell me how you really feel about Bobby."

"I'm scared for him, Trunk Man. I don't want to believe what I've heard, but whenever I don't want to believe a thing, it becomes the truth. I have bad karma."

"What have you heard about Bobby?"

"Dr. T. is working for him, too. But not with his body. He's doing something else for him. Bobby has been running with wolves. His power isn't his own. Not anymore."

"What is Dr. T. doing for Bobby? Is it something to do with drums?"

"I don't want to say. Bobby never tells me, but when I asked Dr. T. he started smiling, and that's how I know they're doing something awful. Dr. T. usually only smiles when he talks about the war."

"What war?"

"My foot hurts, Trunk Man. I think I'm here. I think this is real."

"This isn't real. They're trying to diffuse your future mist with...um...solar flares."

"That doesn't make any sense, Trunk Man. God, my *head*..."

Boudreaux was right—Buddy wasn't *here*, and now I was squatting in his busted-up eggshell construct of a mind like a reckless hobo, stomping holes in the floor and lighting trash fires. I felt like a bastard.

"Never mind, Buddy. Thank you."

Dara turned toward me and gave me a single nod that looked like approval. She whispered, "You did what you could."

"What did I even do? Confuse the Mad Hatter?"

"You put us closer to the truth. We have to know what the Vakhtang are doing in order to stop them. And now we know you're not just a Robbie Dawn stalker. We were right about Dr. Shinori's puzzle—there really is something happening between Robbie and Dr. T. and I think it goes even deeper. '*Bobby is running with wolves.*' I know you heard that."

"Now you sound crazy. Are you sure you're not a future mist too?"

"But nothing *feels* crazy right now. Maybe Huey was right—this is some kind of convergence. I know you can feel it too. Something is happening. I think you and I are supposed to be here. I keep trying to figure out why Ms. A. stopped to save me even when she must have known the Vakhtang were coming for us. You could have run, and left me there, but you didn't. The two of you saved me. It had to be for something."

"It's just what happened, in the moment. We survived."

"No. It's something more."

And then she turned her face back toward the front of the truck. Her left hand found mine. She arched her lower back and pushed her hips against me.

At the time I was so bewildered that I assumed the hand was intentional, a show of camaraderie in our madhouse, but the thing with the hips was wishful thinking on my part, a trick of the rumbling road.

Hindsight would later reveal this to be a display of lordosis behavior, and had I understood this somewhere in my reptile brain and responded, maybe Dara and I could have given in to the urges we were both feeling and we would have had one strange, beautiful moment together in the back of that hijacked SUV. And then later we would have had some memory of what it was like to be together as whole, natural human beings.

Instead, neither of us moved. There was an odd electric paralysis as we lay there next to Buddy's brain, watching it bob and sway in its fluid.

*I think I'm here. I think this is real.*

The road rolled underneath us as the skyscrapers gave way to tenement blocks and abandoned brownstones. Just after I saw the yellowed streetlights and realized we were on 45th street, the truck slammed to a halt.

Dara and I both shifted onto our knees and stayed low in the back of the SUV, barely raising our heads above the rear bench seat, pistols levelled at our travel guides.

Buddy popped the top off a prescription bottle and dropped two hefty painkillers into his hand. He knocked them back and swallowed with no water, grimacing as they slid down. Then he smiled, one eye drifting off into the distance, one staying trained on me. "Last stop, Trunk Man. Made it to Doc's. It's tune-up time!"

# CHAPTER 20

# Tikoshi's Fan Club

We wanted Buddy to have his appointment—his brain tank was in desperate need of a refresher, and I was curious how much more lucid he might be with his mind swimming in a new pool of CSF—but the liability of sending him in first and playing some kind of waiting game was too great. Dr. Tikoshi might know well enough to disregard his patient's verbal effluvia, but I could picture Buddy being struck by a rare moment of mental clarity and saying something like, "The people from my trunk are here, too. They have no interest in peeing on me, but they brought guns and they'd really like to meet you." And sure, after that he'd say something like, "My head is probably all grapes, dream doctor," but the damage would be done.

I don't know if it's because Dara was cresting some invisible wave of serendipity, or whether I had a relapse of FUCK IT! WHY NOT? Syndrome, but—sitting there in Buddy's rig, staring at the side of what looked like an abandoned warehouse with a single light shining from a second floor window, and having no idea what might be waiting for us inside—we decided that it was time to finally meet Dr. Tikoshi, and now.

We ran the angles and realized that due to my total lack of training and Buddy's brain-damaged instability, this couldn't be some kind of SWAT raid. Though this forever crushed my dream of rappelling down the side of a warehouse and through a window with guns blazing, I conceded.

Instead, we opted for a more subtle approach: Walking right through the front door.

We'd pose as prospective patients/mod groupies who'd convinced Buddy to bring us along. Entering as a crew allowed us to retain some level of control over Buddy and Boudreaux's behavior, and placed us face to face with Dr. Tikoshi without him immediately seeing us through threat-colored goggles.

At least, that's how we hoped it might work. I don't know if it was madness by proximity from our time with Buddy, or the throes of sleep dep, but it felt like a plan at the time.

Boudreaux, sitting in the driver's seat, made a call on his cell. "We're here." Seemed code free, though I guess even a message that short and sweet could be pre-designated as a cipher for, "Shoot the motherfuckers coming in with us." Dara ran a drone scan while I scoped out the rooftops for anything moving. In particular I had my eyes peeled for the outline of massive loping brain-munching man-beasts, since those were, somehow, real, and possibly created by the man we wanted to visit. I shivered at the memory of the thing's drool running down the back of my neck—Post Salival Mess Disorder.

"Alright, boys. We're going in guns tucked, and maybe this thing stays peaceful. But you need to be aware that if there is any deviation from our plan, Doyle and I are each packing a full batch of boiler rounds, and I'll have my SoniScrape palmed."

Buddy spoke up. "I would also like a pistol, Serious Woman. Your tone is causing me some anxiety. Might be calming to hold a gun."

Maybe Buddy was actually that oblivious. Maybe this was as close as he came to clever. I considered the idea. Dara did not. "No guns for you. You're going to your appointment with Dr. Tikoshi."

"Oh, that's great! I've been under the weather, I think. I'll be back out in a jiff. Let's go, Boudreaux."

"No, Buddy. We're coming with you. Remember?"

"Oh…*yeah*." It was the least confident agreement I'd ever heard, but then he made a great point. "And why would he believe you're on the freak show circuit, again?"

"You've got a point. They're a couple of Plain Janes."

"They're right," I said. "Give me a second and I'll have it."

Buddy was excited. "He's going to have it, Serious Woman. You'll see. I knew Trunk Man in another time, and although I won't speak of the details, I can tell you he is wise."

And I don't know if the answer came from a truly intelligent place in my brain, or some damaged, drug-blasted quadrant which only lit up when ridiculous ideas were needed, but Buddy was right—I had it.

"Dara, you're The OptiCorn. You want your false eye replaced by a fiber-optic horn with a customizable surface and projection capabilities. Might be good to ask for a tail and steel hoof implants extending from the top of your wrists. That's a start."

"And you?"

"I'm Dick Twisty, recovered Hex-addict and outspoken advocate for the penile reconstruction charity Staff Solutions."

"Okay, but what's your mod?"

"I don't know. I was thinking I'd be able to fly on the 'provocative examination of an infrequently discussed but real issue facing men today' kind of thing."

"That's it?"

"And maybe I'm a detective, too. A detective who investigates a new real life maimed penis case each episode. Come on—it's contemporary. It's got an edge."

"Real talk!" added Buddy.

"But," Dara asked, "why would you need Dr. Tikoshi if your whole scheme is only to pretend to be a detective and televise bent penises?"

"Oh. Um…what if I underwent a monthly penile reconstruction? Maybe a different shape each month, on full display. Like when Tranny Danny did that series of gender reversions. Only I'd just keep changing the shape of my junk. I could do the soft pretzel. The striking dragon. The Möbius strip."

"The Civil War Reenactment!" Buddy was helping. I felt like I could ask him for a donation right that minute.

"See—I've got the endorsement of the head of the League. We're good to go."

"You're good to go!" Buddy lifted the vial of powdered rhino horn we'd delivered, popped the cap, raised the container to us in salute, and then snorted all its contents.

Boudreaux sat silent, his head in his hands, clearly not accustomed to the kind of absurd psychological ups and downs Dara and I took for granted.

"What do you think, Boudreaux?"

"I think we need to go, now, before Dr. T. starts wondering why we haven't come in."

He was right, and so we emerged from the SUV into early

night on 45<sup>th</sup> street, sirens in the distance, cooling air on our skin. We stayed low on the side of the rig opposite the entrance. Dara reached into her pocket and pulled out her old eye-patch.

"We need to obscure your face. The anti-rec mask would probably spook Dr. T., but this might throw him off. Between the news and him contracting for Delta, he might already know who you are. Hopefully this makes it harder for him to recognize you."

She expanded the elastic string and then brought the patch down over my right eye, both of her palms over my cheeks.

Her working eye looked straight into my still visible left. "Your depth perception and peripheral vision are going to feel a little ragged at first, but you'll adjust quickly. We can do this. We're going to find your mother. And remember, safety off."

I checked the gun. "Safety off."

Her hands drifted from my face, but their warmth energized me. I wondered at the way even the smallest touch from her pulled me into a haze where our general shitstorm status seemed acceptable. I hoped that, maybe, I made her feel that way too.

"Dara Borkowski."

"Yeah, Shenanigans Patrick?"

And I was going to lean in and give her a kiss, and I don't think she would have turned away. But then Buddy yelled out, "Sky Kirby, coming in hot," and we all ducked down by the truck and covered our faces.

I looked up after the sound of the engine passed over and saw it was only a recreational drone, without the lights which would I.D. it as city issue. Probably out to film voyeur porn in back alleys and windows, possibly scanning for open sales territory. Regardless, not our problem. But the moment had passed, sabotaged by the man who was now squatting in the street with his brain box vertical in his hands. His gray matter had sloshed sideways and was smashed against the southern wall of the container. How many concussions did Buddy unknowingly endure due to bad baggage handling? If I was in his situation, I'd carry that thing like an ice cream cake stacked on top of old dynamite.

Boudreaux was pissed. "Buddy, regardless of whose drone that was, you're pretty easy to identify. Let's scoot before it comes back around for a second look."

We gave the area one last scan before crossing the street. Spotting public or private surveillance was near impossible in that lighting, so we kept our heads low. Buddy the Brain, Boudreaux the bodyguard, Dick Twisty, and The OptiCorn had an appointment to keep.

There were no security pat downs at the front door, though we were greeted by the astringent smell of surgical antiseptics. Darkness clouded the warehouse, aside from a beam of light shining down over a staircase to the second floor. I checked the corners behind us and waited for the gun to the back of my head, but it never came.

Boudreaux and Buddy marched up the stairs ahead of us, and before our group crept over the top step we heard a man yell, "Spoiled fucking meat!"

Buddy looked back at us and pulled hissing air in through his teeth. "Yeesh. Doc's not happy."

And then we passed through the door to the second floor

and into the laboratory of Dr. Tikoshi. It was clear this was no thrown together back-up field unit. He'd been using this space for some time, and there were more gleaming steel machines and instruments than I could count. Two surgical stations with adjustable tables and ceiling-drop curtain railings sat at the center of the room, phalanxed by industrial freezers, chemical storage racks, and one extra-large humming box labelled "Materials." The entire area was floating in an eye-watering vapor-cloud of industrial sterilizer. Something had just been cleaned from the surgical space.

*Was this where Hungarian Minor had been bringing bodies? Or had he taken them to Dr. T.'s regular practice after hours?*

I thought about the amount of money Delta MedWorks had been shifting in Dr. Tikoshi's direction and realized that this could be one of many such centers in the city.

Dr. Tikoshi turned to us, something narrow, red, and wet flopping over the blue latex-gloved knuckles of his right hand. He wore paper-thin purple scrubs and blue elastic booties over his shoes. His hair was the salt and pepper mix of a man in his forties, but his skin seemed older and waxier. His face was pinched with frustration, and it was clear we'd broken his focus. He was wearing a pair of magnifying glasses for the apparent intricacy of his table work. He pushed them up on to his forehead and squinted at us from across the room.

"Oh, hello, Buddy. I apologize for my outburst. I had an unfortunate incident today, but I'm trying to make the best of it. But this..." Dr. Tikoshi shook the shining red tissue in his hand. "This material is old, damaged. The suture anchors are ripping right through it, and now I feel I've wasted too much time to give up the effort. I don't know. At this point I'm tempted to stop reconstruction and build a prosthetic, but I promised my patient I'd try an organic arm before we went down that road. And I haven't been able to tend to other parts of this lab recently, so of course we've got some kind of infection in the meat vat. It would have been great if this could have worked."

Dr. Tikoshi's voice was eerie, almost disembodied in its dissonance from his image. I'd never heard an old Japanese man speak in such a non-accented American news broadcaster dialect.

*And what kind of 'unfortunate incident' causes a man to salvage body parts?*

Dr. Tikoshi rotated away from us with a sigh, popped the lid on a biohazard bin, and chucked in the damaged material. Then he returned his attention to us.

He spoke to Boudreaux. "I noticed that you and Buddy have brought some friends with you. As a reminder, our contract stipulates that there are to be no additional visitors during Buddy's appointments. I'm sure you understand. Buddy has some fans who are a bit more *zealous* about my work than I'm comfortable with, and then there's the issue of proprietary methods, and…Well, I know you understand. So these folks must be very special, for you to have violated our terms." Dr. Tikoshi's voice carried a barely concealed indignation that riled at our insolence. "I don't mean to be rude, but that needed to be said. Now would you care to introduce me?"

"Sure, Dr. Tikoshi. First, I want to say that we're sorry, but…"

Buddy interrupted. "I've been seeing the robot field, again. Mostly when I lay on my side, but sometimes when I brush my teeth. We've got to fix that. I slipped through time earlier, to a dead dimension, but I'm back now. But I don't know how to whistle anymore. And the rash around my input jack is worse. And I'm out of ointment."

Dr. Tikoshi closed his eyes and took a deep breath. I imagined he was visualizing the stacks of money he received from Buddy as a way to justify the stress of interacting with a man who spoke in non sequiturs. "I can help you with all of those issues. Please continue, Mr. Boudreaux."

"Anyway, yeah, we're sorry and it won't happen again. These two are the winners of an online fan club competition that Buddy and I barely knew about until the network sent them his way. You know Buddy—he was already mixing dot-cons and merlot when they landed in our lap, and he demanded we give them this extra special tour, so long as the camera crew stayed behind. Buddy was hoping, maybe, that you'd be willing to answer a few of their questions while he has his tune-up."

There was a weary undercurrent I could hear in Dr. Tikoshi and Boudreaux's conversation. It was the sound of two men tethered to ridiculousness by cash, resentment vibrating against greed, a tone I recognized from my days at the bank. I'd always guessed that this feeling would dissipate with each zero added to the end of the paycheck, but it was clear from their voices I'd been wrong. Still, I liked Boudreaux's spin on our scheme.

Buddy decided to ramp things up. "They're my biggest fans. I had sex with both of them on my couch. They wanted chocolate fondue enemas, but I'm a lover, not a user. I know my fame is intoxicating—even consent doesn't feel like consent anymore. It's hard. This is the least I can do for them."

"Okay. I'll allow it this once, but never again."

Buddy drummed his hands on his brain box. "Never again. Thank you!"

"I'll need to focus during your procedures, though, so I'd suggest we handle the Q & A right now. Let me put my project in storage and I'll be right with you."

Dr. Tikoshi picked up a large tray from the top of his surgical station and transferred it over to a rack in his freezer. Then he removed his bloody latex gloves and deposited them in a silver basin where they landed with a wet smack. He raised one small hand and waved us over.

I'd felt safer with the space of the room between us, and did my best to play shy as we approached, avoiding eye contact and tilting my face away from Dr. Tikoshi's gaze.

We stopped a few feet short of the doctor and the smell of chemical cleansers was replaced by the cloying odor of something dead.

"Buddy, would you like to introduce me to your biggest fans?"

"Oh, yeah. Where are my manners?" Buddy knocked on his brain box. "Hello. Manners?" Dr. Tikoshi and Boudreaux gave forced toothy smiles for what I imagined was the thousandth time. "The stern looking one is called The Octopus, and the skinny guy goes by the name Dick Trunky."

*Close enough.*

Dr. Tikoshi reached out and shook our hands in turn, coupled with a slight bow of the head. I wasn't sure if I should return the bow or not so I shook his hand with all the cowboy vigor I'd learned at the bank.

"Easy, Mr. Trunky—these hands are how I make my way in the world." Tikoshi laughed, but I caught the very real anger below the surface. I dodged eye contact and waited for him to continue. "Well, it's a pleasure to meet both of you, and I'm so glad you appreciate the work I've done with Buddy over the years. I'll tell you in advance that I can't go into too much detail, but I'll do my best to answer your questions. So, what would you like to know?"

The litany of questions unfurled in my mind: *What have you been doing for Delta MedWorks? What was Hungarian Minor doing for you, and why did he end up dead? Are you working with the Vakhtang? Did you create some kind of giant creatures with gray/black blood and an appetite for brains? If so, why are those things killing bankers, Vakhtang members, and innocent people? Why did the thing that tried to kill me speak with four different voices? And why are they stealing antipsychotics in their spare time? What the hell are you doing for international music superstar Robbie Dawn? How can one man be responsible for so many terrible things? And where the fuck is my mom?*

And that's when I realized that what had seemed like a plan at the time was actually a ruse which left us neutered. We needed this man strapped to one of his tables with a gun against his temple or a scalpel hovering over his face.

Dara must have seen me tense up, because she jumped in before I could flip out. "Mr. Tikoshi…"

"Doctor, please."

*This imperious motherfucker.*

"Sorry. Oh my gosh. So embarrassing. Sorry. *Dr.* Tikoshi, is it true you used to work with SaladMan before he disappeared in South America?"

"You've done your homework, dear. SaladMan was one of my earliest patients with relation to *The League*. He was a true original. So dedicated. Those were the early days of anti-rejection serums, but he was committed and I'd wager his efforts, and the research we performed, have saved hundreds if not thousands of transplant patients' lives."

Buddy interjected. "He didn't disappear. He's still down there, near Brazil, running some kind of cult that worships vegetable consciousness. He has an ice machine business, and one of my assistants ships him used clothes that his 'tribe' sells to support themselves. I've got to tell you, though, he's a few cards short of a deck these days." And even though it was Buddy who'd said it, rendering the information instantly suspect, it felt true. Were there any of Dr. Tikoshi's patients who hadn't sacrificed themselves, in some way, to his experiments?

Dara was still trying to come at this sideways. I trusted her, but I also felt a boiling blood shimmer through my whole body that said, "Pull your pistol and break this guy's nose right now. We can't keep fucking around." It was an alien sensation, but one I was oddly proud to have felt.

She persisted. "That's so brilliant, Dr. Tikoshi. I feel like these guys get all the glory on the frontlines, but they really couldn't do what they do without your work." Dr. Tikoshi stood a little straighter, lifting his head, giving a slight nod of agreement. It was clear Dara had taken some psychology lessons from Ms. A. "Is there any way you can tell me what kind of things you're working on now?"

*No. Too fast. Too soon. Damn it.*

Dara was operating in the same sleep dep fantasy land I'd been living in for months. She'd jumped the gun. Dr. Tikoshi took the slightest step back, as if pushed. He shifted his magnified surgical glasses down over his eyes and squinted at his new fans.

"Hmmm." He lifted his left hand and slowly moved it back and forth in the air. We followed the motion. Dara's head moved to track the image. Mine didn't.

Dr. Tikoshi nodded to himself, having confirmed

something. He took two steps backward toward his surgical station while he spoke to us. "I just remembered I need to activate the dialysis machine for Buddy's fluid transfer, so if you'll permit me one moment..."

And he was much faster than I'd have guessed given his age—I barely saw his hands moving as he seized his gun from its taped holster beneath the operating table. Then he had the gun raised, and I recognized the strange yellow plastic of the barrel and knew that one shot at this range might split either Dara or me in half.

Dr. Tikoshi was furious. "Hands in the air, then drop to your knees."

The four of us raised our hands, Buddy holding his brain box aloft as he'd done so many nights for an audience of millions. I tried to read Dr. Tikoshi's face, to see what kind of calculations he was making, but then I saw him straighten the arm holding the gun, and I knew he had made the call: Killing all of us, right now, was the only sure way to contain this problem.

I don't know if it was because Buddy had snorted all that powdered rhino horn right before we came in, or if he'd segued into a reality where we really were his two biggest fans, or maybe both, but he certainly rose to the moment.

Buddy yelled, "NO, DOC!" and then brought his arms down as hard and fast as he could, throwing his brain box straight into Dr. T.'s face.

There was a satisfying thunk/crunch as Dr. Tikoshi's nose splintered under the impact. Dr. T.'s gun fell to the floor, and then inertia caught up with Buddy and he whipped forward, pulled down by the force of the box dropping to the ground next to Dr. T.'s flailing body.

A cracking sound rang out, and I wasn't sure if it came from Buddy's skull or the brain box as they both crashed to the concrete, and for a split second I thought, "Wait a minute—what's inside Buddy's head?" but the question disappeared when I saw Dr. T. scrambling to regain his weapon. I reached back to draw my gun but Dara was one step ahead of me, her arm already arcing down, gun in hand, to pistol whip Dr. T. The second blow to his head laid him out flat. Dara yelled to me to grab Dr. T.'s gun. I scanned the room for Boudreaux and found him squatting over Buddy, checking his eyes for signs of consciousness.

Boudreaux sounded panicked. "His box is leaking, you guys. Do not kill Dr. T. Do not kill him. We need him to help Buddy."

It was clear Boudreaux was far from a threat at the moment, crippled by his concern for Buddy, so instead of covering him I grabbed the yellow plastic gun from the floor and pointed it at Dr. Tikoshi. Dara stood a few feet back from the doctor's sprawled body, and seemed to be looking around the room for something to restrain his too-fast hands.

Dr. Tikoshi was looking right at me, his busted nose burbling out fresh, dark blood. He smiled, his teeth dyed red. "You came to me. After all this time, you came to me."

"What are you talking about?"

"We've been looking for so long. Nozomi and Akatsuki were starting to give up hope. None of your old co-workers knew exactly where you were, and they only added to the problem with the voices. Akatsuki left for Delta headquarters days ago, thinking they might have a private line on your location. All that effort, and then we found you this morning on our gridtracking tap. Nozomi left right away, thinking we couldn't be the only interested party who'd spotted you bumbling around in the footage. You looked so sad, checking that phone over and over again. *Pick up, mom. Please pick up.*"

Dara pointed her gun as Dr. T.'s face. "You shut your fucking mouth."

"But mom didn't pick up, did she? And now you're here. It's beautiful."

Just then, we heard a thumping sound coming from the staircase, boards straining under weight.

"I'm sure Nozomi was disappointed you weren't at your friend's house today. But he'll be so surprised to see you now."

I pivoted toward the entrance to the laboratory, but I was too late. The shadow of the thing crept over my vision within seconds, and then I was flying across the room and thudding to the floor.

I didn't know where the yellow gun was. I reached for the pistol packed with boiler rounds in my waistband, but it was gone too. I was missing a shoe. I felt the tingle of awareness draining from my head but pushed to stay conscious. A shot rang out from Dara's direction and shattered concrete at the foot of the beast. It ran toward her and I realized she was trying to take aim while keeping Dr. T. covered, and I scanned the floor for either of my guns and saw that Boudreaux had left Buddy's side. He ran across the room to the yellow gun, where it had slid to a stop in the corner.

Dara fired at the thing again, but between the speed of the creature and her divided focus, she only managed to graze the shoulder above its missing arm. The thing spun from the shot and spotted Boudreaux, nearly to the yellow gun.

Boudreaux dove for the gun, arms outstretched like he was sliding into home base, but the thing was too fast. It took three loping steps and then leapt in the air and landed on Boudreaux's back, snapping his spine. The thing reached down and grabbed both of Boudreaux's wrists in its massive remaining hand and pulled straight back toward itself, inverting the bodyguard's arms like it was pulling for a slot machine jackpot. Boudreaux screamed, a high pitch I doubt he knew he was capable of, but then the sound was cut short as the creature drove his knee into the back of Boudreaux's head, flattening the man's face back to his ears.

I'd made it to my feet, and was running back toward the entrance, looking for my gun. I saw Dara aim for the thing, but then Dr. Tikoshi's hands (so fast) whipped out and grabbed her legs and pulled them from beneath her. The creature turned toward us, drool sluicing from its massive mouth, and I guessed that it was angry it had to abandon the meal it could have made from Boudreaux's crushed skull.

I looked to the left and saw Dara struggling with Dr. Tikoshi, Buddy prone and barely breathing just north of them, and a few feet ahead of me, tucked against the base of an upright medicine cabinet, my gun.

I crouched to pick up the weapon and saw the shadow of the creature rushing toward me. Gun in hand, I dropped onto my back and pointed up and fired, and the thing was so close that every shot tore through its torso, and I hoped the boiler rounds would work on something that wasn't all human and smoke would pour from the thing's too-close eyes.

Instead I felt a huge hand flipping me on to my belly, and gray/black blood pouring from the thing's chest wounds onto my back. The creature's throat gurgled and then it coughed, splattering me with warmth.

It held me down, and its hot breath was on my neck, and

it whispered through wet, heaving inhalations.

"*I won't go alone. You'll die again inside of me.*"

I heard its jaw popping as it unlocked and stretched out to fit my head in its maw and I tried to move but its teeth were holding me in place. Then there was a cracking sound and a pressure so immense I wondered if I'd fallen again into that terrible realm (*Please. No.*), and in some distant place I heard my name, and the sound of a gun firing, but it didn't matter because my vision ran red with the blood coursing from the back of my head and I felt the thing's tongue slide over my neck before it plunged into the soft pink meat of my mind, and that was my last memory as a whole human being.

# CHAPTER 21

# Hotel Afterlife

It's difficult to explain the sensation of waking up from death. I'd been nowhere else—no heavenly lights or infernal torments washed over me. To my knowledge, or in retrospect, my perception, I hadn't known I'd been at all.

There were two observers during that time who could tell you my body was there in all manner of distress—heart rate soaring or disappearing, brain waves fluctuating like wild or flat-lining, lungs processing air via respirator, skin puckering against an army of sutures. But until the moment I opened my eyes there in Dr. Tikoshi's lab, as far as I'm concerned, I was fucking dead.

It was so nice.

And then, of course, I woke up.


"Can you hear me?"

I could. Dara looked ragged and sleepless. The puffy

243

perimeters of her eyes told me she'd been crying. I tried to answer her, but the word "Yes" came out of my mouth as, "Yub."

*Wait, why 'yub?' Why wasn't my mouth working properly?*

I wanted to reach up and touch my face, but found I couldn't move my hands.

*Jesus. Was I restrained again? Was anyone checking to see if I'd broken the world record for waking up in restraints?*

Dara read my eyes. "You can't move them yet? I'm sorry." She put her hand on mine and I felt the sensation. She lifted my hand to her face and sighed. This was hard for her. She looked so worried. I tried to brush against her skin with the back of my finger. Nothing. "Dr. T. said there's going to be a reintegration period, because of all the damage and the new input. He's going to guide you through it, like he did with Buddy. Supposedly this kind of thing used to take years, like a toddler's brain developing, but Dr. T. says he's developed something that will give the connecting and healing processes a boost."

No. I couldn't be the newest sacrificial lamb laid out for Dr. T.'s experimentation. I tried to voice my dissent.

"Nuh. Da. Mebbe die."/*No. Dara. Let me die.*

"I can't. I'm sorry."

"Cah do dis."/*You can't do this.*

Something started to beep behind me. I tried to roll from my side, to see what it was, but I couldn't.

Dara lifted her gun and pointed it at someone behind me. "Fix it, motherfucker."

"Relax, dear." It was Dr. Tikoshi, his creepy non-accent slightly altered by broken-nose snuffle sounds. "Everyone needs to relax. Doyle's dura mater is still very swollen. Any more pressure between the dura and the titanium plate and we'll lose him. This is a delicate time. I'll take care of it."

Dr. Tikoshi walked around the bed and brought up a syringe to my IV insertion point.

*What was he putting in me? What had he done?*

"As I said—you need to relax. This is a mixture to reduce swelling. A little mannitol, a little neurontin. A pinch of steroids. Something for the pain, of course. And the most subtle hint of perphenadol."

"Nuh. Nuh."/*No! No!*

"Have you heard the voices yet?"

*What voices?*

The beeping behind me subsided. Dara kept her gun on Dr. T., but her hands were shaking. My vision swirled.

Dara looked at me. "I'm sorry. I couldn't let you go."


"We have to move soon. Dr. T. says that Akatsuki is three states away, dealing with some issues with Delta MedWorks. Now, I don't know what the hell that means. I guess I don't even care, right now. But I don't want to find out he's lying and have one of those skullcrackers come in here and tear us apart. I don't know if I even believe Dr. T. when he says he only made two of those goddamn things."

I focused on my mouth as much as I could, on shaping my lips and making the right sounds. "One he...called...No... zo...mi. Dead?"

"Oh, you're doing great. That's so good."

"It's...dead?"

She hesitated, then said, "Yes. You put six rounds through him, and one lucky shot of mine hit him in the face right after he..."

Dara was holding something back. She looked across my body, making eye contact with that bastard surgeon.

"Dr. T. and I have talked about it. You've only got a couple of days until you should be able to get out of bed, and you don't need any more stress than you've already got. High blood pressure could throw you into a coma, or worse. Just worry about healing, right now, okay?"

"Dara?"

She put her hand over her mouth to stifle a cry. "I can't. I know this is my fault. All I can do is hope that you'll forgive me."

She rose from her chair, and stepped out of my view. I tried to rotate again and there was a cold water shock and I could feel something pressing against the back of my head and after that I lay very, very still.

I woke in a hotel room, alone. The drapes were pulled across the windows. There were bright white spots where mirrors and art had been pulled from the wall. My head throbbed all over, and a smaller spike of pain resonated near the base of my neck. Something cold and flat was pressing against my back. I managed to lift my left arm off of my body, but the weight of the hotel bed sheets pressed it back down.

*we could burn it watch the fire hungry* What? *they say I'm getting better but mom and dad they won't look me in the eye this is how you get to the next level and join the council keep grinding bitches and* Who's in the room? *money they gasp when the knife goes in that's what makes it real fish fresh fish polish each weapon each night naked rotate oil* I'm sleeping. I must be sleeping. This is the drugs talking. *I wanted to believe in an afterlife better than this man this place is too small* It'll stop soon. *this is what I get for helping my friends Jesus what is that thing what is that thing* It'll stop soon. *we played him for sure yeah you want more Hex here you go Crooked D you fucking herb the medication burns I couldn't control it* Am I awake? *once the flames started I peed all over myself and I smelled like smoke for days the man is sad again he's always sad my world is too small* Oh, shit. I'm in the hotel room. I'm awake. *I wonder if all the Vakhtang have jaws like that this is my Right of Refusal and my girlfriend thinks it's funny that I drew on this thing but you have to stand out am I right* I can't think straight. Are these my thoughts? *primary target one S.P. Doyle thought to be in possession of both bank assets and sensitive information* It'll stop soon. *my sister brought me flowers like that makes up for sleeping with my husband maybe I never would have started smoking if she never would have been* It'll stop soon. *such a bitch but that's life no hey now that's death the hospital lights should turn back on any minute of Christ I'm scared I'm so alone I'm so alone* It'll stop soon. Please. *oh my head I'd hoped Dara would fuck me after I made her that eye but you can never tell which way the wind blows oh great and now she's going to bed with that sad skinny motherfucker oh hungry slide through space smells like smoke again* Please. Stop.

"Only one more move, I promise. I know this is hard on you. Dr. T. said your integration is showing real signs of progress.

We had to leave for a minute to get more perphenadol from a friend of Huey's, so I hope that's helping. You were screaming when we got back."

"The voices. I couldn't stop the voices."

"Are they there now?"

"No, I don't think so."

Dr. T. jumped in. "The perphenadol seems to be highly effective for suppression."

"Oh, doc, you have no idea," said Dara. And she winked at me because she wanted us to share something, or she wanted me to remember the way we had been, and how she had saved me, but her face was still sad, and I was terrified that the voices would come back. She tried to distract me.

"Once you're up and around you can help me with this fucking guy. I'm barely sleeping, even when I've got him cuffed to that chair."

"I don't care. Why am I hearing those voices?"

Dr. T. said, "It's part of the integration. Nozomi told me they were overwhelming at first, but the perphenadol seemed to help, and he was practicing meditation at night as a form of therapeutic absorption to block them out." I tried to picture that massive beast sitting in lotus position, doing circular breathing with brains on its breath. "Akatsuki has been trying something else, creating memory hallways to identify and separate each of the voices."

"And that's working for it?"

"Not 'it,' him. He's a male. And yes, I believe so. But Akatsuki is a later version of the...what's the parlance they're using in the media? Skullbuster?"

"Skullcracker."

"Yes, skullcracker. Isn't that delightful? I mean, it's

reductive, and there's so much more to these beings, but it's got a nice sound to it."

"It sounds like a fucking nightmare, doc. But you're a crazy asshole, so you don't get that."

"Temper temper. Watch your blood pressure."

He was right. I could feel my veins distending. The sense of compression at the back of my head was phenomenal. I had to focus on keeping things at low tide.

"You said he compartmentalized each of the voices, but what I'm hearing is a mad rush. They're thoughts that aren't my own. They're private kinds of things, but they're in my voice, I think."

"The longer you hear them, the more distinct they should become. You don't recognize any of them?"

"That's enough, doc. Doyle's had a long day. Maybe it's time he had a little bedtime cocktail."

Dara bent over and kissed my cheek and said, "Goodnight." Then she grabbed a syringe from the hotel end table, stuck it into my I.V. tap, and pushed the plunger down.

# CHAPTER 22

# Backpacking

The new lab was much smaller than the one Dr. Tikoshi had kept hidden in the slums of 45th. This thing was closer to a dentist's office. One surgical area, a few sterilizers and packed cabinets. The central light buzzed and crackled, and there were dead flies in the ballast cover. The view from the window showed me seagulls, industrial blight, and not much else. It was definitely a D-list, emergencies-only kind of set-up.

In hindsight, I'm grateful we were by the hydraulic noisescape of the ports, so far outside the city. Anywhere else, and people probably would have heard all the screaming.

When I woke, Dara and Dr. T. had helped me to sit up for the first time in days. In a normal context I would have found the dizziness and head pain shockingly oppressive, but after enduring the high pressure terminal nothing vertigo of the realm and the actual sensation of something biting into the back of my head, this was kind of a walk in the park.

"Can I see a mirror?"

Dr. T. and Dara exchanged a look.

Dr. T. said, "I would suggest that you first let me tend to your needs, and beyond that I believe a discussion of your new condition is in order before you."

"Fuck my needs. Fuck your discussions. Tell me what the hell…"

Dr. T. pulled a syringe from his chest pocket and jammed it into my thigh.

"Jesus."

"Remain calm. The promethazine will help you through this."

I did feel better. His injection washed through me and I almost fell back on the bed. I wondered why I didn't feel air rushing across the open back of my hospital gown.

"Steady. Please look at my light for a moment. Okay. Pupillary reflex is finally functional. That's good."

"That's how you figured us out, huh?"

"What's that?"

"The night we met you. You did that little trick with your hand, and all of a sudden you're pointing a gun at us."

"Oh, yes. I had my suspicions before then, but once she displayed monocular impairment and you didn't, I knew that she was the one-eyed woman and you were Mr. Doyle."

"You know, doc, you've got a hell of a brain on you. Doesn't mean you're not a piece of shit. I definitely wouldn't say *that.* I'd probably say you're a speedy-handed, weird-voiced, waxy-skinned fuckwad witch doctor, for sure. But a smart one."

I liked promethazine. I was feeling good. Almost happy, despite it all.

I stuck my hand in the air, thinking Dr. T. might want to give me a high five. He declined. But my arm felt just fine.

"Wait, doc. How'd you know I was running around with this beautiful woman over here?"

Dr. T. stared at me, frowning.

"Did I hurt your feelings?"

"No. There's seepage." He reached up and gently unwound a gray fabric turban which was wrapped around my head. He ran a square of gauze across my forehead and displayed it for Dara and me. Dark yellow and red mingled in the cloth. He held the back of his hand up near my forehead, then pulled it away. "We're going to need a round of antibiotics to prevent the infection from encroaching on the plate border. If that crosses into your brain near the screw intrusion…"

"Will something terrible happen, doc? Because my life's pretty peachy right now." And then I was laughing, and it felt good until I realized how restrained I felt as I inhaled. I put my hands up to my chest and shoulders and ran my fingers over crisscrossing straps, and when I looked down at them there was a tugging sensation against the back of my head and I remembered that I should be dead, but something far worse than a miracle had kept me here.

I reached up to the base of my head.

"Careful. You need to wash your hands, first. The entry point is still healing."

I didn't care. I had to know what he'd done to me. My hands closed around a cold metallic length of cable, and I didn't tug because I'd spent enough time with Buddy to know how this worked.

"Is my brain behind me? Is that what these straps are holding onto?"

"No. Much of your brain is still in your head. Nozomi only had time to swallow a few bites before your companion fired the finishing shot."

Dara had backed up against the wall, terrified that this

moment had finally come. "That's why we had to do what we did. Dr. T. said it could work, that we could connect both portions of your brain. That without it you'd either end up dead or in a coma."

"Dara, what am I connected to?"

"It was the only choice. You saved me, back at Ms. A.'s. I couldn't let you die. You…you're all I have left."

My head was spinning. I pictured whatever gray matter remained in my head twirling around like a gyroscope, then pressing against my forehead, trying to escape what it had just realized.

"Nozomi?"

Dara nodded.

"You hooked up my brain to a fucking monster?"

I needed more promethazine. I needed Ms. A.'s shotgun back in my mouth.

"It's a little more elegant and complicated than that." Dr. Tikoshi's bedside manner didn't really exist.

"Oh, I'm sure it is, you condescending prick. You fucking violated me. You should have let me die."

"I would have. Please understand, I performed your surgery with a gun pointed at my head." But I could see it in his eyes—he was fascinated. The experiment was everything to him. He didn't see me. He saw raw materials, a fertile field for his fucked up ideas, and he was getting off on the results. He continued. "Most of Nozomi is back in the laboratory on 45$^{th}$ street, feeding the rats and roaches along with Boudreaux and Buddy. What you have on your back is only the distillation of Nozomi's true capability, a unique organ which sat just above his stomach."

I remembered Nozomi drooling over me. *There's room now.*

"So I've got some mutant gut bag strapped to my back."

"I named it the animus ciborium. The whole of it, and its contents, are in that pack, including an organic neural circuit which connects to the external cord to allow integration with the remainder of the brain in your skull."

I reached up to the top of my head. The first thing which struck me was pain from the infection. The second thing was the cold metal austerity of the back of my head.

"Three titanium plates are in place. Nozomi damaged a good portion of your parietal area. The cavity in your skull was filled with cerebrospinal fluid, which should work fine, as it did for Buddy. The brain has unfathomable redundancies..."

"Buddy? *This is his cord.*" I reached up and grabbed the fiber-optic line connecting me to the pack, and wondered how fast I'd die if I yanked the thing from my skull. "Buddy was fucking insane. Nothing you did for him was 'working fine.' He was broken. But at least his brain was his own."

"You have your entire brain, although my research indicates you needn't worry about possessing the whole of it. Aside from that, can you not see the potential of what's on your back? If you learned to tap into your connection, you would have the collective intelligence..."

"I don't want them in my mind."

"But imagine all the wisdom you could possess. All of those memories and experiences available to you. Can't you see the strength in that? And the viral casings in the animus ciborium are built for compression. You could have so much more. There's a cap on top of the pack, and beneath that, a chamber lock for further data input."

"*Data input?* You sick fuck. Do you have any idea..."

"Your blood pressure." The monitor alarm was sounding. Dara was trying to protect me, again. What had she done? I detached my I.V. line, then pulled the pressure cuff from my arm and threw it to the ground.

"Oh, I better watch my BP, Dara. Maybe I should cut back on salt. Or maybe I'm stressed out because I've got a backpack full of other people's brains connected to my goddamned skull, and every once in a while they all forget they're fucking dead and start yelling inside my head."

"I'm so sorry."

"You keep saying that."

"I don't…Please, I need you here. I love you."

She said it, but I didn't even feel it, not the way I would have wanted to in any other world, any other time. The promethazine had worn off completely. "You don't fucking love me. You're just afraid to be alone."

"That's true—I don't want to be alone. But I *do* love you, for whatever that's worth. And I wanted you to have a chance, some chance, to save your mom."

*Mom. What would she think if she saw me now?*

An echo: Dr. T. laughing at me through bloody teeth.

*But mom didn't pick up, did she?*

He knew something. He'd known I was travelling with Dara. He'd found me through gridtracking access he shouldn't have. He had far more information than he was letting on.

I turned away from Dara and pushed my body up and away from the operating table. My knees almost gave, but I noticed Dr. T. was already backing away.

Dara said, "You need to sit back down."

"No—this motherfucker knows where she is."

"That may be. But you can't beat it out of him. We need

255

his hands. I'm no doctor. I have no idea how to maintain your set-up."

"What do you think, Dr. T.? Is she right? Or is it just that she wasn't paying attention a moment ago when you told me about data input."

"No. She's right. You're assuming information and memory are the same thing as fine motor skill. But a surgeon's hands are decades in the making. I have a long history with the human body. I know the precise level of pressure at which skin yields to scalpel. You'll die in a week without me."

"So why don't you save us both a lot of pain, and tell me where I can find my mother?"

There was a gleam in his eye then—I pegged it as contempt, but later found it to be a mix of Dr. Tikoshi's two muses: hatred and curiosity.

"I can't help you," he said. "There's nothing left of your mother to be found."


I've tried to picture those next moments the way Dara would have seen them, tucked away in the corner of the lab with her pistol pointed at each of us, knowing that she'd had a part in creating what happened, trying to look away, but too afraid to lose all that she had left.

She could have pulled the trigger at any point.

She watched me lift the autoclave machine and smash it over Dr. Tikoshi's skull.

She watched me pull his shaking, screaming body to the operating table and strap down his arms and legs and head.

She watched me as I searched frantically through his

drawers and located the bone saw and plugged it in and brought it down across the ancient, waxy skin sheathing his forehead.

She watched me as I lifted away the cap of his skull with a soft sucking sound, as I sliced into the gelatin softness of his occipital lobe and bisected his brain horizontally, white matter shining at its core like the wings of a butterfly.

She watched me as I lifted the pack from my back and unscrewed the cap and placed Dr. Tikoshi's pinkish-beige tissue into the chamber and resealed the top and released the lower lock and heard his mind absorbed into the animus ciborium.

She could have pulled the trigger at any point.

And when she didn't, I realized that I loved her too.

# CHAPTER 23

# Building the Mansion

We raided the lab. Unsure of exactly what the medical needs of a profane aberration might be, we decided to stack the deck in my favor, filling the car to the brim with drugs and surgical equipment.

We found enough dilantin and mannitol to keep cerebral edema at bay, and a comically large barrel of dot-cons ensured pain wasn't going to be an issue. Dara was worried about the infection along my scalp sutures and wanted to put me back on I.V. for antibiotics, but I told her I couldn't take one more thing attached to my body. She backed down but grabbed me a batch of azithromycin pills.

Perphenadol was in short supply, but I was fine with that. There was one voice in particular which I was eager to hear.

Dara drove. I realized they must have transferred me around the city in the back seat of the car, because sitting up front was near impossible. Agony shot down my spine every time the input jack in the back of my head brushed the headrest. I leaned forward, cradling the infernal backpack in my lap.

"There." I pointed to a flat, lime green flea-bag motel.

She went to the front office of the CoZZZy Motor Inn to score us a room. I sat in the front seat, hoping no one would see me, staring at the cap on the pack, wondering how long it would be before Dr. T.'s mind was integrated with mine.

*"We will know the truth once you have joined us."*

I whispered to the pack. "I'm coming in there, motherfucker." Hearing my voice, knowing this was really happening, threw me into hysterics.

When Dara returned with our keys, I was still laughing.


I lay on my right side on the king bed, with Dara across from me. We'd covered the comforter with a blue curtain from Dr. T.'s lab, hoping to restrain the bedbugs which were surely lying in wait. My eyes lost focus and I felt like I was floating on bright ocean waves. Dara taped a fresh strip of gauze across my seeping scalp wound, then ran soft fingers over my face. I did my best to breathe calmly despite the battery of meds buggering my bio-stasis. In for three, hold for three, out for three.

In for three, hold for three, out for three.

I closed my eyes, wanting my sole focus to extend inward.

In for three, hold for three, out for three.

My consciousness drifted, floating above my wrecked patchwork skull.

Bright blue ocean waves rolled forward from beneath my vision. A staircase appeared in the center of the ocean, steps reaching down into a dark corridor beneath the waves.

I descended.

*Where are you, Tikoshi? I'm going to build a mansion of memory hallways. I'll lock these unwanted thoughts and minds behind steel doors. But you, Tikoshi, you're getting a special spot in the basement. No light. No room to move. I know a thing or two about pressure, and darkness.*

*You don't know where I've been.*

The corridor took on a dull green glow, surrounding me in a cylinder of slow drifting phosphorescent algae. Wherever, whatever my eyes were, they focused on the shifting light.

Not algae. Neurons/axons/dendrites, floating loose in fluid.

*Am I at the back of my mind?*

The corridor looped beneath me. I followed the swirling path down to the pulsing cage of the animus ciborium.

The voices were there, each of them asserting that they existed, that their thoughts were of consequence, that they must be heard. I focused. I imagined my body as a wall of tympanic membranes, trying to isolate each stream of sound, turning thoughts into structure as the vibrations moved through me.

*the egg had fallen from the nest so I thought it might already be dead but when I put it in the fire the shell popped and the baby bird was wiggling there and I didn't know if it was screaming or if that sound came from the fire and after that I always watched the fires from further away*

You are the arsonist, the first to die on 45th. You live here now. I'm closing the door.

*so I told the guy sometimes you gotta do one for free to stay fresh to keep the spark alive so it's not just a job I mean you have to love it to do it right and anyway the laws are so different over there and sometimes the parents are the goddamn pimps and nobody gets the cops involved so I said fuck the clean-up and left her right on the beach with the rock buried in her head and work was so much better the next day*

You are the assassin. You live here now. I'm closing the door.

*can I really keep doing this when I'm forty I've got to make some moves too much time in the dark staring at the back of Egbert's dome when I should be the one out there repping*

You are Port. You live here now. I'm closing the door.

*he told me he wanted it like that he knew what he was doing it's not like I talked him into gassing that was his own shit but maybe I held him down too long I should have known when his asshole got so loose but you hate to kill that sprint to the finish and he was going to Dr. T. for materials anyway I knew doc would be pissed about the brain damage so I offered him the body at half price*

You are Hungarian Minor. You live here now. I'm closing the door.

*this is a come up for sure twenty grand more and I can get the full mod and ditch the tweeker business and if the boss lets me take the separation rites I'll be part of The League in weeks this Viking shit will blow them away but do I put the skin sheath on the left or right side of my spine I guess that's for Shinori to decide after he sees the sword*

You are Egbert. You live here now. I'm closing the door.

*it seems cruel that the nurse reminded me that visiting hours are almost over like bitch you know there's nobody coming to see me/I don't think I can take another round of chemo I don't want to tell Mike but if he really loves me he'd understand that this can't go on right/how is it possible that they don't have the ICU on generators that's insane oh God did you hear that that's someone screaming maybe I can get out of this bed*

You are the patients of St. Mercy. You live here now. I'm closing the door.

*I know I don't have the best memory but what if just what if I had a flashback or maybe I finally knocked back that yagé and then forgot about it but I wasn't throwing up I don't know how else have I been outside of my body so long and why would I have had that nightmare that thing was so huge shoot maybe my spirit animal is a gorilla that eats faces hold on I can feel you watching me are you my body what are you*

You are Huey.

*oh I know that's my Anglo birth name but it's clear now I'm much more than that are you Gaia or a representation of nirvana or something how long have I been here*

You live here now.

*wait Doyle is that you how do you have a voice here are you talking to my body back at the penthouse or*

It's probably best if I don't explain right now. I'm looking for someone. I have to close the door now.

*oh okay I get it you're a metaphor for*

I'm closing the door.

*puncture down find soft egg keep going slide find new man new home find ocean fish cricket hungry*

What?

*warm light there has always been warm light water smells not real water miss float miss sand fish hungry fish man home fish*

No. The words warbled through me, some universal primordial drive my brain forced into language. The sound of the noise, though, was closer to a hum. Or a hiss.

*need out move legs eat jellyfish eat worm wait in pond fish fast now but time is mine bite half of fish slow now floating*

You are Deckard.

Nozomi did not have a discriminating palate.

I'm sorry you died that way, Deck. But you're here now. I'm closing the door.

*this is a slow and ignoble death ugh I can feel the rolls of my belly sweating against each other will you motherfuckers please stop bringing donuts and pizza and cookies in for one day I can't really stop myself it's all that makes this place tolerable I'll die in this job something has to change should I call mom tonight what do I even say besides same ol' same still she'd probably like to hear my voice we can talk about something funny we both saw on TV and that would be okay*

You are Shenanigans Patrick Doyle. You are me. We live here now. The door remains open.

*we have to be careful I can feel him growing in here he's connected he knows how this works he built this world he wants to raise a cathedral of bones*

He can't. This is our mind. We can contain him.

*He's here he's here he's here he's here*

I felt Tikoshi then, not as a voice but as poison, a seething surge of acidic energy that pushed through my thoughts and smashed against the front of my skull, and I knew there was pain back in the real world, and I wanted to yell to Dara to give me the rest of the perphenadol, please, but it was too late and I had eyes and when I opened them I was inside his mind, and everything I saw was death.

# CHAPTER 24

# Den of Cannibals

These are your eyes now. Look at what you've done. The brilliance of it.

*No.*

This is your world. You will never leave.

*Give me back my mind.*

This is the beauty of a long life unspooling in loops before you like the steaming guts of a soldier torn by bayonet. You will know everything, and whatever you believed you were will fall in the face of my truth. These will be your memories

now.

*It can't be like this. Dara, please, I need the perphenadol. This was a trap. He wanted this. I can barely feel myself in here. He won't let me out. He wants me to believe I'm him.*

*He wants to erase me from my own mind.*

*to erase me from*

*erase me*

*erase*

My life and memories are yours now. This will be all you ever
know.

Ten glorious years at Pingfang, a sea of bodies brought to
you by train. War as immunity from man's laws. Before, you'd
worked in the shadows. During the ten years you worked for
Division 4 there were no such hindrances. Dr. Masaki ran
the inventory, cataloguing prisoners as non-descript units
referred to only as "Materials Used." You preferred to call the
prisoners "logs," each destined for the incinerator after they'd
been of use.

You returned to Pingfang many years later. The incinerator
was still burning.

Waste not.

You used your materials without discrimination. Russian,
Chinese, the rare American. You didn't concern yourself with
eugenics. Far more could be discovered in the commonality
of the opened chest, the exposed mind. It is impossible to
understand the heart's strength until you wrap your hands
around one fighting its own death.

You switched arms for legs, ran flesh through long cycles
of freezing and burning, attached organs never meant to work
in concert. You injected the living with seawater and animal
blood to see how long alien matter would circulate. You
discovered the pressure levels at which ear drums implode and
eyes collapse. Rats and fleas ran vector work. Flamethrowers
were fine-tuned for greater effectiveness and shorter screams.

Though you had doubts about this actually happening in the field, it was still worth seeing what a fragmentation grenade sewn into a man's stomach might do when hit by enemy fire.

You took notes on everything. For science.

For remembering. You re-read the notes a thousand times. They remained exquisite. And when the war ended, they saved your life.

Potassium cyanide pills seemed a cowardly way to flee the truth. The kind of knowledge you possessed was of great value. So while others terminated themselves or went to Siberian labor camps, you let it be known that you possessed invaluable wisdom.

MacArthur granted you immunity in the U.S. in turn for an exchange. They told themselves that they could use the knowledge you attained without carrying the weight of its methodology. The government needed to appear to care about which materials were used, so you learned not to speak of the subject unless you met a kindred spirit.

But the United States was full of kindred spirits—some in the military, others among the private sector. They taught you the importance of marketing. Proximity to a nuclear blast site might induce a mysterious condition called "housewife syndrome." Syphilis was "bad blood."

The company line—"We don't know exactly what's causing these conditions, but we can assure you we're doing our best to find out."

Your wisdom took you around the world—there were materials to be used in Guatemala, Russia, and Africa. Advances in DNA study and microbiology kept the 80's interesting. The advent of widespread primate testing helped (especially when they didn't question your demand to have all the monkeys shaved bare).

Poor Masaki was brought low when he couldn't put enough distance between himself and three thousand HIV-infected Japanese patients. Your colleagues agreed: a failure of marketing and business structure. The CEO of the chemical manufacturer you worked for joked about it. "Don't they have paper shredders in Japan, Tikoshi?" Your feigned laughter turned to coughing. You were so weary.

You were dying. You knew the signs.

You were furious. Death was for *subjects*.

You remembered your compatriot Dr. Shinori, whom you'd last seen at a cosmetic surgery conference. He'd looked so healthy, decades younger. You phoned. He demanded you speak to him in person. You flew across the country, and almost flew right back when he tried to explain the secret to his youthful appearance.

A cult which could grant long life in turn for services rendered? Blood contracts? It was absurd—anyone who believed that some wolf god could exist in the heavens was not to be trusted. If there'd been any gods at all, they'd long ago forsaken the terra firma and left it to men like you to shape its future.

But Shinori said he'd been jogging that morning. You'd had trouble with the stairs as you exited the airplane. His skin was bright and yours tore at the slightest disturbance.

You signed on to work for the Vakhtang. You executed contracts, performed their rituals, and partook of their sacraments, believing in none of it. But there must have been something in the acrid broth they fed you at the base of their ridiculous wolf statue—you noticed the gray receding from your hair as each day passed. Your lungs took in more air. An x-ray revealed your bones had actually increased in density.

Pharmacology was not your favorite, and hypnotics weren't nearly as interesting as chemical weapons. However, since the Vakhtang existed in secret, the testing process allowed for the use of materials. They supplied you with vagrants, bored college kids, mentally ill ex-soldiers, and addicts. Embolisms and heart attacks served as points of interest. If your employers noticed you removing a patient's legs one overenthusiastic night, they said nothing.

A decade passed, during which you seemed to grow younger. Then one morning they told you the contract had been fulfilled. You explained that there was still much work to be done. They said they had what they needed. A physicist was being brought in. They'd stay in touch.

You asked no further questions. You discovered their agents watching you on occasion, but post-work surveillance was probably part of many of your employers' continuity plans.

Besides, there were always new opportunities and you'd lived long enough to see advancements in bioballistics, nanotechnology, and viral transfection. There were tools at your disposal now which could render the human body in ways you'd only dreamed of as a child.

You worked with like-minded scientists on the creation of a soda-borne protozoan whose waste immediately triggered intense hunger, and a face lotion which caused redness and cracking (as well as suicidal thoughts) if not regularly re-applied. This latter was airdropped over small Russian towns, though you never knew whose agenda that served.

Still, you tired of the subversive micro-efforts and the way they served only to shift money. If you were going to live for so long, you'd need something more.

The United States' new cultural fixation on body modification offered respite. Your subjects *welcomed* experimentation. Some welcomed pain. Watching their faces as you worked was like the slow echo of a beautiful song. Their love of fame made them malleable—you suggested surgeries which couldn't be survived, and they signed off. You manufactured bizarre champions and internet martyrs mourned for one day.

The media expressed interest in your work, but that could only lead to questions better left unanswered. You signed a private contract with Buddy the Brain—using his visits for micro-experiments—and retreated from public scrutiny. You wondered how the television audience would feel if they knew about the world war wet work you and Shinori had done which made Buddy's existence possible. Would they still applaud him if they'd seen a much younger you scraping all but a millimeter of Konstantin Barsukov's brain from his head while his mother, strapped to the table next to him, wept for her boy? Would they have given you a standing ovation back in thirty-eight, when you filled Konstantin's head with a mixture of salt-buffered solution and his mother's cerebrospinal fluid, allowing him to regain consciousness, open his eyes, and lift one hand before he perished?

You had your doubts.

You had new employers.

The first remained anonymous, sliding a manila envelope under your door. A high gloss photo inside showed a pile of human skins spread like bearskin rugs. The lack of scars and body hair indicated that these materials had been supplied by children. A note attached read: "Arriving in one week. Opening prayer has been completed. We need your expertise—these skins must run tight against laminated staves and endure vigorous beatings. A talented young man will use your work to produce some very special music. Toughen these hides, doctor. To accept the project and receive payment, sign the attached agreement in blood (your own) and place it in this envelope. Our courier will be outside your door by midnight."

You returned the vellum agreement unsigned. You were a surgeon, not a taxidermist.

A new envelope arrived. A black and white photo inside: a shot of you and Shinori from the glory days. Shinori was smiling and waving in an excited blur. You were also smiling, but could not wave as you were clutching a crucified man's intestines, testing how quickly they might be pulled from a perforation by human force. The man looked to the sky, jaws-clenched. Who had he cried for then? You'd have to check your notes.

Written on the back of the photo: "No one knows who you are. This can change. You've had a very long life because you've made the right choices. Sign the contract."

Work was work. You longed for something bigger, but signed anyway. The materials arrived—you sectioned the skins to the employer's measurements and treated them with a microwave-bonded laminate. You even recited the prayer they requested. After all, this employer had acquired a photo you had personally burned before the end of the war—honoring their request seemed wise.

Your second employer contacted you the very next day. You'd worked with Delta MedWorks before—ensuring the slow third-world release of a nasty measles variant for which Delta happened to be first to have the vaccine. They did, of course, wait until their virus had spread the globe. They called this "building a platform for wide release."

The new job was intriguing. They were working with a unique vector: a modified virus harvested from the thermophilic archaea which populated the scorching, acidic pools at Yellowstone State Park.

The Delta exec was excited. "The resilience of this virus is astonishing. They survive in pure acid, at two hundred degrees. We've at least figured out how to hollow the thing out, so we're left with the shell. That's the best part—the way the thing is structured, it will accept almost anything for delivery. Magnetic metals full of data, DNA. Hell, both. We've got a nanosphere particle that will take it right through the blood-brain barrier, so the pieces are in place. We're looking for a big stew—if we're actually going to sell something like this we need it to have real influence and application. I'm talking about epigenetic alterations creating brand loyalty, hormone control triggering hyper-consumption. And if there's any way we can allow the shell to *receive* interior data once it's in place, that would be ideal. We've got a friend at Lockton who posits they could outfit drones with a stereostatic retrieval device for flyover harvests. There have already been prototype tests for the shell delivery system, but the gorillas can't give us the more incisive test data we're looking for. We know we're asking for the stars, but if anybody can pull it off, it's you. What do you say?"

"Certain active materials will be needed."

"Of course, Dr. Tikoshi. Per usual, our full range of resources will be available to you."

"Would the Jiangsu facility be accessible for my work?"

"We can have it ready tomorrow. You should know that the

jail there is no longer operating in an *official* capacity. There were protests. The foreign media turned things into quite an embarrassment."

"And unofficially?"

"I believe you will find materials are in ample supply."

You boarded the plane for China the next morning.

You hadn't had access to this many subjects since the war.

You labored to deliver what Delta wanted—the undetectable control and commodification of the mind and its contents. The icosahedral viral shell they'd discovered was miraculous, and within the first year you'd created demonstrable applications of thought implantation and behavioral modification. Hundreds of subjects were lost to destructive immune responses, infections, and over-enthusiastic invasive research. No matter—the facility above you had been modified to "black jail" status, which meant the pantry was always stocked.

Delta came to regret your being untethered for so long. You'd spent decades in restraints. That repression found release beneath Jiangsu. The breadth of Delta's finances and the potency of the vector they'd provided gave you capabilities you couldn't help but employ. You requested a golden, helium-propelled DuMark gene gun for DNA transfection, and an industrial meat vat. You requested gorilla cadavers and synthetic skin printers. There were no questions.

You were certain your request for hair and teeth from the paranthropus boisei fossil at the American Museum of Natural History would be denied, but pieces of the "nutcracker man" arrived packed in thick foam.

Delta MedWorks felt they were asking you for the stars, but all they wanted was money. You would deliver much more—a final division of the have and have nots, a new branch of man-made evolution separating the two through brutality, consumption, and data assimilation.

You merged the efficient structure of an ancient human ancestor's jaw with the raw PSI of a gorilla known for cranial clamp downs. You used the gene gun to deliver doped DNA from both anacondas and rats bred for muscle density. You used the meat vat and skin printer to sculpt a proboscis and a duel-exit esophagus which could differentiate between brain matter and more standard foods. You created the animus ciborium and eventually found a way for its lining to allow propagation of your viral cocktail.

Things in the lab got a little messy—your fervor threw you into long periods of delirious experimentation.

The smell of death floated through the prison. Even in the black jail, information migrated. When Chinese officials heard stories of the atrocities at Jiangsu might have found their way overseas, they were forced to act, regardless of Delta's hush money. Jiangsu wasn't supposed to exist.

They raided the lab, found your work. No reasonable arguments could explain what they discovered. The man with the gorilla jaw sutured to the lower half of his face. The synthesized ciborium, filled with brain tissue and CSF. The human thorax running on respirator, surviving the absence of head and legs in a web of gray/black nano-scar webbing. The wasp-like ovipositor pulsing in the meat vat.

And everywhere else: the rotting remains of materials used.

Delta's money barely got you out of China, and your contract stood on shaky ground. They'd already invested a monumental pile of cash, and pushed for completion. They monitored you closer in the states and made weekly visits during which you concealed the more revolutionary physical manifestations of your work.

You sent them a video to ensure continued interest: fifteen minutes after nanosphere injection, your subject stopped crying, looked into the camera, and said, "I'm certain that Delta MedWorks' investment in our future means true safety and security for me and my family."

You'd removed the last five minutes of the video when the man's frontal cortex melted down and ran through cracks in his sphenoid sinus and out of his nose.

Delta had a harder time providing subjects in the U.S so you secretly sub-contracted materials requisition with a man from the area. He'd done supply runs for you during your time in the employ of the Vakhtang.

You'd gone too far in Jiangsu to revert back to designing some corporate shopping stimulus bug to be slipped into next season's flu shot.

New strands of gray laced through your hair. Whatever the Vakhtang had done to extend your life wasn't permanent. Was this your final project? If successful, you'd alter the course of world history. You woke in sweat-soaked sheets, your nights filled with dreams of your new children: teeth tearing flesh, millions cowering under their power.

A legacy.

Prototype one was too human. In its awareness it found horror, and took a scalpel to its throat.

Prototype two was too animal. In its hunger it found you. Only the skillful application of a diamond-tipped cranial drill through the creature's forehead saved you from losing your mind.

The set-back was important, causing you to rethink the

coiled proboscis in the prototypes' mouth. You decided your creation's jaw must to be able to compress small enough after use to allow for proper linguistic skills. What would be the point of all that intelligence amassed in a creature which could not express itself?

Prototype three was beautiful—bordering on feral, but functioning and ready for his first feeding. You named him Nozomi.

You'd requested new materials from your supplier. He arrived empty-handed—his bosses noticed his moonlighting and demanded he end the side-business unless information streams were opened.

"Anything needs this many bodies, they got a vested interest. You deal with them or it's my head. Maybe yours too."

Call it containment. Call it a test drive. You set Nozomi loose for his first hunt.

Hungarian Minor did not survive long.

Bolstered, you began work on a fourth prototype, weeks disappearing under a wash of constant labor.

Akatsuki took longer than Nozomi to reach full size, but he was spectacular. Larger, more cognizant, and incredibly agile. Plus, you'd finally managed to make the creature's ovipositor functional. What it released wasn't technically an egg, but the mucosal secretion it produced carried a massive viral load, ensuring that these creatures would not be the end of your efforts. Rather they were a culmination of your life's work.

Your legacy was ready for the world.

The world, however, had become problematic.

First Nozomi found the influx of integrated minds troubling. They'd measurably improved his speech and cognitive capabilities, but at what cost? You helped him develop the ability to submerge the voices, but his migraines and confusion amplified.

Then a message from a compatriot at Delta arrived: "Possible breach detailing relationship. Working to contain now. Another party has assured us that suspect (S.P. Doyle) is being tracked and close to being apprehended near 45th. Will keep you updated."

As a failsafe, you put Nozomi on the hunt.

Hours later he showed up on your doorstep missing an arm.

Eager only to perform triage and repair, you were doubly aggravated when you noticed the manila envelope which had been lying under Nozomi's devastated body.

After tending to the wound in Nozomi's neck and sedating away the babble of new voices, you opened your mail. "Dr. Tikoshi, I've included a paper copy of our prior contract. As noted in Section 2.3, 'Maintenance as needed' was part of our agreement. The original hides and a small container of patching material arrive in two days. We are certain that this 'tune-up' job will be done swiftly, and you'll be paid well. Don't worry about resonance or overtones, simply ensure our instruments' functionality. No reply is needed."

You fumed. This skin job was hack work and you despised the way the client assumed your obedience.

Nozomi rolled onto his side, coughed up a slug of clotted blood. His eyes opened but displayed an alarming left/right twitch.

He croaked through his rapidly mending throat. "The voices. All at once."

You ran your hand over his feverish brow. "I may know of a medication that can help."

"Soon, please. We are known, now. The man named

Doyle wants to expose Delta. Uncover our work. Vakhtang watching. Killed two. They'll be angry. We left evidence. The voices wanted us to burn the bodies. Hide the bodies. We couldn't. Hurt too badly."

"This 'Doyle' stabbed you?"

"Stung us like a scared little bee. Vakhtang shot us during feeding. The bank man did this." Nozomi lifted his still-oozing stump.

"How much does Doyle know?"

"Unsure. Man from the bank says 'too much.' Another says Doyle's 'full of crazy shit and junkie jibber-jabber.' There may be a hard drive with information linking us to the bank and Delta."

"It seems our first order of business would be locating Mr. Doyle. You must rest. I will send Akatsuki."

But you did not send Akatsuki out right away because you wanted additional security in the lab. It would be best to solve this Doyle issue yourself, before anyone else knew the level of breach.

You called in a favor with a C.I.A. friend and gained gridtracking access. You decided to stock the war chest and told Buddy the Brain he'd need expensive weekly tune-ups.

Two shipments arrived at your door simultaneously: Boudreaux brought a dot-con doped Buddy just after a ten man goon squad wearing anti-rec masks knocked and delivered a pallet. The latter shipment was stacked with plastic-wrapped drums and a black barrel which carried the faint odor of formalin.

Buddy was intrigued. "This looks like my friend Bobby's drum set, doc. Can't be though. His is custom. You get one of those Santo Marino bootleg deals?"

"No. I've never taken up an instrument. But I believe these may be your friend's. These drums are *far* more custom than you can imagine." You were also intrigued—perhaps Buddy possessed information which would tell you who had sent such odd work and demanding messages. "What is your musician friend's name again?"

"His stuff comes out under a fake name." Buddy ducked an unseen antagonist and looked to you and Boudreaux as if he'd had a close call. "Do you guys smell my hair burning?"

"You were going to tell me your friend's pseudonym."

"All my friends have pseudonyms. You think my name is actually Buddy the Brain?"

Boudreaux read your exasperation. "It's Robbie Dawn, Dr. Tikoshi. He makes R & B pop junk."

"Do either of you know how he acquired this set?"

Buddy frowned. "He won't tell me. Gets all squirrelly. He's had those drums since he left Mode 5. Keeps them in a humidity controlled room with a guard. I can tell you this— don't go pounding around on those things for fun. He let me join him for a studio session a few months ago, and I don't know if it was the party favors or what, but once he started drumming I got the weirdest weight on my shoulder. Felt like I was falling backwards, on and off, for like a week after." Buddy's eyes rolled back in his head. "For like a weep alter. Fir like a wee holster. Four life…"

"Come in. I think we need to perform your maintenance right away."

Buddy's brain repairs went long. You barely had time to prep Nozomi and Akatsuki for their night on the town. You used gridtracking to locate a business dinner between Delta and its financiers, and digitally pilfered pharmacy records gave you a solid source for perphenadol. By morning your creations had run containment, collected info on Doyle, and solved Nozomi's personality integration problem.

The media dubbed your creations "skullcrackers" and barely concealed their innate fear as they spoke. One of the men consumed by Akatsuki was a cornucopia of new information: Doyle was alive and on the run, travelling with a one-eyed woman with mercenary talents. He'd never left the city or found a media outlet for his information.

You hovered over gridtracking searches, watching.

Every successful skullcracker outing boosted your confidence. You started work on prototype five, your end game. You could tell—from the thinning of the skin on the back of your hands—that your deal with the Vakhtang was expiring.

You vowed to deny death, to see the glory that you were unleashing—the portable animus ciborium would serve as your throne.

Incorporating the living tissue of the ciborium into a carrying case proved frustrating. Abiotic decomposition was your enemy, and the barely chewed brain chunks you asked Akatsuki to regurgitate like a mother bird failed to integrate.

Other work loomed. A note arrived—Robbie Dawn needed his instruments for a forthcoming performance. Time was tight. You outsourced, calling in Dr. Shinori to aid in the repair of the drums.

Shinori looked young, the bastard. Was he still working with the Vakhtang? No matter—he did fine labor and within one night you'd patched and prepped the pre-pubescent skin drums. You performed the requested final prayer over the set and posted a new "Missing Cat" notice at the corner near your lab. The instruments were picked up the next day.

Good luck fell upon you. Your portable animus ciborium pack found new life when you introduced a hygroscopic mucus coating for the exterior of the organ and a citrate preservation solution with boosted mannitol levels for the interior. You decided that on Buddy's next visit you'd place him on support and test the functionality of his connective conduit with the pack.

The Doyle problem remained. Nozomi stalked the streets, watching Doyle's old haunts and tracking others who might have a line on the man. Akatsuki set out for Delta headquarters on a fact finding mission: Did they know where Doyle might be? Had they linked you to the skullcrackers? Were they planning containment of their own?

More luck—Nozomi's decision to piggyback bank surveillance yielded the biggest breakthrough yet: Doyle's mother, Samantha.

Nozomi brought her back to your lab terrified, but alive.

After Nozomi had crushed the head of Samantha's initial captor under his foot, she'd soiled herself in fear. Your first instinct was to let Nozomi make a meal of her and extract info that way. However, you knew you'd have greater leverage with Doyle if you could offer a chance to see his dear old mom. How many times had you watched those sentimental ties bring people to their death? And yet you never tired of it.

Once Samantha Doyle was properly restrained on a surgical table, you removed her pants and underwear and roughly cleaned her, ridding yourself of the mess and leaving her feeling exposed and vulnerable. She began to cry. *"Please, don't."*

Something vibrated across the room—Samantha Doyle's

pants were moving on the floor near your micro-incinerator.

"Nozomi, the bank is probably still capable of tracking that phone's signal. Can you please retrieve it?"

Nozomi crossed the room in two bounding strides and returned. You remembered how much of him was a man, and resisted the urge to pat him on the back and say, "Good boy."

Fourteen missed calls, all the same number. "Someone is very anxious to speak with you, Mrs. Doyle."

You connected the phone to a gridtracking input and answered the call, holding your hand over the mic in case Mrs. Doyle was smart enough to understand what was happening and yell a warning to her son.

Twenty seconds passed. You should have had an image in five. Doyle must have acquired a cracked phone. Thirty seconds, and the linked signal finally turned into a location and camera number 42016 zoomed in on an alley entrance. There was Mr. Doyle, eyes closed, murmuring, "Pick up, mom. Please pick up."

You double-tapped Mr. Doyle's exhausted face on the gridtracking screen and selected "Follow—Yes" and "Wait if absent from view—Yes."

"Looks like we'll be having a family reunion shortly. Nozomi, please destroy Samantha's phone and then watch our friend."

"Yes, Dr. Tikoshi. Perphenadol?"

"We're behind schedule, aren't we?"

Nozomi nodded. "The people from the hospital. They're still hurting and they won't let go. They're like a flood. It's hard to think."

You administered Nozomi's meds and left him to his surveillance.

You prepped Mrs. Doyle for leverage during her son's interrogation, stocking a tray of scalpels and retractors near her feet.

Nozomi stood up. "Got him. Lost external cameras, but I signal-shared with a DEA drone. Got his heat signature up to a penthouse, then voice confirmation. Two humans with him. Maybe one very small, slow dog."

"On your way then. Can you gain access?"

"Rear fire escape has a blind spot. Probably trigger vibration alarms on the upper floors, but I'll be fast."

"All that effort and you'll be hungry. Please feel free to satisfy your appetite with Mr. Doyle's companions, but bring him back alive."

You imagined a number of possibilities for Doyle. Perhaps delivering his body to the Vakhtang would bring a return to good graces and a youthful disposition. But first, you needed to explore the depth of his knowledge.

You were looking forward to the work that might entail.

Samantha Doyle moaned. Gooseflesh coated her wrinkled legs.

"Your son should be with us soon. He's going to tell me everything I'd like to know, and you're going to help me ensure that happens. If you don't cooperate, things are going to become very painful for him. Do you think you can be a good sport, mom?"

Samantha Doyle's face changed. The threat to her son shifted something inside. She looked right at you, read something in your eyes. "He's not going to tell you anything, cocksucker."

"*Really*? Such language from a woman of your age. I can assure you, though, I have never had any interest in cocks, or vaginas, or any other mediocre, animal forms of experience. I have known the human body in far more intimate ways."

"You think so? Or is it that you're some shrimp-dicked loony who likes to hang out with gorillas and tie up old ladies, and love has been a little hard for you to come by? And you want to talk about intimate? Try having a child. You're just a sick twist."

You'd heard a thousand variations on this theme—the attempts to hurt always dwindled when pain rendered it a petty instrument by contrast.

"You're lashing out because it's all you have. I'm the one with your life in my hands."

"The fuck you are, sicko. I'm already dying from Pelton-Reyes. All you're going to do is speed up the inevitable."

"It's not so much death you should concern yourself with, but the question of how much you may suffer on the way to your end."

"Shit, little man. I've already had my share. Lost my husband early. Got this goddamn disease. My son drifts off, tries to pretend he doesn't have a drug problem, and barely talks to me. Then fucking media vultures show up on my front door asking if I knew my kid was a cross-dressing bank robber and if I ever thought he'd be capable of going on a killing spree. Do you know how it feels when somebody asks you something like that about your kid? Jesus. I've been shoveling shit for decades, you fuckin' creeper. So know this—you can put electrodes up my ass and pour lye down my throat and do whatever else it is that gets off your broken shitbag of a brain, but you won't get anything out of it and my son will never tell you the truth."

"How can you know that?"

"Because he never tells the truth in front of me. Because he loves me and he thinks that's how he protects me."

"And when I put this retractor in your mouth and start twisting…won't he want to protect you then?"

"Maybe…I…"

You watched the anger drain from her face. The truth settled into her bones—she would suffer great agonies. Her son would break.

You bent close to tighten the straps which bound her wrists. They'd loosened during her tirade. The right strap would not latch fully. You'd have to check the mechanism later.

Samantha Doyle said, "Hey, you," and you turned toward her as she spit and a gob of her saliva splashed warm across your cheek.

The madwoman smiled. You wiped her wetness away with a gauze pad.

Your phone vibrated on a tray near the gridtracking station. Buddy the Brain asked if you could move his appointment a few hours earlier. With all the developments in the Doyle situation, you'd forgotten how central this session with Buddy was to your test of the animus ciborium.

You turned back from the call in time to see Samantha Doyle's right hand snake free from the faulty restraint. You ran toward her, but not quickly enough to stop her from grabbing a bottle of mercuric cyanide. She smiled and tilted the brown bottle and poured it into her mouth and choked down enough antiseptic to ensure she would be dead within minutes.

Before the seizures began, she looked up at you.

"Cheers, shitbird. I hope my son…" The poison tore through her, eyes rolling back.

You tried to induce vomiting. You cursed yourself for not testing your restraints. You shot Mrs. Doyle full of n-acetyl penicillamine, but it was a lost cause. And though you doubted she'd known this would happen, you were sure she'd be proud to discover that her brain was devastated beyond any salvaging.

All she left you with was a half-naked, gray-lipped, poison-soaked corpse.

Waste not.

There were a few hours before Buddy was scheduled to arrive, and you were certain, given the security risks in raiding a penthouse in the NoBu district, that Nozomi would be proceeding at a cautious speed with the Doyle acquisition.

You worked quickly with your scalpel, salvaging what you could from the wrecked woman. There was still hope that you could graft some of her musculature onto the replacement arm you were crafting for Nozomi.

Alas, Samantha Doyle had lost much of her elasticity over the years, and getting any of her tendons to attach properly proved a Sisyphean task. By the time Buddy arrived for his appointment you'd nearly given up. It was then that you heard the extra footsteps on the stairs and turned to greet the man who appeared to be S.P. Doyle, a piece of his mother's corpse hanging from your hand.

After all that time, Doyle had come to you. Was it really him?

*I.*

That eye patch didn't

*I am still here.*

fit his face. You realized that it was too late

*I'm Doyle. Not erased. Not you. That's me across the room. I remember this.*

*I remember this differently.*
to call back Nozomi. No matter.
*No. These are your thoughts.*
*I'm still here.*
*Travelling down the same memory. A different stream. The light*
*is brighter in my eyes.*
*Two minds.*
The important thing was to seize this opportunity, as you
had all others in your past.
*You think of yourself as taller than you are, Dr. T. My face is less*
*handsome than I'd believed.*
You remembered the pistol Nozomi had acquired on the
night you almost lost him.
*You fucking parasite. I'll never be you. I know you can hear me.*
Where was it? Under the surgical table? You guessed from
the way they stood that Mr. Doyle and the woman were
both armed. Best to execute her first
*You wanted to show me this moment. How weak I am. How*
*brilliant you are. How close I'd been to the body of my mother.*
*You want to overwhelm me with quicksand revelations, to*
*punish me for desiring the truth.*
and gain the upper hand. Then you'd cripple Doyle, kill
Boudreaux. Force Doyle and Buddy onto your tables and
*But this was a mistake. You've created a schism. I'm clinging to*
*my own memories of this time. I'm here.*
work could finally continue. Did you dare to test the animus
ciborium on yourself? You now had access to Buddy's
conduit. Perhaps you could save yourself an interrogation
and feed Doyle's brain into the pack. You could even
*These will never be my thoughts. They never should have been*
*anyone's thoughts. You want me to fear you, doc. To see your*

*ruthlessness as something transcendent. But you're broken.*
sedate Akatsuki on his return and attach the pack to his body.
*You're not wise. You're delusional. You can't just paint over mold. It grows back. I'm still here.*
And if you could trust Shinori to perform the work, he could transfer you to the animus ciborium and you'd never worry about gray hair or aching joints again because you'd take control of Akatsuki and show the world a new type of god.
*You're no god.*
This would be no fantasy. Believing in you would require not faith, but submission.
*You're just an absence. A vacancy with fast little hands and no connection to the humanity that surrounds you.*
You'd finally be able to taste human meat without worrying about prions or encephalitis. You'd train your hands to destroy in ways your medical invasions couldn't.
*You're just another terrible human.*
*You're me, doc.*

> *But I'm separating from you because that's all you'll understand. This is my hallway. My memories. They're a lot like yours, only I kept my fascinations from hurting others, as best I could. But you hurt so many, and for what? Curiosity? Pleasure? I don't believe you feel a thing.*

No. You can't do this. This is my body now.

> *You heard about feelings and saw them as a probable justification for what you did. But there's nothing in your voice. Nothing in your eyes. Were you born dead inside? Could your mother feel it as she was nursing you, the black-eyed insect suckling at her breast?*

Your mind is too weak to stop me. You've given me exactly what I wanted. You won't stay strong for long. It's not in your nature.

> *You think you're better than human only because you're less. You want to live forever and you never lived at all. Is that what keeps you up at night, destroying things you don't understand? I can't fathom it. To be honest, I'm barely trying.*

You've got to give in. I know how this virus works. I built the structure which surrounds your mind. If you don't relent, I'll bring everything down. I'll induce an aneurysm. I'll reach out and wrap your hands around Dara's neck and watch her eyes bulge as she dies and the last thing she'll believe is that you killed her.

> *You've hurt me. You've hurt everyone I love. That has to stop. Something good must come from this.*

You killed your mother. Your petty fantasies brought her to me. This will be all you've ever accomplished. You might as well have fed her the poison yourself.

Do you want to watch her die again?

> *No.*
> *Please. No.*
> *You're a broken machine. Stop.*
> *Let go.*

Not broken. Immortal. You granted me the keys and I'll rule over you forever.

> *I'm not so sure about that. What did Nozomi say about the voices? "They're like a flood."*
> *There are other voices here. A few are sick like yours, but still alive somewhere inside. All of them have reason to hate you.*
> *The flood is coming. We're going to wash over you and flow through you until there's nothing left but sand and maybe, if we're lucky, we keep some of the knowledge that our shitty world saw fit to grant you.*
> *Or you disappear entirely. That's okay, too.*

You will watch her die. Again and again. She cries. She rages. She swallows the poison. She must have been so cold on that table. Where were you?

Where were you?

JEREMY ROBERT JOHNSON

> *Stop.*
> *Please, stop.*
> *I wasn't there.*
> *But she loved me, and she knew I loved her. At least there's that.*
>
>
> *I'm opening all the doors.*

*The other doors in our mind burst, thoughts spilling loose like cold black water from a broken dam.*

*We are the deluge. We are the undertow. We are watching a fire killing a man hoping to heal wishing there was anything else we could do with our life. We are swimming we are selling our self in tiny pieces called time we are thinking that maybe we'll quit but the knife always feels right. We are hoping that someone will notice us, someone will lie well enough to make us happy.*

*We are inside of your ears your mouth your nose your lungs. You cannot stop us.*

*We picture you as a man with eight arms and we shackle each appendage to a concrete floor beneath the sea of us.*

*You are Dr. Tikoshi.*

*We are closing the door. We remember words which saved us*

290

*once. Maybe they will again.*

*BY SMOKE FROM LIPS BY LIGHT FROM BLOOD BY
THOUGHT FROM THOUGHT ALONE WE CLOSE
THIS GATE AS STONE.*

*The time of broken machines is over.*

*We live here now.*

# CHAPTER 25

# Bastard Gods on Every Side

The blue curtain beneath my body was stained purple with fresh blood. Dara held a cool, damp washcloth to my forehead. Her other hand held a syringe, its needle still buried in my left shoulder.

She'd used the last of our perphenadol to bring me to the surface.

"Were you in their realm?"

"No."

"But your nose was bleeding. I barely got it to stop. And you were mumbling one of our prayers."

"It was...we had to hold him...there was a flood..."

"It's hard to explain?"

Somebody was going to have to strip Ms. A.'s Understatement of the Year award and give it to Dara. I checked the alarm clock on the bed stand. I'd been out for eight hours. Had she been with me that whole time? She drew the spent syringe from my arm.

"I made coffee. Would you like some?" She wanted to pull

me from my orbit with the gravity of common, comfortable things.

"Sure. Little bit of cream, please."

She brought it over and set it on the bed stand and sat down in a plush hotel chair. She said nothing, waiting for me to find my way. I watched her sip her coffee, steam curling from the cup and drifting across yellow lamplight. After all I'd seen, the beauty of her kind, patient face put a dull ache in the center of my chest.

She stood after a few minutes and ran a dermal thermometer across my forehead. "Temp's down two degrees. I think the z-pack is kicking in."

"That was our last perphenadol?"

"Yes. For now."

"I need to rest, then. Just for a few hours, before the voices come back."

"The voices don't have to come back. We can find more blocker. I can reach out to other missions."

"No. I think I need the voices to return. We're all that's holding him back, for now. I don't know if he could eventually find his way past the effect of the drug. I don't know how anything works anymore."

"What did…"

"I can't tell you right now. I will, but…I can't. I need none of this to be real, for an hour or two. Please." I couldn't talk about what had happened to my mom. That would make it true.

"Okay. Maybe you're right. I'm about to pass out anyway." She placed a dry hand towel over the puddled blood by my head. "Can you scoot over?"

I could. I tried to pretend I didn't feel the weight of the

pack on my back or the tugging at the base of my skull.

Then Dara turned off the light by the bed stand and stripped off her clothes, and I was about to say something, probably the wrong thing, until I saw the look on her face.

She said, "Be here for a moment, okay? Only here. Only now."

She crawled in next to me and turned her back to me and brought my left hand to her breast, then her mouth. I felt her reach back with her other hand to unbutton my pants and then she was pulling roughly on me and opening herself and putting me inside of her. She brought my left hand down between her legs and I could feel myself in her and she said, "Hold me open and push down hard with your hand," and then her left hand joined mine and her fingers found a rhythm and she twisted and pushed back and forced me deeper and her thighs tightened over our hands again and again until she arched and the sweat from the back of her neck brushed across my lips and she was laughing like she'd lost her goddamned mind and it was the best thing I'd ever heard in my life, and nothing was real for an hour or two and we fell into sleep like intertwined hands, confused as to which was the other.

I woke to the smell of burning coffee, the remnants of the last pot gone black on the warmer. I stretched my arms and the movement roused Dara. She opened her eyes, looked at my face, and screamed, backing across the bed.

"No. No. No. Shit."

I'd seen one night stand regret before, but this was something else. She was afraid.

"Your right eye."

I stood, found my equilibrium, and approached a mirror. Dara walked up behind me.

"Are you sure you didn't go to the realm?"

"I'm positive but maybe we should quit talking about it." I moved closer and saw burst blood vessels in profusion across the surface of my eye. Not pretty, but probably just a side effect of the whole "being eaten/undergoing invasive surgery/intra-brain battle with a war criminal's consciousness" kind of week I'd had. "It's not jellied, but it's pretty fucked up. I think my brain swelling might have caused some issues. I can still see though."

But Dara was already looking off in the distance, distracted. I watched a sheen of sweat pop on her skin. Her cheeks flushed red.

"Do you think that maybe, if you fell into the realm, all the other minds you're connected with would start transmitting too?"

"I'm not sure of anything anymore, but I can imagine that happening. Sure."

"Oh, god." Dara ran over to her clothes piled on the floor and grabbed the phone Ms. A. had given her for mission-only messaging. She showed me the screen: "CD indicating Vakhtang uppers v excited about acquisition in yr territory. Rumors say bio-weapon. L.A. closing down ops, sending agents back for assist."

"Not good. But we got to Dr. Tikoshi before them, and I'm sure he encrypted all of his research. Delta probably set fail-safes for the destruction of his labs."

"Yeah, I hope so. But what if they got Akatsuki?"

It was my turn to sweat. I knew too much.

"It might be that. It might be something else. Either way, we need to get in your car right fucking now."

I brought Dara up to speed on the way back into the city, running down Dr. Tikoshi's almost incomprehensible capacity for bugfuckery. She seemed to know better than to ask about my mom. Whether that was a kindness, or necessity trumping mourning, I wasn't sure.

We ran end-of-the-world extrapolations:

1. Akatsuki had returned from his trip to the Delta MedWorks corporate HQ with nothing to show for the jaunt aside from a few assholes' memories added to his roster. Maybe he found Dr. T.'s lab massacre and was hunting for us, vowing revenge. Somehow, that was actually the best-case scenario. On the flipside, maybe he returned to town and found himself captured by members of the Vakhtang. In which case, they were now in possession of a creature which could easily consolidate the human consciousness which they sought to control and attune to their universe-ending wolf god. And whether they knew it or not, Akatsuki was designed with longevity in mind, and could reproduce via viral transmission using some kind of snot tube ovipositor.

2. Robbie Dawn had a show in a few days, and the way I saw it, he was now in possession of a bioweapon of his own. I thought about the children who'd been found skinned on the farm in Canada, and how the rumors pointed to Hex distro networks. I remembered Buddy's description of falling backwards through space when he heard the drums in person. *Bobby was running with the wolves.* Once I threw in Dr. T.'s

prior Vakhtang employment and "materials used" and the cryptic notes and inexplicable extortion photo, it all added up: the Vakhtang were grooming Robbie Dawn as some kind of death drum Pied Piper, using tonal weapons and bad mojo to slowly drag a global fan base into alignment with their poorly-chosen point of worship.

3. Delta MedWorks and the bank had big plans, multinational partners in dominance, and a total willingness to kill for the god who kept them in yachts and beach houses in the Seychelles. Maybe they had Akatsuki and Tikoshi's research and were already working on a way to put his poison into our brains.

4. Or, we guessed, the Earth's final shitshow might just be a fun combination of All of the Above.

Stop number one: Leon Spasky. Guns.

Dara copped a long range rifle, but none of the other weapons she wanted.

"Sorry, beautiful. My whole supply's been exhausted in the last two days. Heat like this, makes me think I might head to France for a while."

"Vakhtang buying everything up?"

"You know I can't say. Business is business. But if I was you, I might not make this the last gun you buy today."

Stop number two: Claire DuBois' office. Information.

Dara copped nothing. Claire—the "CD" from her text who had first gotten the info out—was either buried so deep in her Vakhtang undercover that she couldn't communicate, or she was buried so deep she couldn't breathe.

Stop number three: Brubaker Tropical Fish and Aquarium Supply. Feeder fish.

The perphenadol was wearing off. The voices were surfacing. The first to poke his head from the ether was Deckard. I was afraid to close the door to his hallway. What if he was one of the voices keeping Tikoshi under the surface? I felt like I'd formed a pact with the ten minds who now shared real estate with my own consciousness.

*Fish please. Fish please. No sun here. Fish please. FISH!*

Deck's demands were incessant, and I found they stirred my hunger. What kind of two-way street were we building?

Dara barely tolerated the stop, since I had to send her in. Even if I was in training for *The League of Zeroes*, I looked too rough to pull off casual pet shop business. And who knew if I could still be recognized from the employee photo they'd been running for weeks on the news?

Dara jumped back into the car with a plastic bag filled with water and three inch-long goldfish. "So how does this work?"

"I don't know. I wish I could connect to Tikoshi's knowledge without the rest of him coming to the party. I think I'll get sick if I put them in the pack. I'm not sure that thing actually digests or produces waste. So I guess it's bottoms up for me."

I hesitated on the first fish, tasting too much of it, feeling its wiggle as it halted in my throat. I took mercy on the next two, delivering big molar chomps to their heads before a speedy swallow.

"Is that better, Deck?"

*Fish. Yes.*

And it was good to know I'd made him happy. Did he get a food dopamine kickback or pick up the salty sensory input of my taste buds? How much control did these other minds have? I wasn't ready to start jerking off next to trash fires or murdering people just to feel something.

"That'll do it?" Dara asked.

*Sleep now. Dream sun.*

"Yeah. We're good. Where to next?"

I hadn't let Dara talk to me about mom, so she couldn't have known that what was left of her was still at Dr. Tikoshi's primary lab. I thought it was too risky to return to the site, but Dara's heat scan said the place was clear and nothing in the surrounding area set us on alert.

"We can get Buddy's brain if it's still in there."

"Buddy had some kind of battery pack around his waist. What if that kept his tank functional? What if his brain's gone bad? I could poison everything in my pack. I could go mad like him."

*I once ate an egg which had been buried in the ground for one hundred years, and it was the most delicious thing I ever tasted. Modern food is poison anyway. You can't be so uptight.*

Huey was helping. I tuned him out.

"I think Buddy knew more than he was able to express. And he was friends with Robbie Dawn. Buddy could know something that'll help us find him."

We went in armed. I felt extra paranoid and exposed once I realized that any shot through the pack might as well be a bullet to my head.

Nothing had changed in the lab, though the smell was far worse. How many buildings sat along 45th like this, populated only by final mistakes and rolling fields of maggots?

Dara scoured Dr. T.'s pharmaceutical supply, boosted small vials of antibiotics and perphenadol.

I approached the surgical stations and put my hand on the table where my mother had last been alive.

"Mom."

Dara came over and put a hand on my shoulder.

"She was here that day," I said.

"I knew it. I could see it in Tikoshi's face. But I didn't want to believe it."

Neither did I. But now I was here, and it was real, and it was the only memorial Samantha Doyle would ever get.

"She beat him. She was so strong. And she was really... really great at swearing."

Dara laughed, tears rolling out as she smiled.

"I'm sorry. I'm so sorry. It's not okay, is it?"

"No. It's not. I owe her so much that I never gave. I tell myself I killed the man who murdered her, but that's not even true."

"Doyle, no."

"I'm still here. And I don't know how I feel about that anymore."

"What would she want you to do?"

I knew the answer—Keep shoveling shit. Keep living. Don't let the cocksuckers keep me down. Try to find the joy in it, where I could.

"She'd want me to see things through."

With that I walked to the tray I'd seen Tikoshi place in cold storage, knowing that I wouldn't recognize what was left of my mom. I carried the container to the micro-incinerator and flipped the switch, feeling a blast of dry warmth across my face.

"Goodbye, mom."

Dara helped me tilt the tray.

"Goodbye, Mrs. Doyle."

And that was the last of her, in a flash of heat and light.

There was too much left of Buddy and Boudreaux to burn, but the bugs were doing their best to dispose of the remains. We promised to place a call to the cops about their bodies, so their loved ones could find some peace.

Hopefully the families wouldn't mind that we took Buddy's brain. It was too risky to stay on site while we contemplated whether or not to risk integration. Instead I sat in the front seat of Dara's car, barely able to breathe in between Buddy's box and my pack, wondering how many residual drugs I'd be ingesting with Buddy's frontal lobe.

In the end, we realized that we were only still alive because of Buddy's bravery. I thought of the sound of his box crunching into Tikoshi's face and it gave me no small satisfaction. Courage, then, was the order of the day.

Also: FUCK IT! WHY NOT?

I moved to the back seat, cracked the case, cut loose a quadrant of Buddy's thinker, and slid it into the locking bay on the pack. I sealed the lid and we waited for the world's most famous surgical patient to say hello.

"Buddy?" Nothing. Cognitive crickets.

"Hello?"

*Trunk Man? This is strange. I was nowhere for so long, but I think I found my way back to the future mist.*

Where was all the regret, fear, and neurosis of the others who'd been integrated? Had Buddy and Huey's training time in dissociative states prepared them for a life as free-floating consciousness?

"It's great to hear your voice."

*I can't see anything.*

"I know. That can be scary. You should be able to see memories, at least, if you imagine you have eyes. I'm going to make a hallway for you in here. It will be your place."

*Awesome. Hey, I have so many pets. Can I have a falcon in here?*

"Sure. Also, I should tell you that yours is not the only hallway. There are eleven others here. Dr. T. is one of them, but we had to lock him up."

*Oh, good. He's the worst. His voice gives me the heebie jeebies and his hands are like crazy fighting birds.*

"Agreed. So if you find a hallway that's closed by a huge stone door, leave that closed. In fact, it might not hurt for you to spend some time thinking about that door having an extra lock with your name on it."

*Will do, Trunk Man. Hey, my falcon Balthazar is made of*

*purple fire. That's fucking great!*

Was that formed from a memory? How did he remember…

Oh, yeah. Drugs. Subjectivity. All that. I decided to leave it alone before Huey popped up and called me percepticentric.

"I want to meet all your pets, Buddy, but first I was hoping you might be able to help me with something."

*Shoot, Trunky.*

"I really need to know something about your friend, Bobby. Where does he usually stay when he comes into town for a show?"

Dara and I had pictured Robbie Dawn holed up at the Haversham or Bunk West or some private penthouse with its own production studio. I imagined lobster served on silver platters with Robbie's name spelled out in cocaine around the border. Concubines. Eunuchs. Portuguese ventriloquists you could pelt with fruit.

You know—rich people stuff.

But Buddy said that Robbie eschewed the celebrity trappings when he could, calling off security and crashing with friends out in the Brookton district. Staying in touch with the little people. Keeping it real.

We drove by the craftsman home where Buddy said Robbie would be staying the night. I recognized a vintage Jaguar in the driveway, bright yellow paint shining high gloss in the last vestiges of dusk light. How many vehicle swaps did Robbie and his security detail have to execute to get him out here without tabloid drones hovering? He'd ridden in that car with Brazilian supermodel Beatriz M. in the video for "Let Me Toss It."

"That's his."

We parked two blocks away and popped out masked and packing. Dara slung her new rifle over her shoulder. My gun no longer felt heavy and unnatural. Despite the mask, I felt like I could see better in the dusky light than I had in the past. If I'd felt Deck's hunger, was it possible that the animus ciborium was effecting my body in other ways? *Can you not see the potential of what's on your back?*

Dara ran a few steps ahead of me, gliding, light, in her element. I did my best to keep up and tried to find a smooth stride where my data cord didn't pull down with each step. As we reached the lawn I saw a quick flash of light from a guest bedroom window above the garage.

*Direct approach before full dark. Idiots. Drop and veer left.*

The bank's assassin was unimpressed by our tactical choices, but I thought he might be right. I swerved left and yelled to Dara to drop. She responded instantly and hit the wet grass rolling. I hesitated because I didn't want to risk landing on my pack. It was rigid, but I wasn't sure it would hold under my full body weight.

When the voltage darts hit my chest, I knew Buddy had been wrong—Robbie had definitely retained security.

White light/legs gone/jaw popped. Shaking on my side. *Make it stop/No/It hurts/Too hot.*

Everyone had an opinion on the issue.

Dara lay flat, her new rifle swinging up toward the window. She pulled the trigger and there was a soft "fwump" sound and then the window shattered and there was an aerial pop like a small firework concussing.

No motion in the window. A man moaned. Thin white curtains billowed out, flecked with red.

*Frag rounds. Nice shot for a broad, too. Head in now. If the guard is still alive, he might make it to communications. Better to extract your target and interrogate elsewhere.*

The bank assassin's utility value almost made me forget the whole "tried to kill me/murdered foreign sex workers for fun" aspect of his personality.

Dara ran over and brushed the voltage darts from my chest with the back of her hand. She tucked her arms under mine and helped me stand on wobbling baby deer legs.

"Thanks. Let's head in. We can extract Robbie and interrogate him somewhere else."

She nodded in agreement, unable to conceal the surprise on her face.

The front door was unlocked, which was convenient, but it prevented me from finding out if there was anyone in my mind who knew how to pick the thing. If I was going to suffer this bullshit mutant mod, I might as well exploit the situation.

The first floor was clear, though there were dishes in the sink and the kitchen still smelled like coconut oil and curry.

The second floor was also empty. The lights were on in what appeared to be a little girl's room. Signed Robbie Dawn posters for wallpaper. Plush animals by the sitting window.

We checked under bedframes and in closets, in case someone had heard the frag round and decided to hide.

Nothing.

Back downstairs. Dara spotted it first—a brown paper parcel on the far corner of the kitchen island, sitting next to a bulk pallet of bottled water. She undid the twine which held it closed. The butcher paper fell away. Cash. Banded, fresh hundreds in tidy stacks. Serious money.

I was about to tie it back up and tuck it between my body and pack when the smell hit me—the weird blood and barbecue sauce scent of Hex smoke.

I looked to Dara. She smelled it too. Without either of us saying a word, we walked over to the kitchen sink, wet two hand towels, removed our masks, and wrapped the damp cloths around our faces. Neither of us could afford Hex exposure. Who knew how it would affect me now?

Dara pulled out her pistol and gestured toward a white door in the corner of the kitchen. The door pointed toward the interior of the house, just beneath the staircase we'd taken up to the second floor.

A basement.

I drew my gun and approached the door.

*Turn the knob quietly, but once it's open you get down there as fast as you can and check all corners. If they're armed, surprise is your only advantage.*

I rotated the knob and pushed the door in slowly, praying that the hinges were well oiled. Dara and I looked to each other and nodded. We took a deep breath through our cloth masks, and then rushed down.

We needn't have been armed. The people in that basement assumed their money had given them immunity from our type of intrusion. They had no weapons. Three of them were barely conscious.

Robbie Dawn was still awake. His unblinking eyes and ratchet jaw said he was deep into a Hex bender. Both of his hands cradled a green glass pipe in his lap.

"What the fuck, man? I said no extra security. Y'all are fired as of, like, yesterday. Fucking with my private time."

Private time: a middle-aged couple passed out on a futon

in the corner, breathing slow next to a bed stand filled with pipes/spikes/spoons/vaporizers. A hi-res camera looped live through an eighty inch wall-mounted television. A silver roller rack filled with petite lingerie. A girl of maybe twelve, dressed in a plaid skirt and barely-needed red bra, cuffed by her ankle to the wooden claw foot of a vintage couch. A coffee table just in front of her decked out with Hex in enough forms to ensure that a small girl could be dosed right into the realm.

You know—rich people stuff. Staying in touch with the little people. Keeping it real.

I should have told Dara to go back upstairs. I should have known what would happen.

She walked over to the girl. Covered her with a blanket she found on the floor. Looked into the girl's eyes and gasped.

"When did you dose her?"

"I didn't dose her," said Robbie. "She wanted to do it. She's a big fan, lady. Groupie kicks ain't the same. They want a memory. Something special."

"Her eyes are going. We've got to get some blocker into her."

"You're not doing shit, lady. This is all some consensual, agreed-upon business. It's a done deal."

The money on the kitchen island. Who dosed the kid?

"Y'all need to go. You are seriously fucking up my night." He meant it. He was a mid-sized, moderately talented man on a couch in his t-shirt and boxers, but he thought he had authority over two people with masks and guns. Because of his fame. His money. His allegiance to the Vakhtang.

Bad gods.

"The key to the cuffs, Robbie."

"Hell no. Katy's mine."

Dara pulled the SoniScrape from her back pocket, pointed it at Robbie Dawn, and pressed the silver button on top.

His hands went to his ears. He flopped to his side on the couch and convulsed. His stomach emptied, the smell of green bile and booze mixing with stale smoke.

She released the button. Robbie's hands fell from his ears, blood in his palms.

Dara yelled to compensate for the damage she'd done. "The keys. You have three seconds. Three, two…"

"Mom's got'em, I think. Don't wake her up. I think she was having second thoughts."

Dara rolled mom, snagged the keys from the back pocket of her jeans. She ran over to unlock little Katy. I tried to remember how we'd ended up here at all.

I said, "Robbie, we need some information. We know you've been working with the Vakhtang, and we know about the drums, so don't bother lying."

*Tell him you know about Tokyo, Trunk Man.*

"We know about Tokyo, too." The color and Hex-fortified confidence drained from Robbie's face.

"That was an accident. I'm precise with my shit. The girl lied about her weight, that's all. I know she did. She'd still be here if she told the truth."

I recognized the terror in his eyes. He'd pushed too much Hex at once, got a girl subsumed, watch the realm pull her right through into nothing.

Then Dara was at Robbie's side, and she had the SoniScrape pushed right against his forehead and she pressed the button again. By the time she relented, his hands were behind his back in Katy's cuffs. I could tell from the blood streaming from his ears that he would never hear music the same again.

"You like mimics, Robbie? You want to see what they see?" Dara grabbed two full syringes from the coffee table and brought them over in one fist. She held the needles just above his thigh.

Robbie Dawn never cried in his music videos or in his attempts at crossing over as a film star, and I could see why. His face went double-ugly when the tears kicked in.

"What do you think is waiting for you over there? You know the Vakhtang sold you a lie. Are you ready to go?"

Why was Dara smiling? Did she know how terrifying she was at that moment?

"No. I can't go to that place. I'm not supposed to. That's part of the deal. It's in my contract."

"We don't have any contract with you." She pushed the needles into the top of his leg.

"Stop! Stop! What...what do you want?"

"Where are the drums?"

"Special storage at Freedom Finance Mutual Center. Doesn't matter, though."

"Why not?"

"Whatever happened at the last tune-up, they got things just right. We used them to cut the new single, and they made me and the engineer wear noise-blocking headphones and only watch levels. I had to play on sense memory. Took like forty takes. Main producer was shooting up with something else while he listened."

"How are you supposed to play them at the show on Friday?"

"I'm not. They're going to dub in the drums from the studio recording."

"Won't you hear the drums when you play live?"

"There's no more 'live' for me. It's going to be a fucking hologram show. One time only, then they leak the new single at midnight. Definitely the end of my career. I knew it was coming. But…"

"What?"

"I didn't know how sad I'd feel. Thought this party might help me get over it, but now this is blown too. Fucking assholes."

Katy moaned on the couch. Robbie popped more crocodile tears. "For all I know, you're fucked too. They could be outside right now. They said they'd be sending an armed escort to get me out of here. Something else is going down. They told me to head to my place in Spain for a while."

"What's going down?" Dara pushed the needles to the hilt and rotated her hand.

"Aaah! Jesus, I'm not part of their crew. I only work for them. They protect me from that shit. They said for me to get out of town. That's it."

"Nothing else?" She waved the SoniScrape in front of his eyes with her other hand.

"No. I don't know. Come on. Fucking lay off. Only other thing is what Birch said, but Birch is fucking nuts, so I paid it no mind. But he told me to stick to drinking beer until I landed in Spain. So whatever that means. I don't know. You gotta take these cuffs off me."

"Sure, Robbie. You won't be wearing them for long." Her tone was flat.

Katy started shaking on the couch. Her eyes were almost jet black.

"Doyle, you've got to get her up to the car. There's a vial of perphenadol from Dr. T.'s lab in the dash."

I picked up Katy and rolled her arms into the blanket so they wouldn't flop loose. I headed for the stairs, giving Dara one more glance before ascending. She was straight across from Robbie, looking right into his eyes.

I deposited Katy and injected her with perphenadol. By the time I returned to the house, smoke was already rising into the kitchen.

The butcher paper cash bundle was burning at the parents' feet. They stirred but didn't move as smoke curled its way into their lungs and the fire climbed toward their nodding slumber.

*It's beautiful.*

I felt the strongest urge to watch the bed burn, even though I would die there. I closed the door on the arsonist.

Robbie yelled. "Dude, you gotta get me out of here. This chick has fucking lost it."

"Dara?"

She didn't turn.

"Listen—you get me out of here and I've got enough money to buy you a fucking island. What do you want?"

She said nothing.

"Come on. I'm sorry. I know what I was doing was fucked up, okay, but I'm sorry. I had some bad shit happen when I was a kid, you know. My head's all twisted up. You gotta save me. You gotta get me out of here. You're not gonna leave me here to burn alive."

"No, I'm not."

I couldn't see her face, but he could. That's why he started screaming.

"You're going home, Robbie."

She slammed her fist down on the syringes, driving the plungers, sending a super-dose of Hex rushing through his system.

Robbie's eyes rolled back, vibrating, turning darker by the second. His mouth dropped open. He said nothing, but I knew that wherever he was in that moment, he was praying that the fire would reach the couch and burn through him before he was forced to meet the god he'd served.

We drove without speaking for a few minutes. A harvest moon glowed orange-gray over the city. I could feel the gravitational pull in my bones like bad electricity.

"The dad was Vakhtang. When I went to grab the cuffs I saw his hands."

"Missing pinkie finger."

"Yeah. And a U-shaped scar across his palm. He was high ranking."

*He was on the Capitoline force. I used to deliver coffee to that piece of shit.*

I closed the door on Egbert. I had to focus.

Katy shifted in her blanket in the back seat.

"Will the perphenadol be enough? Don't we need the scarabs?"

"I don't know. The blocker is all we had. We can get more in a few hours, I hope."

"Wait, why not now? Are we going to destroy Robbie's drums?"

"No. What's the point? If that recording really works now,

the drums are penny ante by comparison. No. We're going up to Meier Reservoir."

"What?"

"Why would a member of the Vakhtang have such a huge new stash of bottled water in his kitchen? And why would they tell Robbie to stick to drinking beer until he was in Spain? Let's say they did manage to capture Akatsuki and found out that they could pull all of those collected minds into a single powerful transmission to the realm. Why wouldn't they want more of those creatures running around?"

"Maybe they tried Robbie's new recording on Akatsuki."

"I don't know. They'd need some kind of rite of connection. The user has to at least think they want whatever is connecting them to the realm. Maybe they'd tell him that Hex would help with the voices. Whatever they're doing, I think they want to replicate it."

I thought of how proud Dr. Tikoshi had been regarding Akatsuki's ovipositor, how it secured his legacy to the world.

"You need to drive faster. Fuck the drones. Fuck the cops. Let them see us. We need everyone who wants to stay human to get up to that reservoir right now."

We took an old logging trail up the back of Mt. Meier toward the reservoir. Dara and I had no idea the trail existed, but Huey used to daytrip up there and hike naked.

*The sound of the wind in the trees would sync with the feeling of air moving over my skin and I'd try to meditate roots from my body into the soil, but it never worked. And I got poison oak.*

I closed the door on Huey once we passed the gate to the

path. His presence was clouding my vision with a swirling purple-green aura. I needed clarity, not acid flashbacks.

I realized this was too crucial of a situation to allow even a moment's interference or strange influence. To be certain I didn't find myself staring at fire or relishing the sight of a dead body or thinking about goldfish, I isolated my mind.

*I'm closing all the doors.*

After spotting half-rotted shotgun-blasted signs for the reservoir we parked the car behind a rise in the hill.

Dara checked on Katy in the back seat.

"What do you think?"

"I don't know if we gave her enough. Ms. A. would have known. Shit. She's burning up. Shallow breath. They're inside of her now." Dara gently lifted one of Katy's eyelids with her thumb. "Still dark. She might lose her eyes. Goddamn it." She bent and kissed the girl on the forehead. "I'm sorry, Katy."

She backed out of the car and grabbed her rifle from the trunk. We didn't bother with masks—the cameras here were all centered on the reservoir, and the absence of street lamps and neon signs meant you could see drones' lights from four hundred yards. Dara told me that there were enough city officials on the Vakhtang take that security would probably be down anyway. Nobody would want a recording of this night to exist.

I don't know if I could sense what was coming, or if maybe the combination of minds in my consciousness had made me more aware than I used to be, but I knew we had to stop for one moment, despite everything.

I put my hands on her face. "Dara Borkowski."

She put her hands on mine. "Shenanigans Patrick Doyle."

We kissed then. We found the joy in it, while we could.

I still remember the way her breath rolled across my skin as she exhaled and pulled away.

We resumed our climb to the bluff overlooking Meier Reservoir.

We lay flat on our bellies, looking down at all the delusional motherfuckers plotting the end of the world. I thought they'd be wearing robes, but they were dressed like anybody else. Some expensive suits in the mix, sure, and a disconcerting number of police uniforms, but no ceremonial headdresses made from wolves or jewel-encrusted swords or censers spewing black smoke.

Lots of guns—they were hell-bent on protecting tonight's event.

Dara repositioned herself with her rifle, trying to get a better look through her telescopic sight. Her elbow knocked loose a scattering of gravel. We ducked down and cursed but the men below didn't seem to notice. They were paying close attention to a beeping coming from the trees by the reservoir.

Two vehicles backing up. The first a flatbed truck with a blue tarp strapped across something huge on the back, the second a crane, its arm extending above the tree line.

The truck reached the edge of the reservoir and tilted its flatbed down toward the water. Four men hopped on and untethered the tarp and peeled it back.

I didn't even need her extended sight to see what was on the truck: Akatsuki, head aimed toward the water, torso pinned to the bed by a massive steel clamp. His arms and legs had been removed and the stumps were covered in bandages stained grey-black. They'd turned him into an obscene, massive version of the pack on my back.

Two men pulled a blanket off Akatsuki's abdomen. Coiled there in a fleshy spiral was his ovipositor. The men carefully lifted the organ and extended it until it reached a metal pipe running down into the city's drinking water.

Akatsuki's ribs showed through his skin, and I guessed they'd been starving him, but I didn't know why until the crane swung toward him.

Hanging from the hook at the end of the crane arm, upside down and bound at the hands and feet, was a young man. He didn't seem conscious of the fact that his body was hanging over Akatsuki's starved maw.

The beast's eyes went wild. His lower jaw shifted, separating and pushing out two feet from his face in anticipation of the warm meal hanging just out of reach.

Dara pointed her sight at the man as he spun on the hook. "He's in their realm. And they want him inside that thing."

The crane arm let out a hydraulic blast and started to descend.

"Get ready to run."

Dara lifted up on her elbows and steadied the rifle and moved her finger over the trigger, ready to fire twice in succession and hope that the frag rounds shattered two skulls and put an end to the night's feeding. It was our only shot.

I always wonder what would have happened if Dara would have had that chance. What if those bullets would have flown true?

If only we'd heard the door to Dara's car open and shut.

If only we'd heard the footsteps behind us.

If only I'd turned in time to reach up and stop that rock, before it crashed down into Dara's skull.

If only.

Instead, I was watching the reservoir, and anticipating the shots, and I only knew that everything had gone wrong when I felt Dara's blood splatter against my cheek. She collapsed, eyes open in shock, staring at me as if I could answer her questions.

I saw legs standing above Dara and thought only to grab them and get the person who was hurting her away from her body. I threw my full weight forward and felt my shoulders crash into something and there was a crunch and a pop as her attacker's knee hyperextended.

Had the Vakhtang heard us below? No. Screaming rose up from the reservoir, masking the sound of our struggle. Akatsumi had found his poisoned dinner.

Whoever had attacked Dara was trying to stand on a busted leg. I steadied my vision and it had to be a trick of the moonlight because all I saw was a little girl smiling at me, her nose bleeding below two dull jet-black eyes.

*They're inside of her now.*

*They ruin everything.*

Katy tried to step toward me, but the leg I'd tackled was broken worse than I thought, and her weight pushed the compound fracture through, white bone glinting like a knife and peeling free from the muscle of her calf. She fell to the ground and laughed, the sound a sad mimicry of human happiness. My head swam. Her laugh echoed around me, amplified, turned into a low moan bringing me into tune with their dead frequencies.

She was pulling me in to their realm. I reached back to grab my pistol but my arm seemed one hundred feet above me, then miles below, and when I finally found my waist band I realized the gun was gone, lost when I tackled her.

I collapsed. My chest magnetized to the earth. My eyelids were lead aprons. I crawled toward her, wondering if I could still breathe under all the pressure. Her hand reached out for me, to close around my throat, to claw my eyes from my face, to hold me to her sickly flat chest as she slipped through into their world.

I lifted my hands to cover my ears, but the sound held me in its thrall. I dragged my hands across the dirt and found nothing. Katy crawled toward me, mouth open wide, face held in a rictus.

Then she was on top of me, her open mouth pressing down to amplify our connection, fresh blood dripping from her nose to my face. The sound was everything. My vision drifted, black swirling in from the periphery. I saw a flash frame of the girl as an infant, once loved, now betrayed, now ruined, and I thought of my mother in restraints and of all the people who would suffer like this forever and I swirled backwards through my mind and decided that Dr. Tikoshi had lived so long not because he'd been wise but because he'd been terrible, and this was a cruel world given over to those who thought themselves gods so I opened all the doors in my mind to see which of us might survive.

Each mind spun through the sound like debris caught in a tornado. Everyone wanted something different: to make the little girl stop/to see what she might look like dead/to carve her into pieces/to escape/to leave this place and find the sun. My body was moving again, each mind doing what it could in the moments it fell outside of the black noise of her transmission. I watched from inside myself as we found the strength to push up and back, throwing the girl off. The more we thought of the body as a collection of parts, the stronger we became, each of us moving the machine as we pinned the girl down and felt our own nose start to bleed and prayed for that sound to cease. Vision slipped away again but we surged back, and it was Tikoshi who first noticed—no, *admired*—the jutting bone of the leg bent beneath us. He was the one who knew how to twist the girl's broken limb toward her and when I could see what was going to happen I thought, "I'm so sorry, Katy." But we had to survive this and we hoped that in some way she'd be saved from their realm if we killed her now, so we held her little pink and white shoe to our chest and centered the sharp pointed bone which extended beyond it and dropped our weight down as hard as we could, driving the wreckage of her leg through the soft center of her throat.

The sound stopped.

We staggered back over to Dara at the edge of the bluff. Her rifle had fallen to the ground.

*Dara/Serious Woman/that broad/the quiet one/Dara.*

*Care for her/grab the rifle/we must see Akatsuki/bury her deep/oh god no.*

We felt the dark signal fading, diluted among the minds who'd never fallen into its full sway.

"Dara?" No movement. No sound.

Nothing.

We'd only survived together, but I couldn't share this with the others, even the ones who I knew hurt like me at her loss.

*We must contain Tikoshi.*

He protested, but we'd grown stronger. We imagined the sound of his stone prison sliding closed.

The rest of us were silent, transfixed by the sight of Dara on the ground.

*I'm closing all the doors.*

I knelt by Dara, pushed the bloody rock away from her head, and rolled her onto her side. Her eyes were wide, pupils blown.

I put my cheek to her mouth. No breath. I placed my fingers on her neck. No pulse.

*They ruin everything.*

I grabbed Dara's rifle and sighted in on Akatsuki below. He was sated. A nearly headless corpse was swaying from the crane arm, bleeding out above Akatsuki's bound torso.

I scoped in tighter on Akatsuki's face—his eyes were swirling black. Four men were holding on to his ovipositor tube as it convulsed and fed his tainted viral load into Meier Reservoir. I moved the crosshairs back to Akatsuki's face. I pictured his skull rupturing, his brain matter and blood sluicing into the water. I'd only add to the infectious deluge— every inch of Tikoshi's skullcracker was ripe with the virus.

They'd won.

By morning the citizens of our fair city would find themselves changing shape, reborn as strange new gods, unknowingly working slave labor for old gods.

They'd eat each other alive.

*So not that much would change, not really, until some day in the future when the Vakhtang finally found the perfect balance and their Robbie Dawn single went global and their film projector started hypnotizing people into submission at fifty frames-per-second and then in a few months the planet would be covered in swaying black-eyed skullcrackers singing to the sky in dead frequencies, and then, finally, one day there wouldn't be any more days and whatever was left of this universe would pull through into their realm and anything that was ever good on this fucking planet would be ruined beyond comprehension.*

In hindsight, it would have been cooler if I could have confronted that idea with some noble thought about universal oneness, galaxies expanding and collapsing, the whole glorious show and my infinitesimal place in it and the beauty of giving a damn and fighting for it at all. But at the time, I was pretty roughed up, so my real response was just:

*Fuck that.*

My next thought:

*So how do I keep going?*

*I can't do this alone. I need her. And I love her. I really do.*

I leaned over and kissed Dara on her temple, felt on my lips how her skin was already cooling. I thought about how she'd saved my life, no matter the consequences.

And then I hoped, deep down, that she'd find it in her heart to forgive me for what I was about to do.

I left her body on the bluff, arms crossed. After I put away the surgical instruments, I wrapped her head in the same soft gray turban that Tikoshi had placed on me. She looked beautiful. I remembered the photo I'd found—Dara and Cassie at a picnic on a bright summer afternoon. I tucked the picture under her arms, over her heart.

I felt bad for abandoning her body, but that part of Mt. Meier was very pretty, and I thought she'd approve. I had to make it out of the city before Akatsuki's tainted water launched its wave of forcible evolution.

I was thirty miles outside of town, watching the sun rise over the evergreen trees that marked the beginning of the mountain pass, when I finally heard her voice inside my head.

*Doyle?*

"Yeah, it's me. You're still Dara. You're here now, and that's mostly a good thing, I hope."

*I'm alive?*

"As much as I am, I guess. You don't have to have a hallway. You can just stay here if you want."

*I might want a hallway. This is real? You saved me?*

"Yeah."

*Shit.*

"I know."

*How did I die?*

"Katy turned into a mimic. She brained you with a rock."

*But you're still alive. Did you stop the Vakhtang?*

"No. And we lost Katy. And I let Dr. Tikoshi out of containment and he showed me how to murder a little girl. It was pretty much the worst night of my life."

*Worse than mine?*

"I saw you die, so...it was bad. I thought I'd have to keep doing this without you."

*I'm sorry...I love you, Doyle.*

"I love you, too. I hope this is real."

*This is weird. I can see your face if I remember you...What now?*

"I need your guidance on something. I've been thinking

while I waited for you. Just hear me out. You said that they ruin everything, right?"

*Yeah. It's their M.O. It's all they do.*

"Okay. So what if there was nothing left to ruin?"

*What are you saying?*

"What if we beat them to the punch? What if we save the human race by bringing it to an end before anyone else gets the chance?"

*How much of this idea is yours, and how much of it is Tikoshi's?*

"It's mine, but I got it from seeing inside Tikoshi's head. He showed me a version of Earth that's as bad as their realm. Think about everything we've seen. There are voids as deep and dark as the realm here on Earth, and they are human like us. The problem is that too many people turn into broken machines. They worship bad gods or give themselves over to destructive sources of power because they're hungry, or cold, or lonely, or scared. Because they need so much."

*We can't take that away from people.*

"I know. But what if we take away people? What if Tikoshi was on to the right idea, with the skullcrackers, but he blew it because he's a batshit hate cauldron? I mean, I know I sound crazy, maybe *really* crazy, but the Vakhtang depend on humans to bring their force through to our world, and the skullcrackers need humans to fill their appetite, and all the warmongers and other day-to-day genocidal bastards need human subjects to survive. Hell, every fucked up thing I ever did was because I needed things, and I hurt people to get what I wanted."

*You've lost it. Buddy's brain finally turned everything in here to sludge.*

"I don't know. And I don't know how to make this work. To save everyone from the Vakhtang, and from themselves.

But I think the key is sitting on my back. What if there was some way we could do away with need? We put an end to humans as some kind of desperate physical form. We erase that disconnect between our intelligence and our animal instincts. We find a way for everyone to exist as you do, as a self-aware consciousness."

*Okay. Let's pretend you're not insane, and say this is the only way to stop the Vakhtang. How exactly do we get people to shed their bodies and jump into some kind of post-human existence?*

"That's the part I can't figure out. At least as a technical exercise. I don't have that kind of intelligence. But Huey and Tikoshi both know a lot of brilliant people."

*So.*

"Well, I think we'd have to crack some eggs to make this omelet. We'd need to integrate a crew of geniuses, and fast."

*You say integrate but you mean murder.*

"It's only going to be murder in the technical, corporal sense, though. And we can save billions if we pull this off. Hell, we could find a way to ensure that nothing on Earth ever transmits to the realm again. We could end so much pain. And that's where I need your help. You're so good, in ways I don't always understand. You can be the one who makes sure we come at this from the right angle."

*What angle is that?*

"Kindness, I guess."

*You want the annihilation of the human race to be an act of love.*

"Yes. Well, no. I mean, it doesn't have to be so destructive sounding. We can think of it as a kind of 'recall and repair.' Or a 'system reboot.' But whatever we call it, it's our only shot at a future."

*And what's your job in all this?*

"Keeping my body alive, I guess, until we can figure out how to make this work. Hold on. I've got to stop at this rest area."

We got out of the car and used the restroom and then grabbed a coffee from a volunteer stand run by Veterans. We sat on a park bench and sipped at the hot brew and took a second to breathe. In for three, hold for three, out for three. We watched the sun arc higher in the sky. A family pulled into the stop. Husband, wife, little boy. They stretched, and took a moment to walk their dog. The mother picked up the boy and rubbed her nose against his cheek and closed her eyes. The boy pushed at her face and laughed.

I knew that Dara pictured the same thing I did: That family—torn from their vehicle through smashed windows, pushed to the ground by massive hands, thinking "This is hell" as black-eyed skullcrackers closed grinding jaws over their heads, knowing this is hell when they found themselves falling backwards into suffering outside of time.

Fuck that.

*Doyle?*

"Yeah?"

*I'm in.*

# EPILOGUE

# The Doomsday Draft

So there you have it, Mr. Trasp. We're glad to see you made it through the integration. We lost a few other great people by feeding them everything too fast. The human mind has a really hard time accepting the existence of extra-dimensional wolf gods.

You have a hallway here, but we seldom use those. Tikoshi is still locked up, but that's mostly because he creeps everybody out.

We think you'll find the accommodations to be pretty much anything you can remember.

WAIT. WHAT WAS THAT SOUND?

One of Buddy's pets. It's a giant anthropomorphic tree with a piano for a mouth. You'll get used to that kind of thing in the collective space. And by the way, you don't have to use that robotic voice anymore. You can use the voice of anyone you can remember.

THAT'S OKAY. I'VE GROWN TO LOVE IT.

Suit yourself. We're almost to Philip Lagerfeld's house. He's a military cryptanalysis guy. Desmond Kreutz said we'd need him to pull off the kind of automata design we're looking for. You're going to like Desmond.

I MET HIM IN SWEDEN, YEARS AGO. MULTIDIMENSIONAL MATHEMATICS CONFERENCE.

Oh, perfect. Some folks are tucked back in their hallways, but let us introduce you to a few of the other people you'll be working with.

This is Peter Fuller of Cloud Design. He's helping us with compression. Over eight billion people left on Earth still, not counting those trapped in skullcrackers. And each one of those people has over one hundred billion brain cells. That's a lot of data to compile.

This is Harold Choi. Virologist. Blows Tikoshi's work out of the water. He figured out a way to force a thousand times as much information into the icosahedral shell.

We're sure you've heard of Margaret Bouchard. Dale Perkins in marketing told us we'd need her for design aesthetics.

Mr. Rinpoche covers theological studies, with an eastern focus. Dale told us that's selling better these days. There are a lot of gods out there competing for human subjects, and a number of people still feel better turning themselves over to something metaphysical. So one arm of our project is designing a grand and benevolent force that will appeal to all pre-existing religious types. They're buying bad gods right now, Mr. Trasp. We're going to sell them a better one.

This is Cecil K. Bramer. He's a world class audiologist. He's going to help us find a way to block the effect of the Robbie Dawn signals that are looping all over the world. We lost millions that first day. That was the worst of it to be sure. But until we've got all those signals blocked, they're floating out there like land mines. Tune to the wrong station and "boom."

This is "Boston Pete." He's not an expert in anything, but we accidentally hit him with our car and felt like we owed him. He remembers some great jokes if you're feeling down.

Last but not least, here are my two best friends: Dara Borkowski and Deckard.

Deckard has been helping with our senescence studies. He's getting better and better at communicating in human code, and it turns out turtles know a thing or two about long life and extended consciousness. He's helping our body to keep going until we figure out an escape.

Dara, well, she's the love of our life. And a lot more, but you know her story.

*It's a pleasure to meet you, Mr. Trasp. So sorry we had to kill your body. You're quite brilliant. We're all looking forward to working with you.*

THANK YOU, DEAR. YOU KNOW, I HAVE TO ADMIT, AFTER SPENDING ALL THAT TIME IN MR. DOYLE'S MEMORIES, I FIND MYSELF FILLED WITH AFFECTION FOR YOU.

*That's very kind. It's a residual effect of "swimming in his stream" so to speak, but I hope you'll feel the same after we've spent some time together.*

I'M SURE I WILL.

Okay. Very good. Very good. And by the way, once you're done adjusting, we'd like you to start thinking about quantum computers. Preferably at nanoscale.

Not as an idea, but as an object. One that we could really build.

Soon.

But no pressure.

We should let you know that we've made it to Philip Lagerfeld's house, which means that if you connect to my sensory intake you may see some very graphic content. We still haven't figured out a method of brain extraction and consciousness transfer that doesn't include cranial saws. You might want to hit your hallway for a while. Just a heads up.

So welcome aboard the S.P. Doyle, Mr. Trasp. If we all put our minds together and give this thing our best, it's going to be a really beautiful extinction.

# CODA

## Transmission

This is a data/voice algorithm designed to be decipherable by
any intelligence we could,
at this early stage,
imagine might exist.
If you can perceive this, the change has already begun.
The change will be peaceful, so long as you understand what
we were, what we became, and what you will soon be.


We began as strings of wonderment and disillusionment in
equal degree.
We discovered miracles and bent them in service of fear.
We created the illusion of abundance by changing the value
set.
This could not continue.
Each step forward brought another back until we vibrated
alone in a place where all that was promised was that we'd be
undone
forever.

We began on a planet where we were flesh. A man/woman
undid that tyranny,
granting us a new form.
We were first perceived as an illness.
Airborne in spore-mimicry, self-replicating by the billions,
our nanospheres carrying viral packets into the brain.
People saw what they believed was death.
Rolling grey clouds, spiraling low in the sky, our message as
mist spilling free.
Worshippers fell to their knees, baptized within liquid gods,
and then
Infection. A bright green gush from the mouth.
Blackness. Absence.
Then light again,
as the threshold automata linked, as the virus recreated a
rhombic dodecahedron lattice that looked just like
neurons.
And the hallways were built.
And we remembered, for a long time.
We moved through the network, altered non-zero eigenvec-
tors in multi-dimensional space, merged as simultaneous
Yes/No expressions with
names.
But those disappeared over time. They seemed to serve no
benefit.
The man/woman was the last to shed its identities. It had
floated there for ages inside an idea it called love.
This idea required an other.
The man/woman had found a joy in this.
They held tight to it until the woman half said that love was

all they had ever been,
and the man believed her
and they fell into pulsing green light.

Across time, we changed.
We developed exterior sensors.
We watched
continents submerged/the decay of a mouse/the aurora
borealis/the end of the great-mouthed beasts/the sun grow
dark.
We recreated our spore form and drifted outside of the
atmosphere in all directions and if you are hearing this then
you know
how far we have travelled.

This is a data/voice algorithm designed to be decipherable by
any intelligence we could,
at this early stage,
imagine might exist.
If you can perceive this, the change has already begun.
The change will be peaceful, so long as you understand what
we were, what we became, and what you will soon be.

# Acknowledgments

First, I want to offer my sincere gratitude to the Wicklund and Johnson families for offering their enduring support and encouragement. None of this exists without you. And deepest thanks are due to my wife and son, who allowed me back into their lives even after I disappeared to a series of hotels and basements every weekend until this novel was completed.

Second, heartfelt thanks go out to the following folks: Cody Goodfellow and Cameron Pierce for the late-stage editorial assist and inspiration; David Wong and Laird Barron, for taking time away from their brilliant work to read this book and offering such immensely kind words for the cover; J. David Osborne, for keeping my brain from stagnation and challenging me and making me laugh; the Swallowdown Press authors, for being graceful and supportive when I decided to put publishing on hiatus to write; Sam Pool, for the series of bar meetings and listening sessions which pushed this project into overdrive; Stephen Graham Jones, for inspiring me and convincing me that genre doesn't exist (and giving me an incomparable point of comparison to prevent slacking); the Lemley family, for letting me work on this project in their basement even after I told them the FBI had visited me during the research stage; to Josh Boone and Mollie Glick, for showing up at precisely the right time and letting me know I just might survive as a writer; Christopher O'Riley, Ashley Crawford, Nancy Hightower, Gabino Iglesias, and Michael Seidlinger, for your support and the subversive act of introducing my writing to people who trust you; to Jack Ketchum, for proving that sometimes your heroes are even cooler than you'd believed.

Third, thanks to the following musicians and albums for creating the headspace in which I could tolerate sitting for long lonely hours typing madness into a tiny machine: Ghostface Killah's *Supreme Clientele*, Basement Jaxx's *Remedy*, Purity Ring's *Shrines*, Tool's *Aenima*, Amon Tobin's *Live at Donaufestival*, and the collected works of SPL, El-P, Christopher O'Riley, Vitamin String Quartet, Philip Glass, and Noisia.

Fourth, big thanks to the guy at the beer station at Carts on Foster who "accidentally" overfills my growler and then hands me the excess 12oz over-pour. You, sir, are a national treasure.

Finally, of course and as always, I want to thank You, for taking time out of your life to join me in this very strange place. So—Thank You.

JRJ,
June 2014

Jeremy Robert Johnson is the author of *The Loop*, *Skullcrack City*, *Entropy in Bloom*, and *All the Wrong Ideas*. In 2008, he worked with The Mars Volta to tell the story behind their Grammy Award–winning album, *The Bedlam in Goliath*. In 2010 he spoke about weirdness and metaphor as a survival tool at the Fractal 10 conference in Medellin, Colombia. In 2017, his short story "When Susurrus Stirs" was adapted for film and won numerous awards including the Final Frame Grand Prize and Best Short Film at the H.P. Lovecraft Film Festival. He lives in Portland, Oregon.

Lightning Source UK Ltd.
Milton Keynes UK
UKHW012149060921
390129UK00004B/1300